THE DREAM

OF

DANTE O'SHEA

D.A. D'AURELIO

PublishAmerica
Baltimore

ISBN: 1-60441-627-0
PUBLISHED BY PUBLISHAMERICA, LLLP
www.publishamerica.com
Baltimore

Printed in the United States of America

DEDICATION

*To my wife, Barb: your encouragement, love and acceptance of my
goals, have made this dream come true.
To my children, Jenny, Karen, Mary, Emily and Katie:
your example of making the most out of life has encouraged me to
do the same.
And to my stepchildren, Brian, Mickey and Colleen:
thank you for making me a part of your lives.*

This book is dedicated to all of you.

Dan D'Aurelio

PROLOGUE

It wasn't the answer he wanted to hear or needed to hear. Especially not tonight. He coasted down the hill, downshifting as he neared the red light at the bottom.

"Bye," she had mumbled as he headed toward the door. There had been minimal conversation before that.

No 'good luck' or 'hope you do good'. Nothing like that. God, how he hated her monosyllabic responses. He wanted to slam the door as he left, but didn't.

He turned left from Smith Road and quickly pushed the Beemer into second, third and then fourth gear. The speed limit was thirty-five. He pushed sixty very quickly.

The conversation, the all too frequent dialogue, played again in his mind.

"It wasn't always like this," he lamented to himself. "We talked a lot, not that long ago. But now she seems intent on keeping to herself. What's that all about?"

He negotiated a curve, tires hugging the road, softly squealing. He didn't care.

"I need to forget about her for now. I need to focus on the task at hand. God, why can't she just be more open with me? It's like she's playing some mind game of hide and seek. Like she's trying to hide something from me."

"I'm not a mind reader," he stated out loud to his steering wheel.

He glanced at the speedometer and decided to decelerate. It was suggested by the yellow sign that the next curve be negotiated at thirty miles per hour. He was slowing down to fifty.

The bicycle lay in the middle of the two lane highway just out of his vision. Its dazed rider sat next to the mangled bike.

Just around the bend.

He sped into the curve and had a decision to make. Swerving, he chose to negotiate the loose gravel on the berm.

A tree stopped him twenty feet off the road. He had nearly flown into it, hitting it six feet above the ground.

"Dammit, I'll be late for work," was his last thought.

CHAPTER 1

The whistle blew and Dante O'Shea did not get up.

"Dang it!" he yelled to no one in particular. He clutched his throbbing ankle. Little did he know that this foul by Daryl Varnell would dramatically alter the course of his life.

Attempting a twisting, turning layup, O'Shea was thrown to the floor of the Cleveland Coliseum by the overzealous Chicago defender. The Cleveland Musketeers' leading scorer writhed in pain. The capacity crowd stood in silent disbelief. The six-four guard was averaging thirty-one points, twelve assists, and seven rebounds throughout these NBA playoffs. The second year All-Star was Cleveland's future franchise and he would not finish this game, the seventh and final game of the National Basketball Association's Eastern Conference Finals.

Lisa O'Shea watched helplessly from her seat three rows behind the Cleveland bench. As two teammates helped her husband of two years off the court, tears of compassion flowed from her soft blue green eyes. She sat down and buried her face into her hands, hoping that Joey Riggs, the Cleveland trainer, could work a miracle with tape and painkiller, and get Dante back into the lineup. The sweat-drenched player slouched in pain on the bench. Thousands of eyes focused on him and the trainer.

John Avery, the Musketeers' coach for the past decade, called timeout. Riggs conferred with him for a brief moment and turned his attention back to Dante.

"This isn't good, Dante," Riggs informed him. "You need an x-ray. Let's get to the locker room."

"Keep me here 'til it's over," pleaded O'Shea. Riggs pursed his lips in thought. The short, plump trainer complied.

Robbie Dulik, a five year pro and Dante's backup at shooting guard, stripped off his warm up suit and advanced to the scorer's table to report into the game.

Bobby Hale, the Musks play-by-play announcer, summed up the situation for his radio audience.

"It appears that Dante O'Shea is done for this game. I don't know the extent of his injury, but judging by the reaction on the bench, I'd be surprised if Dante came back in. Joey Riggs is working on him, but it doesn't look good for the Musketeers."

"Robbie Dulik is replacing O'Shea. He will be shooting two foul shots. Let's see, he's an eighty-two percent foul shooter for the season, but has made eight of eleven during his limited time in the playoffs. Tonight, he's played two and a half minutes, all in the second quarter. He didn't score, but had one steal."

"Chicago is up by three, 103 to 100. There's one minute and eleven seconds to go in the game. The ref has handed the ball to Dulik. Here we go, folks."

The crowd groaned as Robbie Dulik's first foul shot hit the front of the rim and fell harmlessly to the floor. His second shot swished cleanly through the net. 1:11 remained in the game. Chicago by two.

Having won the last two NBA championships, the Chicago team was used to winning pressure games. Daryl Varnell, their latest superstar guard, calmly walked the ball up the court and across the time line at half court. Looking to his left, he deftly lofted a lob pass over the heads of the Musketeer defenders and into the waiting hands of Chicago's German-born seven-foot center. Hesitating a moment, the German vaulted his 285 pound frame into the air, and stuffed the ball through the hoop with malicious authority. The Cleveland crowd groaned with disgust and frustration. Fifty-seven seconds remained. Chicago now led by four, 105 to 101.

The Musks needed offense and they needed it now. Henry Pickett, their six-eleven power forward, saw Coach Avery signal to move the ball quickly. Taking the ball out of bounds, Henry Pickett threw a long pass ahead of the running Robbie Dulik. It hit the tip of his fingers and rolled harmlessly into the feet of a Chicago fan sitting in the courtside seats.

"You're gonna lose," shouted the obese supporter as Robbie Dulik retrieved the ball.

Swiping dark hair from his forehead, he gave the mouthy fan a look of disdain and vowed to himself to play the best he could the remainder of this game. Fifty seconds remained. Chicago still had a four-point lead.

Daryl Varnell, hounded furiously by Dulik, dribbled the ball up the court. He reached the top of the key with forty-one seconds left in the game. Dulik kept up his relentless defense, causing Varnell to lose his concentration for a brief moment. Henry Pickett, sensing confusion in Varnell's eyes, moved up quickly to double-team the Chicago point guard. Daryl Varnell did not see Henry advancing toward him as he bounced a pass to the center of the key. Pickett moved in front of the Chicago center for whom the pass was intended and snatched the ball as it caromed off the bounce. He dribbled the full length of the floor and dunked the ball for two quick points.

The frenzied crowd went wild as their beloved Musketeers closed the gap to two points. The red numbers on the scoreboard, mounted high above the center of the court, indicated thirty-one seconds to play.

Varnell once again worked the ball up court. Dulik stayed with him step for step, darting his hands back and forth, in and out, in an effort to disrupt the Chicago point guard's dribble. After crossing the center court line, Daryl Varnell called timeout. Twenty-two seconds remained on the game clock; fifteen seconds showed on the twenty-four second shot clock. Chicago's lead was two, 105 to 103.

"Defense!" implored Coach Avery. "Deny them access underneath. Stay in their face. No shots. And no fouls."

The Musketeers huddled together placing their hands, one on top of the other, in a show of team unity. Dante O'Shea was on his knees in the middle of it all, fire in his eyes, the will to win spirited to all of his teammates.

"Defense!" they shouted as one.

"DEFENSE! DEFENSE!" shouted twenty thousand loyal fans. Almost every seat was empty as each Cleveland fan stood and screamed in support of their team.

Inbounding the ball, Chicago's center patiently waited for his teammates to move from their assigned formation and get in the open. At the very last moment he bulleted a pass to Varnell as Daryl used a screen to lose his defender. Varnell had his back to the basket on the right side of the key. He was Chicago's go-to man in pressure situations and everyone expected him to work against the inexperienced Robbie Dulik and take a shot. He didn't.

After passing the ball in bounds, the German center stood at the sideline and looked for an open spot on the court. He saw that the right side of the baseline was not crowded with neither teammates nor defenders and dashed toward that area. Varnell smoothly bounced him a pass as he cut to the baseline. Henry Pickett saw the action and raced to help his beaten teammate. The wide body German received the pass and in one fluid motion shot the ball over the outstretched right hand of Pickett. The shot hit the side of the backboard and bounced into the row of Musketeer cheerleaders at the baseline. A whistle blew.

"Foul!" shouted veteran referee, Earl Seifert. "Number 31. He hit his arm. Two shots."

Henry Pickett felt it was a cheap call, he had barely touched him, but he held his cool.

Coach Avery called his final timeout. He did not want his players to lose their composure and play helter skelter offense in an effort to catch up. He looked down the bench at his star player and shook his head.

The Musketeer players joined their coach on the sideline as he instructed them on how he wanted the final fifteen seconds to be played.

Standing at the foul line, the Chicago center caressed the ball as he prepared for his two foul shots. The Cleveland crowd became more vocal, screaming louder and louder. Their booing sounded like a locomotive rushing through a tunnel. The fans sitting behind the Chicago basket waved their arms, signs, foam #1 hands, anything they had to distract the Chicago center.

His first shot banged off the back of the rim, as did his second. Henry Pickett scooped up the second miss and quickly got the ball into the hands of Robbie Dulik. Thirteen seconds remained as Robbie advanced the ball purposely up the court.

Coach Avery's instructions were simple. Work the ball to Henry Pickett or whoever might be open inside, and if that wasn't there, create a shot from outside. Simple to listen to, hard to do.

Robbie Dulik worked his way to the left side of the top of the key and waited as Pickett cut towards him for a pass. Henry moved gracefully through the center of the blue painted key and waited for the pass.

Robbie released a lob pass over the head of Daryl Varnell and into the hands of Pickett. Henry faked left, then right, then made a move to his left towards the basket. Six seconds remained as he started to make an arching left-handed hook shot.

Daryl Varnell, who had made the NBA's All Defensive Team four years running, reacted quickly to Robbie Dulik's pass and hustled over to double team Henry Pickett just as the Cleveland player started his shot. Seeing the ball being held only by Pickett's left hand and almost in his face, the Chicago guard swatted at it.

The ball caromed from the force of Varnell's swipe and hit the backside of a Chicago defender. It rolled toward the out-of-bounds line deep in the left corner of the court. Robbie Dulik scrambled toward the sideline and in one motion, scooped up the elusive ball, jumped, and while in mid-air, turned his body toward the basket. Squaring his shoulders as well as he could toward his target, he released his desperation shot.

The referee raised one arm to signal that the shot was a three-point attempt. Releasing the ball, Robbie snapped his wrist toward the basket, then the floor, in a perfect follow through of his shot. SWISH! The ball hit nothing but net. The referee raised his other arm, signaling a made three-point basket. The scoreboard read: Time remaining: 0:00. Cleveland 106, Chicago 105.

The crowd erupted. Bobby Hale went berserk on the air.

"The Musks WON! The Musks WON! The Musketeers are going to the Finals!" That's all that the excited veteran broadcaster shouted over and over to his radio audience.

The jubilant Cleveland crowd swarmed onto the floor, hugging strangers, players, even the referees. Except for one. Earl Seifert. He was too busy having an animated discussion with the official scorekeeper.

CHAPTER 2

In the exclusive loges high above the Coliseum basketball court, Paul Pallibio celebrated the victory with several of his cronies. Sipping champagne and gorging himself with yet another bite of stuffed shrimp, Pallibio and his guests discussed the outcome of the Musketeer victory and what it meant to them.

"When O'Shea went down, I thought it was over," commented one inebriated guest.

"It's about time some Cleveland team got lucky," added another. "It's been years since we've been in any kind of championship game. I hope we fare well in the Finals."

Benny Vetera, the only one in the crowd not happy with the outcome, stared at the dark-haired, slightly overweight owner of the prestigious loge. Benny swiped a hand through his slicked-back hair.

"Your lucky, Pauly," he stated. "I guess we're even."

Pallibio looked out the large loge window, down at the celebrating crowd, and thought to himself how much he had to lose if the Musks had lost. At halftime, when the score was tied at fifty-two, he had bet Benny double or nothing on an existing gambling debt. He owed the Chicago native $150,000 from a poker game four days earlier. But tonight he felt lucky. The night before, he hit four numbers on the lottery. It was only worth eighty dollars, but more importantly than the meager winnings, it meant his luck was changing.

"That's how luck is," he thought as he sipped more Dom Perignon. "Ride out the bad, because the good is right around the corner." Kind of a gambler's creed.

"Now," he continued to himself. "I can collect all my winnings, which he quickly calculated to be a hundred thousand dollars profit, and leave the country for a while."

No one in the lavishly furnished loge had any idea how close Paul Pallibio had come to losing it all. Because of his recent gambling misfortunes, he had to cash in on some investments, and had all but closed his savings accounts. And that hadn't even covered Benny Vetera's debt. At one time, he had almost three-quarters of a million dollars in the bank. But gambling and his extravagant style of living had been eating away at his ready cash. He needed this one big hit to get it going again.

"Thank God for Robbie Dulik," he said out loud to his friends.

All but Benny Vetera agreed. The diehard Chicago fan grew up in the rough neighborhood on Roosevelt Avenue. He learned his illegal trade as a kid, thirty-five years earlier, running numbers for the neighborhood mob. It was well known among the heavy hitters in the underworld, that a monetary debt to Benny Vetera had better be paid in seven days, his terms, or else. It was the 'or else' that scared the forty-eight year old Pallibio.

Earl Seifert had been raised to do the right thing. His father had died when Earl was fifteen years old. But he had instilled many values to his son, ever since Earl was old enough to understand.

When his father passed away, Earl dropped out of school to take care of his mother, sisters, and the farm his father had loved. It was the right thing to do.

In '68, he volunteered to serve his country in Vietnam. He came home with a Medal of Honor for saving the life of a fellow soldier. It had cost him part of his right hand, but it was the right thing to do.

In '75, he finished school and began his apprenticeship as a referee. Two decades later, he was one of the most respected refs in the game. He had a history of making the unpopular call in tough situations. Especially when he knew it was the right thing to do.

Earl had spoken to the head scorekeeper and was now conversing with each head coach and the two other referees. They stood near the scorer's table, out of earshot of most of the fans and players. Five minutes after the game, the meeting broke up.

"No way!" shouted the Musketeer floor announcer. "I'm not gonna make that announcement."

With a look of irritation, Earl Seifert grabbed the microphone from the quivering announcer's hand.

"May I have your attention, please?" he asked the celebrating fans. "May I please have your attention?" he shouted into the mike.

Earl continued his request until the Coliseum became as quiet as a wake. With everyone's attention focused on him, Earl firmly grasped the microphone and resolutely stared straight at the Cleveland crowd. It would have been easier to ignore what he had seen and just let things be. But this was the right thing to do.

"The last shot of the game has been disallowed," he calmly stated. "Time had clearly expired before the release of the ball. Chicago is the winner of the game."

Before the crowd totally absorbed what had just transpired, Earl and the other referees ran, with police escort, to their locker room.

"Folks," stated a beleaguered Bobby Hale to his listeners. "You are not going to believe this one."

Up in his private loge, a crestfallen Paul Pallibio sunk into an overstuffed leather chair. Benny Vetera leaned over, his thick mustache tickling Pallibio's ear.

"Three hundred thousand dollars, Pallibio," he whispered. "And I better have it in seven days. No more double or nothings. Seven days."

Paul Pallibio lost all color in his face. He was in trouble. Big trouble.

CHAPTER 3

Lisa Veronica Callahan worked at the bookstore on the campus of Ohio State University to help defray the cost of her education. She was the second of four children, all girls, and her father did not plan on any of his daughters attending college.

He had made a good living as an engineer working for General Electric in Cincinnati, but he enjoyed spending his money on their home, on the golf course, on extravagant family vacations, and in the corner pub, especially when his beloved Bengals played football on Sunday.

Lisa wanted to be a teacher ever since she could remember. She was in her third year at Ohio State when Dante O'Shea walked into her life. One look at the tall, blonde, muscular athlete and Lisa knew her life would never be the same.

Dante had gone to the bookstore late one evening to purchase a book he needed for his Philosophy course. Not being able to find the exact book he wanted, he asked Lisa for her assistance.

It was her soft, blue green eyes he had noticed first. Her naturally curly dark brown hair outlined the soft features of her face. But it was the eyes that attracted him. In them, Dante saw a determined person who was caring and compassionate. He was not wrong.

Lisa and Dante saw each other often during the next year and a half. They were often seen at campus functions, working out at the campus recreation facility, in the library studying together, in the campus chapel on Sundays. They were inseparable and knew that once their college days were over, they would marry.

After they had both graduated, they were married at the chapel on the campus and, two months later; Dante was drafted in the first round by the Cleveland Musketeers.

Dante emerged as one of the top players in the league in his second year as an NBA player. In his first year, he was the Rookie of the Year. Good management on the part of the Musketeer organization surrounded Dante with the winning combination of seasoned NBA veterans and second and third year players. The veterans fed off the exuberance of the younger players and the newer members of the team looked at the veterans for guidance on and off the court. During this season, a chemistry had developed among the players, a winning chemistry, and the dismal seasons the Musks had been having, were replaced with the hope that a championship caliber team was in the making. Possibly this year.

Cleveland seemed to be the league's bridesmaid, never the bride. When things were going well for the franchise, it appeared that somehow, something would happen to alter their course for success. There were unexplainable and untimely injuries and, more often than not, seemingly inept officiating. Considering the history of sports in Cleveland, it was no major surprise to Dante O'Shea that Earl Seifert made the call that he did.

Dante grew up in Akron, Ohio, twenty miles from the Coliseum where he now made his living. He was an avid Musketeer fan as a kid, and he loved the Browns, Cleveland's professional football team. He had a season ticket in the fanatic Dawg Pound for as long as he could remember. And after the basketball season was over, unfortunately, usually quite early for the Musks, he loved to watch the Indians play baseball. Of all the players on the team, Dante understood more than anyone how important a championship would be to the fans of northeastern Ohio. To him, the NBA championship wasn't just bragging rights, or a ring on his finger, or more money, or a trophy or two. It was a quest, not only for him, but also for the hungry and zealous fans that paid good money, year after year, to see their Musketeers play basketball.

Like most of the stars of the game, Dante would go out of his way to sign an autograph, or talk to the fans, or be involved in giving to the community. In the malls around Akron, Canton and Cleveland, he would shop and stop, always responding to the needs of the fans. He realized that as much as he liked the attention, the fans needed to know that they were important to him and to the team. They wanted his attention, too.

It had been a two year love affair for Dante. But for Lisa, it was harder. Even though she was his wife and she wanted to be supportive, she sometimes felt that she got in the way. When they came around in droves, which they did often, Lisa would eventually loosen her arm from Dante's and wander off to another store. It was never hard to find Dante, she just looked for the crowd.

Fans sometimes came to their home in Fairlawn, an Akron suburb. Dante always catered to them, but Lisa was becoming more and more concerned about his safety. She asked him more than once to ignore the people who had wandered up to their home in search of autographs, or worse yet, souvenirs from their yard. But Dante felt an obligation to the fans, always the fans.

Being an NBA player's wife was not as glamorous as it seemed. Sure, there were the trips with the team to New York, L.A., Orlando, Phoenix, a nice change from the winters in northern Ohio. But after a couple of years, even those trips became cumbersome. A night here, a night there. Hotel rooms. Late suppers, usually after the game. Lisa stayed home more and more. Unlike her husband, she didn't like the attention. She wanted a normal home life. She wanted to raise a family and do all the ordinary things that made a house a home.

"What I need is a child, no, three children," Lisa lamented to herself. "I wish I didn't have such a problem getting pregnant."

She knew in her heart that Dante wouldn't always be playing basketball, that they would have a real life some day, and although she enjoyed what Dante did, because he enjoyed it so much, she still wanted to settle down and start a family. If they ever could.

Lisa had other issues with her husband, some things he should know about, but were hard for her to bring up. Not fond memories. From not so long ago.

It had been three days since "The Call" as it was now known all over America.

"It just isn't fair," Lisa said to her husband. "I mean you guys had won the game. How could he make that call five minutes after the game was over?"

"He made the right call, Lisa," Dante calmly stated. "Believe me, I hated the call, but all the replays I've seen on ESPN proved that Earl made the right decision."

"You know, Coach Avery and the team talked about it afterwards," he continued. "We all felt cheated at first, but after seeing the replays, well, Robbie just didn't get the shot off in time. It wasn't his fault, we just ran out of time. We shouldn't have gotten into the position of having to make a desperation shot. It happens."

Dante was positioning his right foot on the pedal of his exercise bike. He wore a cast, the injury turned out to be a minor fracture. He would heal, but it would take a few weeks in the cumbersome cast. Being a workout junkie, he had outfitted the basement of their home with more exercise equipment than most health spas.

The team doctor, Doctor Ernest Kavalecz, had told him how lucky he was that he only had a minor fracture. After seeing on the replays how he had landed on his foot, Dante felt fortunate that he would be in a cast for only six to eight weeks.

"I just wished the Musketeers had won," Lisa lamented.

"We'll be there next year," promised Dante.

His wife gave him a reassuring kiss, long and tender, and announced that she was going shopping.

"Don't forget the game tonight," Dante reminded her. "We're supposed to meet the Dulik's at the Indians game at seven.

"Great," thought Lisa to herself. "More fans."

"I'll be home at six," she stated. She left her husband trying to maneuver the huge cast on the small bicycle pedal.

"See ya, hon," he said to a closing door.

CHAPTER 4

The Warehouse Bar and Grille rocked with the sound of loud music and inebriated patrons. The former steel warehouse had been converted to its present format as part of the renovation of downtown Cleveland. Located on the banks of the Cuyahoga River to the west and Lake Erie to the north, the Warehouse Bar and Grille was a natural meeting place for the many blue collar and office workers that lived in the area.

Out on the wooden deck overlooking the river sat twenty-three year old Eddie Burson, his younger brother Vince, and their large friend, Carl Plath. A pyramid of empty beer cans stood in the center of the table like a monument to their friendship. Eddie and his twenty-one year old brother had met "Big Carl" in high school six years earlier. Since they were not large in stature, the Burson brothers used Carl to bail them out of fights, which the hotheaded Vince Burson usually started. Especially when he drank. Carl Plath was not known for his intellect and accepted the conditions of their friendship without question.

"We got screwed," exclaimed Vince for the umpteenth time since 'the Call'. "I don't care what the replays show, we won that game. If I see some idiot with a Chicago shirt on, I'll kick his ass."

Eddie Burson agreed but kept his mouth shut. He realized that his younger brother was always trying to prove his manliness to him. Usually by getting drunk, loud, and into fights. Eddie had been an outstanding athlete in high school and Vince seemed to always be trying to impress him. It was better not to bait his younger brother into yet another fight.

Eddie had good potential in football, even had a scholarship offered to him by Kent State. But he got his girlfriend pregnant, ended up marrying her when he was eighteen, divorced her two years later, and now just scrapped around doing odd jobs to pay his share of living expenses and child support. He, Vince and Carl shared an old house on East Fortieth Street.

Vince Burson had decided early that school wasn't for him. He dropped out when he was seventeen, joined the Navy for two years, and returned to civilian life eighteen months ago. He had been a hospital corpsman in the Navy and used what he had learned to get a job at the Cleveland Clinic. His life was a contrast. By day, he was a caring aide, helping the nurses and patients, giving sponge baths, running errands, helping out. At night time, he drank much beer, vulgarly mouthed off to anyone who crossed his path, picked fights, and usually woke up with a hangover.

The Burson brothers, in their own fashion, cared for each other. Being the same size, which was not big, they shared the same features. Pug nose, brown eyes, the same short hair. They were often mistaken for twins, even with their age difference. Temperament was one thing they did not have in common. Eddie was cool and levelheaded, somewhat a leader. Vince was just the opposite. Especially when he consumed alcohol. He became mean and vulgar. His temper was well known in his Cleveland hangouts.

Carl Plath, Big Carl, was huge. His six foot ten inch frame supported three hundred and twenty pounds. When he was in school, the football coaches tried to make a player out of him. Carl had neither the desire nor the ability to play the game. He suffered from dyslexia, which was not discovered until he somehow graduated from high school at age twenty. Big, dumb Carl was what most people called him, except Eddie and Vince. When they offered him their friendship, although he didn't understand their motive, he accepted it wholeheartedly. He protected his friends when they needed it, and contributed more than his share to the needs of the house he shared with them. He didn't mind. They were his buddies. Carl became a machinist when he got out of high school. He was proud that he was able to run a big Cincinnati CNC Machining Center. He was not unhappy with his life.

"When's Pallibio coming?" asked Vince. He guzzled his seventh can of beer and added it to the pyramid.

"Any time," replied Eddie.

"I don't understand why he wants to meet us," Vince stated.

"He just told me he had an opportunity he wanted to throw at us," explained Eddie for the third time. "Probably some odd jobs around his house or something."

"I hope he comes soon," slurred Carl. "I gotta get up early for work."

"We all do...Carl," Vince declared. He wanted to call Carl something else, but refrained. Since Carl's dad yelled at him out a lot, Carl didn't like being called names or cussed at. That was something that could upset him.

Twenty minutes and two more beers later, Paul Pallibio ambled up to the table and joined the threesome. He looked out of place with the trio, dressed in tan pressed pants and a blue golf shirt with the colorful shark emblem displayed on the left breast. Greg Norman, the PGA's "Shark" was his favorite golfer, and Pallibio bought anything he could find with the logo. Even his vanity license plates declared to other drivers, in big blue letters, the word "SHARK". To Paul Pallibio, it also epitomized how he led his life, the sharp businessman, able and willing to make tough decisions, especially if it meant making more money.

And he had made a tough decision. Now he had to put it into action.

CHAPTER 5

The Cleveland Indians had not won a championship since 1948. Even then, a questionable call by an umpire on a foul ball dictated the outcome of the game. Cleveland was in a one game playoff with Boston, who had tied them for first place during the regular season. A ninth inning hit down the right field foul line was ruled a home run by the first base umpire. Others saw it as a foul ball, but his decision reigned, and Cleveland won the game. They went on to win the World Championship. As a punishment to the franchise and the city, it would be the last championship for any Cleveland team for decades.

Their new home at Jacobs Field catered to the fans of baseball. Smaller by far than the ancient stadium they had shared for years with the Browns, Jacobs Field offered uninterrupted views, modern restroom facilities, souvenir shops, many off-the-field activities, and the feeling of closeness between the fans and the players.

Dante, Lisa, Robbie Dulik and his wife, Alise, sat in the box seats behind the Indians dugout. When they were recognized, fans asked for and received autographs. Lisa noticed that they weren't hounded like they normally were.

"Maybe the fans feel sorry for Dante because of his broken ankle," she thought. "Or maybe they're just finally leaving him alone."

Actually, the fans felt like they were at a wake when they saw a Musketeer player. They wanted to say something consoling, but didn't know how to approach the subject. Their real feelings were left unsaid.

The Indians were struggling to stay above the five hundred mark, again. But they had an exciting young team to watch. With Rodriguez and McCurdy and the new kid, Tommy Benner, they were a team that never quit. They were trailing this game 1 to 0 in the bottom of the ninth.

The ageless McCurdy, worked his way on base via a walk. Benner strode to the plate and promptly lifted a fly ball to deep center, but it was caught. With two outs, Jesus Rodriguez advanced to the plate and got down in the count with two quick called strikes.

The next pitch, a hanging curve, never reached the catcher's glove. Instead, Rodriguez parked it four hundred and twenty feet into the second deck of right field.

The thirty five thousand fans continued to call for "HAY SUS! HAY SUS" even as the grounds crew covered the infield. It was almost a religious experience.

"This is what it's all about, Robbie," Dante shouted to his friend and back up. "Just listen to these people, they love this."

Robbie Dulik grew up in San Diego and had been a diehard Padres fan. But this Indians team had grown on him and he hollered for Jesus Rodriguez with the rest of the fans.

"You gotta make the fans believe in you," stated the Musketeer All-Star. "Then they'll back you and support you no matter what you do. Good times and bad times."

"Thanks, O Great One," Robbie joked. But he knew his teammate wanted him to appreciate the people of this area as much as Dante did. They had been through so much, not only sports wise, but economically, and even nationally, as the butt of many jokes.

The crowd swarmed out of the stadium still buzzing about Rodriguez's timely home run. Dante and Lisa made a half-hearted offer to the Dulik's to join them at their home, but Robbie and Alise declined.

"Since my parents are flying in from California tomorrow," Alise explained. "We have to get up early to make sure everything's ready. Don't forget, you two are coming over tomorrow night. Remember? Dante's gourmet pizza?"

"That's right," Lisa replied.

She wanted to get Dante alone anyway to discuss another matter. He seemed to be more open to suggestions after a sporting event, especially when his team won.

"I'll call you in the morning, or call me if you need any help, ok?"

The Duliks got into their white Jeep Cherokee and the O'Shea's dodged cars and people to find their dark green BMW. It wasn't exactly a walk in the park for Dante. But he seemed to have mastered the crutches and the extra weight on his right foot.

Lisa maneuvered the Beemer into an outgoing lane and waited patiently with other drivers as Cleveland's Finest directed traffic.

"You know, Dante," she started. "I see the doctor tomorrow for another exam. She may want you to come in for some tests, too. Would you be ok with that?"

"I've heard about those tests, Lisa, and well, to tell you the truth, having my sperm tested isn't a big deal. It's just how they get it that gets me."

"C'mon, honey, it can't be all that bad."

"Well, it's kind of demeaning to me," he stated. "Let's see what tomorrow brings, all right?"

"But if the doctor said it would help, you would do it, wouldn't you?"

Dante didn't answer. He knew that Lisa wanted to have a child more than anything. He wasn't convinced that there were any physical problems with her, or him. And he really didn't want to have to go get tested. He's not sure where that fear came from, but he didn't want to have to deal with it unless he really had to.

"Getting pregnant is a natural thing," he thought. "It shouldn't have to be turned into some clinical medical thing."

His lack of emotional support hurt Lisa. But she didn't let those feelings show. She had become good at disguising her real thoughts and emotions. Sometimes too good for their relationship.

The dark green BMW pulled into their paved driveway an hour later. Although the automatic garage door opener hadn't worked all week, Lisa pushed the button of the remote control affixed to the visor.

As it had all week, the door remained closed. Lisa was getting in the habit of leaving the door open when she left to run errands. Dante wanted to say something, but thought better of it. Especially since she had actually closed it this time.

"I'll get the door," he offered.

"Is it ok for me to call a repairman?" his wife asked. "I know you can fix it, but it probably wouldn't be too wonderful to do in a cast, on a ladder and all. I'll call one tomorrow."

"No problem-o," mumbled Dante as he maneuvered out of the car and pulled up the white aluminum door. He didn't like others doing what he should, or could, but she was right. Why chance an accident and really screw up his foot?

"What time's your appointment tomorrow?" he inquired.

"I couldn't get in until 4:30."

"I'll get the pizza dough done by the time you get home" countered Dante. "You know how I pride myself on my secret formula."

"I wish you'd pay as much attention to my needs," thought his wife.

The words never came out and another brick of spite was added to the wall.

CHAPTER 6

Pallibio Machine Shop opened its doors in 1942. Vince Pallibio and his immigrant father, Pasquale, started the machine shop and it quickly flourished, regarded by the Defense Department as one of the better manufacturers of tank parts, jeep parts, and other war supplies. During the war years, Pallibio Machine ran three shifts.

Pasquale Pallibio had become a successful grocer his first ten years in America. When it became apparent that his two sons, Vincent and Anthony, were not interested in the grocery business, he fronted the twenty thousand dollars needed to buy a building and some machinery. The banks took care of the rest. With his proven business mind, Pasquale helped make Pallibio Machine successful.

The building they purchased was located on the East Side of Cleveland, on East Fortieth Street. It stretched from the street eighty feet back, where twenty feet of open area separated it from an adjacent building that was currently being used as a warehouse for frozen foods. The two-story building was a natural for a machine shop. The downstairs had a wooden floor that was well oiled for preservation. It had ample room for lathes, milling machines, and secondary operation machines, such as surface grinders and drill presses. The upstairs had a large open area that was used for the office workers. It easily had room for twenty or more desks. Toward the back of the building on the second floor were three fifteen foot square offices with windows that faced the larger room. A bathroom had been added by the Pallibio's in the corner of the large office near the three executive offices.

Vincent and his father settled into two of the offices. Anthony, the younger of the two sons, would have occupied the third office, but instead went off to serve his country with the army in Europe. He never came back. His death was a blow to the widowed Pasquale, and he, too, succumbed to death from pneumonia in 1945.

Vincent continued the company as best he could without his father's sharp business mind. Vincent was a talented machinist, not a businessman, but he learned. In 1969, he brought his only child, Paul, into the business. Paul Pallibio had been weaned on the machining business since he was seven years old. He did not desire to go to college. He did not desire to protest or become involved with the Vietnam War. Nor, because of his father's influence with the local politicians, did he worry about being drafted into the army. Paul wanted to make money. Lots and lots of money. His father's machine shop was his financial salvation. Like a sponge in water, Paul absorbed all that his father could teach him about machining and running a business. Through the years, Paul and his father had surrounded themselves with talented machinists and office personnel. With the successful machine shop providing him quite well, Paul Pallibio became used to a lavish lifestyle.

When Vincent Pallibio died of cancer in 1979, Paul was more than able to continue the business. He eventually expanded its machining capabilities more and more into the automotive area, manufacturing parts for General Motors, the Ford Motor Company, and the Honda plant in southern Ohio.

One of the curious aspects of Pallibio Machine Shop was the tunnels. The building had been erected in1918 and was used for storing parts for the new Model T's that Henry Ford was manufacturing en masse in Dearborn, Michigan. It was suspected back then, that the warehouse was a front, and that the building was also being used to store illegal products, such as whiskey, rum and beer.

The reason for this rumor was that the tunnels led to several houses in the area. It was not uncommon, when the warning of an unwanted visit by the local authorities was to take place, that the illegal inventory was hastily relocated through the tunnels and into the basements of several houses across the street. Many times, the warehouse 'employees' would sit on the porches of the houses, not a hundred feet away, and watch the cops enter the warehouse and find it empty, excepting for automotive parts.

Paul Pallibio knew of the tunnels. His father and grandfather had boarded up or filled them in shortly after buying the property. Paul remembered how he had once removed a decaying board and, with flashlight in hand, discovered where that particular tunnel had led. It was to the house directly across the street. The house he now owned and rented to the Burson brothers and their friend, Big Carl Plath.

CHAPTER 7

As Dante and Lisa were sleeping in the master bedroom of their sprawling home in Fairlawn, Paul Pallibio was concluding his meeting with Eddie, Vince, and Carl.

"Do you boys know how much a million dollars is?" he asked. "You could live anywhere in the world, have whatever you want, all the beer you could drink, a different woman every night of the year."

He didn't wait for their reply. Their alcohol enhanced faces brightened at the prospect of living the good life.

"Even with conservative investments, you could live well and never touch most of the million," he whispered. "Think about it. And all you have to do is follow my plan. One week from now, you could all be millionaires."

Paul paused and studied their reactions.

Vince looked at Eddie and Carl. After consuming ten beers, the easy life sounded real good to him. He nodded toward his brother.

"Whaddaya think?" he slurred.

Eddie was usually levelheaded and his brother depended on him to make the big decisions. He was the one who convinced Carl and Vince that they could afford to rent the house. He was the one who usually declared where they would go each night. Eddie was the leader. Paul Pallibio sensed this and showed his last card, his ace in the hole.

"Here's the key to my Lexus. It's parked across the street under the light. Before you make a decision, I want you to drive my car. Because next week you could have one just like it. Or better," he added with a wink.

Eddie looked at his brother. Then Carl. These guys would follow him into hell if he led them. He knew that. Pallibio's plan seemed faultless. He could see no way they would get caught.

"A million bucks," he thought. "No more lottery tickets. Hell, no more crappy jobs."

Carl sat glassy-eyed and tried to comprehend all that he had just heard. He understood his role in the plan and that in a week he could be in Europe or Australia or someplace he really didn't want to be. But if his buddies said they would do it, he would be there, too. Real friends stuck together. And he was a real friend to the Burson brothers.

"I'll leave my key right here," stated Pallibio as he laid the Lexus key at the base of the beer can pyramid. "I'll come back here tomorrow morning. If the car is gone, I'll know you're in. If it's here, I'll know you're not interested. You ok to drive, son?" he asked Eddie.

Eddie nodded.

"If you decide to join me, the supplies you'll need are in the trunk. A million dollars for one week of work, boys. It doesn't get any easier than that."

Paul Pallibio rose from his seat. Dusting potato chip crumbs from his lap, he turned abruptly and walked confidently from the deck to the bar where he eyed a redheaded beauty.

Deciding against involving himself with yet another stranger, Pallibio went outside and seated himself into a waiting cab.

"I'm going to Shaker Heights," he told the driver.

"That'll be about thirty dollars," the cabby informed him.

"Drive, my man, drive," he instructed with a smug smile on his face.

In the Terminal Tower in downtown Cleveland, a meeting was taking place at the Federal Building. It involved Special Agent James Sweeney, his partner, Special Agent Len Gill, and two employees of the Internal Revenue Service.

Their discussion involved one Mr. Paul Pallibio.

CHAPTER 8

"So you're telling me that this clown hasn't paid any taxes for three years," started Special Agent Sweeney. "And you're just now getting around to auditing him?"

Lillian Chamberlain stared at the tall FBI agent and bit her tongue. She pushed aside a stray strand of auburn hair that had fallen into her eyes.

"If these guys would listen once in a while," she said to herself.

"No, what I am saying, what we are saying," she continued, nodding to her partner. "We had sent Mr. Pallibio notices and he ignored them. His accountant was supposed to be working with us, and we got the "check's in the mail" routine, every time we contacted her. When that happens too many times, we pay a visit. We went to Mr. Pallibio's home. He has a lavishly landscaped yard, a brand new Lexus in the driveway, what appeared to be a classic Corvette in the garage, and," she hesitated.

Sweeney cut her off.

"I don't understand you people," he stated harshly. "Millions of Americans are struggling to make ends meet and you wait three years to collect taxes from some deadbeat who thinks he's above the system."

"Listen, Mr. Sweeney," interjected the IRS employee. "There are thousands of people just like Pallibio. They skirt the system, take chances on questionable write-offs, and if they get caught, they pay. If not, they laugh all the way to the bank."

"Ok, ok, I'm sorry. I guess twenty years of catching criminals, or at least trying, has made me a little cynical of the system I'm trying to protect." Sweeney shifted his weight in the leather chair. "Please continue with what you saw."

"When we were at the house, which was a couple days ago, we spotted Mr. Pallibio on the phone in what appeared to be a heated argument," she explained.

"And before I even knocked on the door, he slammed the receiver down, and before I knew it, he was in the Lexus speeding down the street," added the second IRS agent.

"Didn't he see you?" asked Special Agent Gill.

"Apparently not," Lillian Chamberlain responded "He was definitely in a big hurry when he left."

"You say he was in his house when you saw him?" Len Gill queried.

"Yea, he was in what I guess was the living room," came the reply. "We kind of scout things out before we announce our arrival."

"Where was your car?" asked Sweeney.

"I parked down the street," Lillian Chamberlain replied. "It's the policy in these situations. With government plates, we don't pull into the client's driveway. It saves them potential embarrassment and also doesn't warn them we're coming."

"Sounds like us," joked Sweeney half-heartedly.

The two FBI agents and two IRS employees laughed at Sweeney's attempt at humor.

"There are some other interesting facts about Mr. Pallibio," stated Lillian Chamberlain. "When he owned his company, Pallibio Machine, he reported income of less than fifty thousand a year. We believe he made more in the area of half a million a year."

"That's not uncommon," pointed out the other agent. "With all the loopholes in the system, a good accountant, or at least a creative accountant, can make some of these owners qualify for food stamps."

"But, in Mr. Pallibio's case," continued Lillian. "He was called in for not reporting sales of scrap metals. We believe he made more than a million dollars through the last several years that his shop was in business, just from scrap. And he never reported it as income. When all was said and done, he paid a mere pittance in back taxes and penalties compared to what he made."

"So you're saying the guy is capable of being dishonest," added Gill.

"I guess everybody is," Lillian retorted. "But when you look at the complete picture, something isn't right."

Lillian's partner lit a cigarette, then quickly snuffed it out as he noticed the "No Smoking" sign on the wall behind Jim Sweeney's desk. Sweeney had added a rough drawing of a hanging man and the words, 'smoke and die', below it.

"The guy makes big money for many years, he squanders it on wine, women and song, or actually, on cars, a lavish home, and gambling. It's no big secret in Cleveland who his friends are and what their habits are. He closed his company three years ago. Yet he continues to live as if he still made three hundred G's a year. Something's not right."

Lillian had laid out all of her ideas and waited for the FBI's reply.

"That's why we're involving you," she added.

"It does seem suspicious," concluded Jim Sweeney. "I suppose he could be into drugs or something like that. Does he still own the building where he had the machine shop?"

"Sure does," Lillian quickly replied. "But it's empty, he's not leasing it or using it."

Standing up, Special Agent Sweeney said, "Well, I agree that Mr. Pallibio might be up to no good. We appreciate your input and Mr. Gill and I will take it from here."

Lillian Chamberlain and her partner smiled at each other and stood up. They had done their job, satisfied that they may have helped cure at least one of the evils of society.

"Do you need us to do anything else?" asked Lillian as she put on her blue lightweight jacket.

"We'll let you know if you can," concluded James Sweeney.

He escorted the two Internal Revenue Service employees to his office door. As soon as they left, he turned to Len Gill.

"Lenny, do we have a surveillance van available for tomorrow morning?" he inquired.

"I'm sure we do, but I'll double check."

"I think we might have something on this guy, Len," continued Sweeney. "This morning I got a call from Bill Fitzsimmons. He told me that one of his informers had told him that a lot of money was lost by some of the big hitters in town when the Musketeers lost the championship game. Big money, too. The informer wouldn't name names, but he told Bill that one guy had lost almost a half million. And the word on the street, according to Fitzsimmons, is that the guy didn't have the bets covered."

"You think it could be Pallibio?" asked Gill.

"It's worth checking out," Sweeney retorted. "We know he gambles with the big boys, he has no apparent income, and the IRS is on him. The boy's in trouble and may do something crazy. Especially if he's in debt to the wrong people."

"I'll requisition the van," stated Len Gill.

"Let's set up for six A.M.," ordered Agent Sweeney. "I'll bring the donuts."

After Len Gill left his office, Special Agent James Sweeney made a call to the Los Angeles FBI office.

"Special Agent Menegay speaking."

"Bill? Jim Sweeney here. Hey Bill, how'd you like to come to Cleveland?"

"You a mind reader?" retorted the LA agent. "Susan and I are catching a flight to come see my daughter tomorrow morning."

After a brief conversation, one that changed the plans of Agent Menegay's visit to his daughter, Alise and her husband Robbie Dulik, Special Agent James Sweeney sat at his desk, opened the top drawer, and pulled out a cigarette.

Ignoring the sign on the wall, he lit up.

CHAPTER 9

Early Wednesday morning, Paul Pallibio drove his second car, the rarely used '67 Corvette, downtown to the Warehouse Bar and Grille. His Lexus was gone. He smiled, turned around in the parking lot and drove home.

Eddie Burson woke up and lay in bed. He thought for a long moment before noticing the Lexus key on his night table. He realized that he and Vince and Carl had made a decision that would change their lives forever. One did not go back on his word, especially to someone like Paul Pallibio.

Eddie had no doubts that the plan could work. It seemed to have been well thought out by Pallibio and whoever else was involved.

As instructed, he stayed around the house. Vince had gone to his job at the Clinic, and Carl had left early to go run his machine. Neither has said anything to Eddie to make him think they shouldn't do this.

He was brushing his teeth, trying to remove the cotton ball taste from his mouth from the previous night's drinking episode, when the phone rang.

"Burson," he simply stated into the mouthpiece.

"Eddie? Pallibio here," came the reply. "I see you took my car. Everything's a go, right?"

"Yeah, right," Eddie numbly replied.

"We move in three days, on Saturday, ok?" asked an excited Pallibio.

"We'll be ready," sighed Eddie Burson reluctantly.

"You guys are going to be rich, Eddie, understand? RICH! No more bosses or rented houses. No more hassles."

"Whatever you say, Mr. Pallibio."

"You do understand, Eddie, there's no turning back, don't you? I mean, we're in this together, we're a team."

"I, uh, I mean, we all understand that, Mr. Pallibio. We'll hold up our end. You do your job and we'll all be happy."

Eddie wanted to believe what he had just said.

"Good, Eddie, good. I'm going on a trip for a couple of days. I'll call you Friday to go over last minute details. We should meet at the shop. I want to see what you did with the place when I get back. And, Eddie, don't forget to use the tunnel, ok?"

"Ok," Eddie mumbled.

He hung up the phone and wandered out the front door of the yellow rented house. He walked a block and a half to a corner bar on East Fortieth and Saint Clair Avenue. He needed a pre-noon drink. A stiff one.

Paul Pallibio grabbed his suitcase, his passport, and a gym bag that contained a tape recorder and several blank cassette tapes. He had three hours before his flight to Rome, Italy. Once there, he would continue to fill in the details for the job.

After making sure the house was secure, Pallibio threw his baggage into the trunk of his beloved 'Vette. He slowly eased it out of the driveway and down the street. He had passed, but not really noticed, a white van with 'Cleveland Cable Company' emblazoned in large blue letters on its side. The occupants of the van had certainly noticed him.

Lisa O'Shea finished her third cup of coffee that morning and found Dante in the den watching replays of the championship game.

"Reliving old horror stories?" she queried.

"No, actually, I'm planning new ones for Chicago," he replied. "I want to know everything about them for next year. So I am going to study these tapes 'til I know their moves and tendencies better than they do."

"You're unbelievable," Lisa told her husband. "Do the other players work this hard at the game?"

37

"I hope so," he replied.

"Well, I'll let you work in peace. I'm going to the Dulik's to help Alise make some appetizers for her dinner with her parents tonight. My doctor appointment is at 4:30, I should be home at six o'clock.

"I'll have everything ready to go for tonight," he promised

"Thanks, hon," she acknowledged. "Oh, by the way, I called the repairman for the garage door, and he can't make it until next week. Ok?"

"Ok," he muttered as he watched Daryl Varnell make a steal against him on the television set.

Lisa O'Shea backed the BMW out of the garage and down the drive. Down the street she remembered that she hadn't closed the garage door. Again. Ignoring it, she sped off to the Dulik's.

CHAPTER 10

Paul Pallibio sat in the first class section of the Boeing 747 and immediately took his tape recorder out of the gym bag, inserted a blank tape, and began recording. Throughout the seven-hour flight, he recorded the various sounds of the flight as he flew from Cleveland to Rome.

He read a little, slept a little, but was always careful not to speak when the recorder was on. After filling two ninety-minute tapes with the sounds of jet engines, murmured conversation, snoring, flight attendants serving meals and drinks, and announcements from the captain of the flight, Pallibio was satisfied.

Sitting back in the leather seat, he stared out of the small rectangular window at the clouds. He started thinking about his life and how he had it planned out and how it had actually gone. Back in the seventies, with his dad there to oversee the machine shop and make sure he didn't make too many mistakes, life was much simpler, much more safe. He remembered how he couldn't wait for the old man to retire so he could run the company his way, a little more progressive, and a lot more profitable. But after his father's death in '79, he realized that maybe he wasn't as ready as he had thought.

He trusted his dad's decisions and advice, but never learned to trust outsiders. In the early eighties, when America was in one of its worst recessions, he did not listen to his accountant or his banker. He continued to spend his money lavishly on cars, trips, and big boy toys. And gambling.

"That's been my downfall," he deduced in an honest moment of self analysis.

The gambling started with friendly poker games on Saturday nights. Pretty soon the five-dollar antes became fifty dollars, then a hundred. Paul had lost tens of thousands of dollars in a night, several times each year. Added to that was his obsession with betting on sporting events. Sometimes he won, won big. Twenty thousand here, fifty thousand there. But most times he lost. Just as big.

Pallibio Machine had helped to sustain his habit for years, but in 1991, when some of his customers quit subcontracting work to his shop for various reasons, Paul closed the doors of Pallibio Machine for good. At that time, after selling the machinery, the various cutting tools and machinery supplies at an auction, he ended up with close to three quarters of a million dollars in the bank. But investments didn't pan out, his gambling continued, and his extravagant spending wasn't curtailed. The result was that he was cash poor. He still had assets with the building and some rental properties, but it did not make for the ready cash that he needed to offset his imminent debts. That was why he desperately put everything on the line in the championship game just five days ago.

Now, not only did he not have much cash, but he was in debt to his cronies whose backgrounds and job descriptions he didn't want to acknowledge. Plus his accountant had told him that he was again getting many calls from the IRS.

His debt to his 'friends' was nearly five hundred thousand dollars. He figured the IRS was a couple hundred grand. The IRS he could handle. The others, he feared. He needed money, much money, and soon. Before he got another reminder, like the call from Benny Vetera's 'banker' earlier this week, he had to take care of the situation. Get control.

"I'll get them their money," he mumbled to himself. "Or die trying."

He arrived in Rome in the early evening, rented a car, and drove to his hotel on the Via Della Conciliazone. He passed the familiar sites on his way: the Aurelian Wall, the Colosseum, and Arch of Constantine, and the Spanish Steps. He had seen most of this city many times. His father, Vincent, had made this very trip with him half a dozen times, before the Vietnam War had influenced their decision not to travel abroad.

"Americans weren't very popular back then," he remembered.

But he came back to Rome after his father's death at least twice a year, using it as a base for other European destinations.

Crossing the Tiber River, Pallibio looked for the cobblestone street where his hotel was located. He turned left, carefully, the Italians were not the most courteous drivers in the world, and parked his rented Fiat in front of the hotel door.

"Mr. Pallibio, we've been expecting you," greeted the voluptuous Georgina from behind the check-in desk. "Was your flight satisfactory?"

"Si. Wonderful," he tiredly replied. "Will I be in my usual suite?"

"Of course, of course," she answered with a forced smile. "Antonio will carry your luggage for you."

"Grazie, grazie," he replied.

He followed the slow moving Antonio to the ancient elevator and continued in silence until he got to his room.

Handing the elderly bellboy a twenty-dollar bill, he demanded he not be disturbed.

"I want no room service, no cleaning ladies, nothing. Capisci?"

Antonio nodded and shuffled away.

"Crazy Americans," he thought. He stuffed the twenty into his pocket. Pallibio would not be disturbed.

Once he was alone, Paul opened a window that faced the noisy street below. He placed the tape recorder on the sill and installed another blank tape. He pushed the pause button, then depressed the record and play buttons. He checked the time on his travel alarm clock, 9:30 P.M. He pushed the pause button once more and watched satisfactorily as the machine began to whir. He quietly walked to the bed, set the alarm for eleven o'clock and lay down. In his ear he placed a small earpiece so that when the alarm went off, only he would hear it, and not the tape recorder.

41

"Glad I took that electronics course in high school," he thought. Then dozed off.

At eleven o'clock, he awoke to the dull buzzing in his ear, sleepily walked to the window, shut off the recorder, replaced the cassette tape that was now filled with an hour and a half of Roman street noises, and began the recording process all over again.

He did this every hour and a half throughout the night. At seven-thirty in the morning, he awoke for the day. He now had six cassette tapes full of the surprisingly active city. Many nights he had laid in this very room and listened to street vendors, motorbikes, children running and laughing, cars squealing around the circle where Michelangelo stood, and the funny sounding sirens. Rome awoke at nighttime, it seemed, which is why he chose the evening and nighttime to record its sounds.

He showered and shaved, then joined the other travelers and hotel guests for breakfast. He had two more projects to complete. Then he could go home.

At eleven o'clock, siesta time in Rome, Pallibio dialed the phone. A familiar voice answered. Johnny Rosetti.

"Johnny, Paul Pallibio, how are you?"

"Pauly, how good to hear your voice, I'm good. I'm good," replied Rosetti. What brings you to town?"

"Here on business, as usual," Pallibio lied. "I have to leave this evening. I wondered if we could get together."

"Sure, sure. Be happy to," responded his friend. "Are you at the usual place, 'cause I'm free right now and I can drop over."

"That'd be great," came the reply.

He didn't really want to drive anyway, not having gotten a good night's sleep and not wanting to play dodge-em with the Italian drivers.

"I'll be there in twenty minutes, ok, old buddy?"

"That's great, Johnny. I'll meet you in the restaurant."

"All right. See you in twenty."

Johnny Rosetti had gone to high school with Paul Pallibio. While Paul was busy making money at his father's machine shop, Johnny was catching the traveling fever. He hitchhiked across the United States twice, then decided to do the same in Australia. Six years later he toured Europe and fell in love with Rome. He lived there ever since. Paul always made an effort to visit his former high school chum.

One never knew when one might need a friend.

CHAPTER 11

John Rosetti arrived at the hotel café and spotted his old friend sitting at a corner table.

"Don't get up," he ordered as he leaned over and shook Paul Pallibio's hand. "As always, it's good to see you, Pauly."

"You too, Johnny. So, how's the Roman from good ol' Cleveland doing?"

Rosetti sat down opposite Paul.

"I'm doing ok. I guess I'm getting a little antsy, I may be ready to move on."

"How's the little woman?" asked Paul.

"Marie's all right, I guess. We're getting along ok. She still wants to tie the knot and all that, but I don't know, I just don't want to be tied down. You know how it is. Her parents still aren't too fond of me. The ugly American syndrome, I guess."

Paul felt the amenity part of the conversation had been covered, and he was anxious to discuss the real reason he wanted to see his friend, so he took control.

"Johnny, how'd you like to make a hundred grand in five minutes?"

"Who wouldn't?" came the expected reply.

"Well, I've got a little project going and I could use your input. But it has a condition."

"What's the project, Pauly? What'd you want me to do? For a hundred G's, you want me to knock off someone?"

Reaching down to his side, Paul picked up a large brown envelope that he had leaned against his chair. He handed it over to Johnny.

"I want you to mail this envelope by special courier on Friday night."

"You're kidding, right?" asked a surprised Johnny. "A hundred thousand dollars to mail a letter? What the hell's in there, Pauly? Naked pictures of the First Lady?"

"Its contents are of no concern to you," replied Pallibio harshly. "Either you do it or you don't. I'm sure I could get some dago around here to handle it."

"No, Pauly. Don't misunderstand me. I mean, you just want me to mail this and you'll hand me a hundred thousand big ones?"

"That's it in a nutshell, Johnny. And, of course, you will deny we ever met if someone should ask. Understand?"

"Perfectly," replied his confused friend.

"I will be returning to Italy in about one month. If all goes well and you don't screw up this little assignment, I'll pay you then. We got a deal, John?"

"Yea, sure, no problem. We got a deal, Pauly."

Paul backed his chair away from the small round table and stood up so he could look down on his chum.

"Make sure this will arrive at its destination on Saturday evening, ok? And not before. Here's twenty bucks to offset the mailing expense."

Tossing a twenty-dollar bill at Johnny, Paul Pallibio did an awkward side step and walked away. He turned toward his friend.

"See you in a month, Johnny. And remember, we never met."

Johnny Rosetti nodded his head. Thoughts about his friend's project and the contents of the envelope filled his head. But he quickly dashed them from his mind as he speculated various ways to enjoy a hundred grand.

Pallibio walked through the lobby to the elevator and returned to his room on the fifth floor. He shoved his clothing into his overnight bag, then laid all the cassette tapes he had recorded on the cherry desk near the window.

With a black felt pen, he carefully marked each cassette. Airplane ride #1, airplane ride #2, Rome #1, Rome #2; he marked them all in the order he wanted them to be played.

When this little project was done, he went downstairs and checked out of the quiet hotel nestled near the Vatican on the Via Della Conciliazone.

"Be back in a month," he muttered to no one.

Pallibio drove the rented white Fiat to the airport and left it at the Avis return area. He was shuttled to the terminal where in an hour and a half, he would begin his return to America.

"One more call to make and the puzzle will just about be completed," reflected the fatigued Pallibio.

He sauntered to a pay phone near his departing gate. Making sure no one was within hearing distance, Pallibio punched in several digits before hooking up with an operator in Sidney, Australia.

"I'd like to make a person-to-person call to Mr. David Huddlestone," he advised the operator.

After a few moments, he heard the familiar voice of his Australian friend.

"David, Pallibio here," he started. "Did you receive the package I sent you?"

"That I did, Pauly," replied Huddlestone. "Somewhat confusing, mate. What is it you want me to do with it?"

"You didn't open it, right, David?"

"No, of course not, those were your explicit instructions, Pauly."

"Good. Do you have the package in front of you?"

"Aye, mate, now I do."

"You can open it now," Pallibio ordered. "Inside is a brown envelope addressed to Mrs. Dante O'Shea. Got it?"

"Got it, mate."

"I want you to send that letter to Mrs. O'Shea to arrive on Sunday morning. Understand? Sunday morning in the States."

"Gotcha, Pauly," confirmed Huddlestone.

"I will send you a very nice payment for your services in two weeks. Ok?"

David Huddlestone had a million questions to ask, but sensed he wouldn't get any answers. So he didn't bother. He had received the package just yesterday and Paul's instructions were to let it sit until he was contacted. He would make fifty thousand dollars if he cooperated.

"Everything's under control, mate," offered Huddlestone. "I look forward to hearing from you again."

"One last thing, David. If anybody asks questions, play dumb. Got it?"

"Got it, mate."

Playing dumb is how David Huddlestone made his living. He ran an underground warehouse for drug dealers and weapons dealers.

He could be very dumb.

Chapter 12

Paul Pallibio arrived back in Cleveland Friday afternoon. He took a shuttle bus to the Park 'N Fly parking lot where he had left his Corvette two days earlier. He drove the twenty miles to his house going over in his mind all of the details of the plan.

"My end is almost covered," he thought. "As long as the boys do what I told them, in a few days I'll leave all of this behind."

Driving down the tree-lined street towards his home, Pallibio noticed the white Cleveland Cable Company van parked across the street from his driveway.

"Wish I had invested in cable companies," he grumbled as he eased up his long concrete driveway.

He gave no other thought to the van's presence.

Inside the van, Special Agents Sweeney, Gill, and Menegay patiently waited for their man, Pallibio, to get into his house. They had reviewed the only phone conversation Paul Pallibio had made from his house on the previous Wednesday morning. It had been to some kid named Eddie. And, unless Pallibio was going to have a partner in a new machine shop, it appeared to the trio that he was setting up a big heist. Jim Sweeney had had such a hunch after the meeting with the IRS on Tuesday night, which is one of the reasons Jim Sweeney called his friend, Bill Menegay. These sort of situations were Bill Menegay's forte.

"If you could guess the outcome of horse races like you do the moves of these scumbags, you'd be a rich man, Bill," joked Sweeney.

"These guys are more predictable," retorted Menegay with a smile.

Lenny Gill, the technical man on the job, put large headphones on his balding head. The headphones were designed to pick up any noise within a hundred yards of the two-foot diameter dish that sat on the roof of the van. It seemed like old technology, but as Agent Gill had earlier informed Jim Sweeney, it was the only available van. Lenny pushed a button on the antiquated control panel and directed the white saucer directly toward Pallibio's living room, where Paul Pallibio now sat.

"You hear anything?" Menegay asked Gill.

"Sounds like he's shuffling papers, maybe opening mail or reading the newspaper. I can tell you this, whatever he ate doesn't totally agree with him. It sounds like he's sitting on a whoopee cushion."

The agents stifled a laugh.

Inside the house, sitting on his well-worn, comfortable recliner, Paul Pallibio smiled with glee. He had just opened a formal looking envelope addressed to him from the Cleveland Musketeers organization. Inside he found an invitation. It read:

Dear Mr. Pallibio,
You are cordially invited to celebrate
with us a SURPRISE birthday party
in honor of our All-Star player,
Dante O'Shea. The party will be held
this Saturday evening, at 7:30 P.M.,
at the O'Shea residence. As an owner
of a loge, and big supporter of the
Cleveland Musketeers, we would be
honored if you could attend. We apologize
for any inconvenience because of this
short notice. Your presence is the
only gift needed for Dante.

The invitation also included a short note from Lisa O'Shea explaining how her husband needed a little morale boost after his injury in such a key game, and how nice it would be if selected fans and the organization could attend. Another page included directions to their home and some detail about how the surprise was going to be pulled off.

"Perfect," muttered Pallibio to himself. "Just perfect."

The only detail he had not figured out satisfactorily was his own alibi when the plan unfolded. Now it was complete.

Paul Pallibio spent the rest of the afternoon packing clothes and getting personal belongings together. He would be leaving Sunday morning for Los Angeles, then to the Cayman Islands, then to Rome. He would carry what he could, and eventually, send for the rest, if he so desired.

At 6:30 P.M., the van occupants decided that they would call it a night. They were collectively frustrated that they did not get a single lead from their surveillance. They chose not to put a tail on Pallibio, and take the chance of discovery.

"Hey, don't fret," offered Bill Menegay to his cohorts. "If something goes down, we'll react. This is how these things go. You can't arrest a person for having gas."

He smiled at Jim Sweeney and Lenny Gill. Both agents appreciated his attempt to minimize the time wasted that they felt they had just spent.

"Jimmy, I have a dinner engagement at my daughter's tonight. Guess I'll be meeting the great Dante O'Shea."

"Get me an autograph, will ya?" requested Agent Gill. "And get one of Robbie's, too, if it isn't too much to ask."

"No sweat," Bill promised. "I'm sure my son-in-law will be happy to oblige.

The trio of agents drove the van back to the basement of the Federal Building in downtown Cleveland.

Paul Pallibio drove his Corvette to his old shop on East Fortieth Street.

CHAPTER 13

The Dulik's lived on a five-acre parcel of land in Copley, Ohio. They had purchased the old farmhouse shortly after Robbie had been traded to the Musketeers two years ago. Robbie Dulik loved to work with his hands and planned after his NBA career to open a carpentry shop back home in Southern California.

He and Alise spent most of their off-season days fixing up the old house. They stripped painted, sanded and refinished the oak trim from around the doors, bringing the elegant wood back to life. They tore down walls, enlarged rooms, added a hot tub, refurbished the large kitchen, and made the old place into their home.

Robbie and Alise made a nice team. All they wanted now were children to make their dwelling place a real home. Alise had thought she was pregnant earlier in the month, but not this time. Her doctor told her she was pretty fertile and it wouldn't be long before her wish came true.

"I wish Lisa would get the same news," she reflected as she remembered her best friend's problem.

The O'Shea's arrived in the early evening and joined Alise, Robbie, and Alise's parents, Bill and Susan Menegay for the informal pizza party. Dante immediately commandeered the kitchen.

Carry out pizza was not a part of this party. Dante had insisted he be allowed to show off his culinary skills and make the pizza from scratch.

"I make the best crust this side of Chicago," he bragged.

Robbie helped his best friend in the kitchen, measuring out the ingredients as Dante ordered. Finally, when the pizzas were assembled with just the right amount of pepperoni, Italian sausage, mushrooms, olives, onions and Dante's own special sauce, he and Robbie joined the conversation in the living room.

"Be twenty minutes," Dante announced to the others. "Unless you want well done pizza."

"Well, Dante, it sure is a pleasure meeting you," Bill Menegay offered. "I've been a fan of yours ever since you were a freshman at Ohio State."

"Thanks," Dante responded in his humble manner. "As I've told Robbie many times, we've got the best job in the world."

Robbie Dulik and Dante O'Shea became best friends moments after they had met. Robbie was with his fourth NBA team, in five years. Dante saw a good person who had a lot of potential as an NBA player. He wanted Robbie to succeed. Dante knew that a good backup, even if it meant taking precious playing time minutes away from his own game, was necessary for the Musketeers to advance to the next plateau of success.

"If I go down, you have to step up your game, Robbie. It's important for the team that you learn all you can as fast as you can. I can't play every minute of every game; you'll get your playing time. Be patient. But above all, be a Musketeer, a team player."

He told Robbie this early in their relationship. It would be good for the team, although that was not his only motive. He definitely liked his teammate and friend from Southern California.

It was a strange relationship, as Dante was the younger of the two, but Robbie Dulik took his friend's words seriously, very seriously, and worked at his game incessantly. At practices, he played as hard as he could, and he learned. Robbie considered himself extremely lucky to have a teacher like Dante O'Shea. Not to mention, a friend. And the fact that their two wives had become best friends cemented an already good relationship.

"Alise tells me that you're an FBI agent, Bill," said Dante as the three couples settled into the various chairs in the living room. "That's got to be interesting work."

"Daddy's been with the company twenty-five years," proclaimed his proud daughter.

"Do you specialize in any area?" asked Lisa. "I've heard the FBI has special agents for special problems."

"Well, yes, I guess I am kind of a specialist," Bill replied. "I seem to be more involved in cases involving bank robberies, art gallery heists, even kidnaping."

"Isn't that kind of dangerous?" Lisa queried.

"Whenever you work with the criminal mind, it gets a little precarious at times. But remember, these guys, and girls, don't want to get caught, so I seldom see the criminals we catch. I let my co-workers take care of the messy part," Bill grinned.

"Remember that newspaper editor who was buried underground in New York a few months ago?" Alise asked her guests. "They brought Daddy in to solve the case. Right, Dad?"

"Well, I was there, but there were many minds piecing that puzzle together. It's just like you guys on the court. One player doesn't make it happen. Teamwork does."

"I guess my employer feels I have a criminal mind, so they call me in to think like a criminal," added Bill Menegay with a smile.

Forty miles north on East Fortieth Street, Paul Pallibio, Eddie and Vince Burson, and Carl Plath were having a party of their own. On the second floor of the former Pallibio Machine Shop.

"This looks good, Eddie, real good," complimented Pallibio as he shined his heavy duty flashlight around his darkened former office.

While Paul was in Italy, and Vince and Carl were working their jobs, Eddie was getting the room prepared. He had covered all of the walls and windows with three inch thick padded foam. On top of the foam covering the windows, he taped dark green garbage bags to keep out any light, or to keep any light from escaping the fifteen foot square office.

An eight foot table stood on one side of the room against the wall. On it were two tape recorders, several cassette tapes labeled "Airplane

Ride #1, Airplane Ride #2, and Rome #1, #2, #3, #4, #5 and #6". Several packs of AA batteries sat next to the recorders. A new roll of the highly flexible duct tape joined the other items on the table. Paul handed Eddie one more tape titled "Italian Car Ride". He had made the tape on his way to the airport in Rome.

In the middle of the room, an old rocking chair sat motionless, waiting for an occupant. The seat, arms and back were covered with foam for extra padding. Under the rockers, Eddie installed another set of wooden rockers that ran perpendicular to the first set. A rope was attached to the back of the rocker and on the side of the right arm rest.

Another roll of duct tape sat on the floor nearby, as did a fifty foot roll of nylon rope. Ten five foot lengths of nylon rope lay in a neat pile near the chair.

On the other side of the room near the doorway, three folding chairs and a green card table were leaning against the foam-covered wall.

The last object in the room was an old army cot Eddie found at the East Side Army-Navy store on East 72nd Street.

On one of the outside windows in the room, on the wall opposite the door, Eddie had left the window cracked open about one inch to let some air into the dank smelling office. Since Pallibio Machine had closed its doors in '99, the only occupants of the building were mice, spiders, insects and an occasional rat. There was no electricity or running water. Eddie had decided against running electrical cords from their house through the tunnel and up to the former office. They would have to rough it, without a fan or air conditioning, in the hot and humid room for just a couple of days. Then off to paradise.

One more look around the room and Paul Pallibio was satisfied. Eddie had followed his orders to perfection. The former shop owner became more and more excited and encouraged that the plan would be pulled off.

"Well, boys," he stated. "Everything here looks in order. Let's go back to the house and go over tomorrow's details."

Shortly after, Paul sneaked out of the house on East Fortieth Street. He had told Eddie, Vince and Carl that he did not want them drinking tonight. That they should go to bed early, get up early, and eat a good breakfast. He wanted them to be as sharp as possible on Saturday.

He walked down the street to Saint Clair Avenue. Turning left, he walked two more blocks before entering the Spaghetti Place, another converted warehouse, now a restaurant. He walked through the restaurant, and out to the fenced in parking lot at the back of the building.

It was the safest place in this neighborhood to park his coveted Corvette.

CHAPTER 14

The bright sunlight filtered its way through the oak and maple trees, through the wooden venetian blinds in the O'Shea bedroom, and into Dante's eyes.

Glancing at the clock, he yawned, stretched, and rolled over to look at his beautiful wife. Lisa could sense his stare. Without opening her eyes, she mumbled 'happy birthday' to her husband.

"That's right," he said in mock surprise. "Today's my birthday. Got anything special for me?"

She caught his wandering hand under the covers.

"Yes," she whispered. "But not that. At least not now. How about a good, healthy breakfast? What would you like?"

"For you to stay in bed with me," Dante quickly responded.

"So that's eggs, over easy, and meat, any kind," quipped Lisa.

"Whatever," he replied in a mocked hurt tone.

Lisa planted a quick kiss on his forehead and rolled out of bed. She fetched her royal blue robe and waltzed into the bathroom. Soon she awoke for the day with a steaming hot shower.

As she was drying her hair with the soft cotton towel, Lisa asked Dante what he had planned for the day.

"Well, I figure I better eat that healthy breakfast," he started. "Then I better work out the knots in this old body of mine. Robbie said something last night about coming over after lunch and getting me out of the house. You wouldn't know anything about that, would you, dear?"

The three plus years that Dante had known Lisa, she had always made a big deal over his birthday, days and, sometimes, weeks before the actual day. This year, she hadn't. He suspected she was up to something, something like a surprise party, and he was going to make her suffer a little for the embarrassment he would later endure.

"So Robbie's coming over, what's so strange about that?" Lisa asked, trying to downplay Robbie's role in her scheme.

"He's usually so busy on Saturdays," retorted her husband. "I just thought it weird he would spend his Saturday running me around. Almost like it was being planned or something. Anyway, aren't Alise's parents still here? I thought they said they weren't leaving until Tuesday. I'd think Robbie would spend his time with his in-laws, don't you?"

Lisa knew of her husband's suspicions, so she threw it back at him.

"Hey, Robbie probably feels that you've been cooped up in the house all week. I mean, you can't drive, you're kind of stuck here, so he's just trying to help out. It's not like he's purposely trying to get you out of the house. Is that what you think?"

Dante sensed it was time to withdraw from the sparring episode. Why ruin her plans and make her unhappy?

"I'm just teasing," he confessed. "So weren't you taking Mimi shopping?"

"Well, I did promise Mimi I would take her to some flower shops and maybe a nursery or two. And I have a couple of errands to run, like to the library and such," she lied.

"Sounds like you'll be gone most of the day. Tell you what. We can have a nice quiet dinner tonight. Ok? Just you and me, a couple of steaks, some potatoes, and corn. Sound good?"

"Sounds good," agreed Lisa. "I'm going to start breakfast."

Mimi and Fred Wilson were the O'Shea's neighbors. They had a brick ranch home similar to the O'Shea's. It made it easier for the elderly couple to get around. Mimi loved to shop for flowers. And Fred learned to love to plant them. Neither could drive, so Lisa tried to make a habit of checking in on them to see if they needed to run an errand or get anything from the store. They liked the O'Shea's. With both of their daughters living out of state, they treated Dante and Lisa as if they were their own. It was a mutual blessing for both sides of the fence.

At ten in the morning, Lisa kissed Dante on his sweaty forehead and headed up the basement steps. Dante stopped pedaling his stationary bike.

"I'll see you around fourish," he blurted out to her.

"Four it is," his wife shouted back before closing the door that led to the garage.

She backed their green BMW out of the garage and was halfway down the drive when she again remembered the opened garage door. Dante had reminded her that morning that a lot of thefts occurred because an open garage door was an invitation to trouble. Even in their nice neighborhood.

Lisa started to ease the BMW forward up the drive when she noticed Mimi walking slowly down her sidewalk towards the street. Deciding not to keep her neighbor waiting, she ignored the open garage door and backed out of the driveway.

Lisa helped her elderly neighbor into the car and started to drive slowly down the street.

"Well, Mimi," she stated in a satisfied tone. "I think we pulled it off. He acted like he suspected something, but then he gave up. He will be so-o-o surprised. And Robbie Dulik promised me he would keep Dante busy 'til eight o'clock. I hope everybody gets here on time tonight."

"Don't worry, dearie," assured Mimi Wilson. "I'm sure everything will be just fine."

At the yellow house on East Fortieth Street, Eddie, Vince and Carl were making their last minute preparations for what they hoped would be a successful day.

"I feel like a million bucks," joked Eddie to his brother.

"You'll have a million bucks pretty soon," replied an optimistic Vince. "I still can't believe we're going to go through with this, Eddie. What if we get caught?"

"I've thought about that. If we do, we deny everything. Pallibio's the one who will get the heat. It'll be ok, Vin. We'll do fine."

Carl awkwardly entered the room trying not to run into furniture. The two brothers looked at him and started laughing. Dressed in a gorilla suit, Big Carl Plath looked every bit as impressive as King Kong.

"This sure is hot," he complained.

Eddie and Vince stifled their laughter. The outfit was part of the plan and they didn't want to discourage Big Carl by making him feel too self-conscious.

"Fits you great," Eddie told his hairy friend.

"Always said you were a hairball," chided Vinnie.

"Wait 'til you get yours on, you ape," challenged Carl to Vince.

One hour later, at eleven a.m., Vince and Carl, dressed as a monkey and gorilla, walked into the deteriorating garage next to their house and got into Paul Pallibio's Lexus. Eddie walked with them to the car administering last minute instructions.

"You got the cake?" he asked.

"Yea," they replied in unison.

"The pouch?"

"Right here," answered Vince, touching the black purse attached to a belt around his ape waist.

"Your masks?"

"Check," replied Vince.

"Check," added Carl.

"You got the syringes and tape, right?"

"In the pouch," Vince impatiently responded.

"You feel ok about the shot?" Eddie asked his brother.

"Practiced on oranges last night," Vince declared. "It'll be a piece of cake."

"Birthday cake, right?" added the usually humorless Carl.

"Well, guys, this is it. I should see you here in about two hours, ok?"

Carl and Vince gave him a thumbs up sign as best they could in their outfits.

"You guys really do look authentic," he yelled to them as Vince backed the Lexus out into the street. "Be careful, you hear?"

They didn't hear as Vince floored the pedal and screeched down the street.

CHAPTER 15

"Hey, you're early," admonished Dante as he let Robbie into the house.

"Yea, I know," Robbie replied. "I forgot that I had to take the Jeep in for some new tires at one. So I thought I'd come here first, scrounge up some lunch, and make you wait with me at the dealer's."

"How thoughtful of you," his friend sarcastically replied.

The two teammates sauntered into the kitchen and sat at the counter.

"Cup of coffee?" asked Dante.

"Sounds good," answered Robbie. "But, please, no pizza. Your specialty last night hasn't totally agreed with my system."

"Poor baby," joked Dante.

Robbie added sugar to the mug of coffee Dante had served. Dante drank his black. The two friends talked a few minutes about trade rumors they had heard involving a teammate or two. A few minutes later, Robbie declared that Montezuma was again getting his revenge. As he walked down the hall towards the "little boy's room" as he called it, the doorbell rang.

"Have a nice dump," shouted Dante to his friend as he maneuvered his cast foot and limped to the front door.

Minutes earlier, while Dante and Robbie argued over who was tradable from the Musketeers, Vince and Carl had slowly driven up the long cemented driveway. Noticing the white Jeep Cherokee, they balked about going through with the plan. Deciding instead to adapt to the situation, they drove the black Lexus into the open garage. Before leaving the safety of the luxury car, Vince opened the glove compartment and produced a thirty-eight special.

"Just in case it gets out of hand," he told a surprised Carl.

Dante had heard the car enter the garage, but was in the middle of making a point about the value of his trade idea with Robbie, and figured Lisa and Mimi had returned early from their shopping trip. When Lisa didn't enter through the kitchen door, he figured she was helping Mrs. Wilson to her house. He was a little surprised to hear the front doorbell ring. Glancing through the small window on the large oak door, Dante saw a very tall gorilla and a considerably shorter monkey.

"So it begins," he thought as he opened the massive door. Separating him from the two primates was a glass storm door. Peering out at his visitors, Dante quickly surmised who they were.

"Hello, Joey. Hello, Henry."

His guess was that Joey Riggs, the Musketeer trainer, was the monkey. And Henry Pickett, his six eleven teammate, posed as the gorilla.

"You guys look better than ever," he commented.

Vince and Carl, feeling foolish, grunted and scratched themselves, as Paul Pallibio had suggested.

Dante opened the storm door, allowing his guests to enter into the foyer. Vince entered first and handed Dante a white box containing the cake. Carl lumbered in behind him and stood awkwardly, awaiting his cue from Vince.

"Well, guys, since I know who you are, why don't you take off those ridiculous costumes and have a cup of "

Before the word coffee left his lips, Vince shouted, "NOW!".

Carl reacted to the command with amazing quickness. As Dante stood holding the cake box, the gorilla swung his left fist squarely hitting the Musketeer star on the jaw. Dante reeled backwards, and before he fell into a heap on the carpeted floor, Vince grabbed the box out of his hands. Dante lay on the floor. He was unconscious.

Vince reached into the black pouch attached to his waist and pulled out a syringe. Pulling the plastic protective cover from the needle, he knelt down beside the fallen player. He roughly twisted Dante's arm so that he could give him the injection. Pushing the needle hastily into Dante's upper arm, Vince slowly pushed the plastic piston down, releasing the Versed into Dante's bloodstream.

Pallibio had told him that O'Shea would be out for about three hours. When he awoke, and was still groggy, Vince would administer more of the sleeping medicine, according to the plan.

Vince and Carl stood over the sleeping body. Pulling out a large roll of silver duct tape, they hurriedly taped Dante's feet together. Then his hands behind his back. And over his eyes. And finally his mouth.

"Let's get him out to the car," ordered Vince. "I saw a door in the garage that must lead into the house from somewhere. I'll go look."

Robbie Dulik put down the latest issue of Sports Illustrated. He flushed what he hoped was the last of Dante's pizza, then washed his hands.

"Did you hear that?" Carl whispered through his gorilla mouth. Vince was walking toward him from the kitchen. He, too, had heard the flushing noise.

"Hell," mumbled Vince. "Somebody is here."

They stood in the hallway, perfectly still. Listening. Waiting. Vince reached into the pouch and pulled out the black handgun.

"Come with me," he murmured to his friend.

With Vince leading, the two men walked through the kitchen and down the hallway where they thought they had heard the noise. Seeing a closed door halfway down the hall, Vince made an educated guess that it was the bathroom. Running water from behind the door confirmed his assumption.

Robbie opened the door and was greeted with a vicious right upper cut from Carl. He tried to shake off the tremendous blow to his chin, but Carl quickly followed with two more strikes. Robbie collapsed to the bathroom floor.

"I think that's Robbie Dulik," stated Vince. It struck him how ordinary Robbie and Dante looked off the basketball court.

"What're we gonna do with him?" Carl nervously asked. "Should we take him, too?"

"Shut up and let me think," answered Vince. "If we take him, we could get twice the money. But then, we're not set up for two guys. I don't know. We can't leave him here. What do you think, Carl?"

The Burson brothers always did the thinking for Carl Plath. That's one of the reasons he liked hanging with them. It made his life uncluttered.

"Well, Carl?"

"I d-d-don't know," he stammered. "Why don't we hide him?"

Vince thought it over for a long moment.

"Let me look around," he stated. "Stay here. Tell you what. Take this and tape him up. If he comes to, hit him again."

He handed Carl the duct tape and began scouting the house. Vince was impressed with the simplicity of the O'Shea home. He had expected it to be more lavishly furnished. He thought how he'd eventually have a nice house like this when he and Eddie settled down in Australia. On the Gold Coast, Eddie had promised him.

Vince toured the upstairs and was not satisfied with any good place to hide Robbie. In the kitchen, he found a door to the basement. Descending the steps, he looked in awe at the workout gym that Dante had assembled. On the far end of the exercise room, he found a door that led into a laundry room. He opened it and canvassed the small room. Then he found the place. Off the laundry room, near the washer and dryer, was a narrow louvered door. He opened it. A hot water heater was located on the far wall. The room was maybe five feet wide and three feet deep. The only other occupant was several cases of beer neatly stacked against the back wall.

"This'll do," he thought.

He raced through Dante's gym, dodging workout equipment like a running back darting through a defense. He ran up the steps and found Carl impatiently waiting for a decision.

"Let's get him downstairs," he excitedly ordered. "And bring the tape."

Carl put the tape in his gorilla suit pocket. He lifted Robbie over his left shoulder and followed Vince to the cramped laundry room closet. While Carl held Robbie in a standing position, Vince taped the backup guard from head to toe. Looking like a silver mummy, Robbie only had the space under his nose uncovered with the duct tape. The two kidnappers placed Robbie on the floor of the closet, bending him to conform to what little space there was. Closing the door, Vince rolled a white clothes hamper in front of the closet.

"That ought to do it," he announced to the gorilla.

Upstairs, they found Dante in the same position they had left him. Big Carl picked up the limp body and followed Vince through the kitchen and out to the Lexus in the garage. He laid the Musketeer player on the gray cement floor.

"Quick, Carl, close the garage door."

Vince got a little excited over his oversight. Carl closed the door as ordered, then easily hoisted the body up onto his shoulder and maneuvered the sleeping ballplayer across the backseat of the car. Vince threw a wool blanket over the unconscious body. The two kidnappers removed their outfits and threw them on top of Dante. If they were stopped for any reason, Dante would appear to be a pile of costumes.

"Get in the car," ordered the younger Burson. "I'll be right back."

He once again entered the O'Shea residence, this time through the kitchen door. Vince retraced his steps throughout the house, making sure everything was as it should be. He stood at the top of the basement stairs and listened for any sound out of Robbie Dulik. There was none.

In the front hallway, where twenty minutes before he and Carl had been invited in, he noticed the front door wide open.

"Another freakin' mistake," he muttered.

He closed the door and locked it. Then he joined his friend in the garage.

CHAPTER 16

Lisa O'Shea and Mimi Wilson had whizzed around Akron for three hours, shopping at several stores to buy the needed decorations for the party. They stopped at Graf Growers, where they purchased potted yellow daisies, violet, purple and white pasqueflowers, and magenta and violet fleabanes to put on the serving tables and around the living room and outside deck.

They stopped at a craft store and purchased blue and orange streamers and table covers. Another store had a cardboard Musketeer, the same as the emblem on the Cleveland uniform. It was the final touch.

They then stopped at the Caterers in the Valley to make sure that everything would be ready for the party. The caterer assured them that their choices of appetizers and finger foods would be on time and delectable.

"The only surprise I want tonight is Dante's birthday party!" exclaimed Lisa to her neighbor.

She was getting very excited over pulling one off on her husband.

"Before we go home," Lisa stated. "I want to call and make sure that Robbie has "kidnaped" my husband for the day.

Mimi Wilson loved to shop. But not at this whirlwind pace. She tiredly nodded to her exuberant friend.

Lisa remained parked at the caterers and phoned her home.

"There's no answer," she informed Mrs. Wilson. "That means we can go home and decorate. Alise Dulik will be coming over around three o'clock. Will you supervise us?"

Mimi tried to duplicate her young friend's excitement, but at seventy-four years old, it got tough.

"Three o'clock's my nap time," she stated in a soft tone. "An old lady like me needs all the beauty rest I can get."

The two women looked at each other and laughed.

"That's what I like about you, Mimi. You tell it like it is."

It was a trait she wished she had, too. At least about some subjects she needed to face and then bury.

Vince slowly backed the Lexus out of the garage.

"Oh, man!" he shouted.

"What?" asked Carl hesitantly.

He didn't like it when Vinnie got upset.

"That," responded Vince, pointing to the white Jeep Cherokee. "I'll bet that's Dulik's car."

"Oh," muttered Big Carl. "What'll we do?"

"Can't leave it here, peabrain," Vince retorted.

He pulled forward into the garage.

"Close the door, Carl. I'll be right back."

Once again, Vince entered the house through the kitchen door. He hastily looked for the keys to the Jeep. Not finding them hanging on the walls where other keys hung, he quickly glanced on the kitchen counters and the hallway table by the front door. Nothing.

Running down the steps to the basement, Vinnie rushed to the laundry closet door. He pushed the clothes hamper out of the way and thrust the louvered door open, almost tearing it off its hinges. Robbie heard the noise but was too groggy to react. He felt someone feeling his jeans pockets. He tried to struggle, but couldn't do anything to hinder his attacker.

Vince found the Cherokee keys in Robbie's left front pocket. He ripped some of the duct tape off to access the tight opening. He squeezed the keys out of the pocket and looked down at the slumping Musketeer. Placing a hand on each side of the closet door frame, Vinnie kicked the hapless victim squarely in the face with both feet. Robbie slouched even further against the cases of beer.

Vince closed the closet door and again slid the hamper across the tiled floor in front of the louvered door. He raced through Dante's workout room and up the stairs, two at a time. He joined Carl in the car. Carl sat in the passenger's seat, letting life happen around him.

"Here," Vinnie thrust the keys toward Carl. "Take the Jeep and follow me. We'll dump it at the Mall."

Carl complied. Ten minutes later, he parked the Cherokee in the crowded parking lot of the mall. Not knowing what to do with the keys, he threw them under a parked car down the aisle. Vinnie pulled up in the Lexus and Carl again took his position in the front passenger seat. He was shaking.

The black Lexus with the SHARK license plates traveled at speed limit north on Interstate 77. Vince took no chances by exceeding the speed limit, his normal habit. For once, he was the cool one.

As he drove, Vince reviewed in his mind the previous hour of his life. He thought of each step, each action, that he and Big Carl had taken. Robbie Dulik being there was a bad break, but he felt that they had hidden him well enough to give he, Carl and Eddie enough time to follow their plan. Then it hit him. Like a ton of bricks.

"Son of a bitch!" he shouted.

"W-W-What's the matter?" asked his shaken cohort.

"Fingerprints. That's what. Freakin' fingerprints."

Vince was visibly upset and that scared Carl. Vinnie slowed the car and pulled over to the side of the road. He sat and gripped the leather bound steering wheel until his knuckles were white.

"When I went back into the house the first time, the front door was wide open. When I closed and locked it, I wasn't wearing my outfit. Sure as hell, I left fingerprints on the that friggin' door."

"You're not thinking of going back?" Carl queried.

He just wanted to get back home. He didn't like what they were doing and even started to question in his own mind why he had gone along with it. Friendship was his answer.

"I don't know. Jesus. I don't know."

Officer Kenny Trumphour was cruising south on the interstate when he noticed the black Lexus stopped on the shoulder on the northbound side. He saw a turnaround about a half mile ahead. He would go help the troubled motorist.

Carl saw the black Chevy Caprice cruiser slowing down on the other side of the grassy divide that separated the north and south bound lanes.

"Vince," he blurted. "We better get outta here."

His friend followed his stare and saw what he saw. His decision had been made by a courteous state cop.

Eddie had watched his brother and friend drive down East Fortieth Street and turn onto Saint Clair Avenue over two hours ago. He had gone into the house, flicked on the television, and sat. He waited. And then he waited some more.

"Something's not right," he thought.

He scurried into the basement and through the tunnel to the previously boarded entrance into the machine shop area of Pallibio Machine. He walked across the oil preserved wooden floor noticing for the first time the distinctive outline of where heavy machinery had once churned out thousands of parts. It reminded him of murder scenes on TV, where the cops outlined the dead bodies. He walked up the creaky, over-sized steps, wondering why they had been built so wide. He reached the second floor, where it would all soon happen, and gazed at the dust covered desks that remained as a monument to the once successful machine shop.

He entered the room, as they now called it, and for the millionth time that week, checked and double-checked everything in it. It was his last trip there before Dante O'Shea would be arriving. Something was missing. They had overlooked something. He looked at the modified rocking chair, the rope, the cot, the folding chairs and card table. He looked at the table against the wall that had the cassette players and the tapes.

"A clock," he thought. "We need a friggin' clock. How are we going to time the tapes and medication without a damn clock?"

Doubts raged in his mind as he raced through the office, down the stairs, through the dark tunnel and into his own basement.

"If we forgot a detail like that," he reasoned. "What else could we have overlooked?"

He didn't like having doubts this late in the game.

Paul Pallibio spent his Saturday on the golf course. He and his cronies met most Saturdays and spent the late morning and most of the afternoon on the course.

"Nothing relaxes a man's mind more than golfing," he thought. "Except maybe fishing. Or sex."

There were a hundred ways to relax. Paul's second favorite was golf.

He was uncharacteristically somber during the entire round with his three best friends. Fred Durzak, who owned a tool and die shop, was Paul's closest friend and confidant.

"You've been mighty quiet today, Pauly," he commented as they walked off the seventeenth green. "Are you under the weather?"

"Yea, a little, I guess," he replied.

He was feeling very melancholy. In all reality, this would probably be the last time he would golf with his friends. They'd been playing together longer than he could remember. And now, all of that would change. His life would never be the same. He would be a criminal, even if he was never traced to the kidnapping. In his mind, he would always be looking over his shoulder. He'd probably never be able to stay in one place, and make friends like these, ever again. He probably would never be able to trust anyone again.

"Like Fred," he thought.

Fred Durzak was ten years older than Paul. He had taken the young shop owner under his wing and helped guide him.

"If I had listened to Freddie ten years ago, I'd still have my shop," he lamented to himself.

Like his accountant and banker, Fred had implored him to cut back on his spending during the lean years. Paul, of course, hadn't listened. Not to that advice, nor to Freddie's warnings about his gambling partners and his gambling habit.

"You're still going to that O'Shea party tonight?" Freddie asked him after the final hole of the day.

Fred Durzak also owned a loge.

"Yes, I plan to make it."

"Good," Freddie replied. "You want me to pick you up around seven, right?"

"Seven's good."

Twenty minutes later, after a quick beer at the nineteenth hole, Paul got into his Corvette and drove home.

"By now, the boys have O'Shea at the shop," he thought. "There's no turning back."

He felt empty inside. The reality of his life hit him like a Tyson uppercut. Everything he had worked for his entire life would be gone. And for what? Gambling debts? Fear of thugs like Benny Vetera? He had set what he thought to be a well thought out plan in motion at a time of monetary despair. He was not a bad person, he was just caught up in a bad situation. One caused by his love of money. He was finally beginning to figure it out.

He returned home to the comfort of his living room. Looking around, he stared at the old, worn Lazy Boy chair sitting in front of the big screen TV. His father had given him that chair shortly before he died in '79. Paul Pallibio did something he hadn't done since his father's death. He cried.

"I'm sorry, Dad," he sobbed to his father's spirit. "I'm sorry that I've let you down. That I'm not the man you wanted me to be. For being greedy and so…stupid."

He sat in the soft, leather recliner. In a few hours, he would attend a party for a person who wouldn't show up. And tomorrow, he'd fly to Los Angeles to finish the plan. His plan.

Paul Pallibio cried himself to sleep.

CHAPTER 17

The black Lexus turned into the grass-covered dirt driveway and stopped abruptly in the dilapidated garage. Eddie heard his brother and Carl return and raced outside to meet them.

He swung the creaky wooden garage door shut and joined his fellow kidnapers in the dark single car garage. The May sun worked its way through the cobwebbed, greasy window and provided the only light for the three young men to continue their job.

"How'd it go?" Eddie anxiously asked his brother.

"Let's get him in the house, then I'll tell you," advised Vinnie. His voice sounded strained.

They removed the gorilla and monkey outfits and the woolen blanket and tossed them in the trunk of the car. Dante was still out. Carefully, Carl and Vince pulled his body out of the back seat toward the side door of the garage. They had a twenty foot walk, in daylight, to the house. Eddie went out first and scouted the area for any unwanted observers. The coast was clear.

Eddie opened the house door, holding it for his cohorts as they quickly dragged Dante, like a drunken friend, into the kitchen.

"Let's get him to the room," Eddie ordered.

Carl loaded Dante onto his right shoulder and followed the Burson brothers down the stairs to their dank basement and into the tunnel.

"We had a little surprise at his house," Vinnie told his brother. "But we handled it."

"What happened?" Eddie asked. He had concerns about Vinnie and Carl doing this right and hoped that the surprise Vinnie spoke about wouldn't cause a problem for them.

The three young men advanced through the dark tunnel, only Eddie had a flashlight. His brother and Carl stayed close behind him.

"Well," started Vinnie. "Dante O'Shea had company when we got there, so we took things into our own hands and took care of him."

"Took care of who?" Eddie was getting impatient.

"Pretty sure it was Robbie Dulik," continued his brother. "Carl gave him a couple shots to the face and then we taped him like a mummy with duct tape and hid him in a closet in the basement. He won't be a problem."

"Did he see you?" Eddie asked.

"He saw a gorilla and a monkey, and the gorilla beat the shit out of him," came the reply. "He won't be a problem."

"We even ditched his car at the mall," added Carl.

"So you think he didn't see you and nobody else did and everything's cool, right?" Eddie concluded.

"I said there won't be any problem," Vinnie retorted.

"What about his wife? She wasn't there, right?" Eddie nervously asked.

"Didn't see her," his brother proclaimed. "The green Beemer Pallibio told us they drove wasn't there either."

"Ok, ok," Eddie replied. "Just want to make sure we got everything covered. That's all. You did good, Vin. You too, Carl."

Five minutes later, Big Carl gently placed Dante on the modified rocking chair. As Eddie held him upright in the chair, Vince and Carl tied him to the back of the wooden rocker. They then tied his arms to the padded armrests.

Dante stirred slightly during the proceedings, but was still in a deep drug-induced sleep. One leg dangled two inches above the floor, his cast foot barely reached the dusty deck of the former office. Dante's head rested on his chest. Vince roughly removed the duct tape from Dante's eyes, pulling several of his eyebrow hairs off in the process. Dante didn't feel a thing. He replaced the tape with a black blindfold.

Vinnie then tore the tape away from Dante's mouth. In its place, he shoved a rolled up red scarf. There would be no screaming for help by the Musketeer guard.

"How long before another injection?" asked Eddie.

"Pallibio told me each shot would last three hours, and it was about 11:30 when I gave him his first dose. I'll give him another around 2:15."

"Ok, good," replied his brother.

Eddie glanced at the round kitchen clock he had positioned on the table an hour earlier. 1:27. He mustered as much confidence as he could and looked at his brother and Big Carl. He still had doubts. But they relied on him for leadership. He couldn't let them share his doubts, not at this point.

"Let's get those chairs in position," he ordered. I know this will be real boring, but Mr. Pallibio said it was real important that Dante thinks he's on a plane."

Vince and Carl nodded in agreement. They each grabbed a folding chair. Carl positioned his behind the rocker and Vince put his chair on the right side, two feet away.

Satisfied that everything was in order, Eddie moved to the eight foot table and inserted the cassette tape labeled "Airplane Ride #1" into the tape player. In the second tape player, he inserted the second airplane ride tape. He depressed the play button and a few moments later, the room was filled with the sounds of a Boeing 747 flying to its final destination in Rome, Italy.

"Whenever he moves or looks like he might be waking up, make sure you rock him," Eddie reminded them. "He has to believe he's on a plane to Rome."

"We know, we know," Vince whispered. "Remember? We were there when Pallibio explained the plan. Jesus, Eddie."

"I'm going to take care of the car," declared Eddie. "If there's any problem, call me on my cell phone. Or just handle it. Like you did Dulik."

Vinnie smiled with pride. It appeared that his big brother actually appreciated something he had done. Although Eddie might have done things a little differently with Robbie Dulik, he lauded their effort. He thought it would boost their confidence. And his.

"Don't forget the shot, Vinnie," Eddie reminded him. "I should be back by 3:00."

As he closed the door to Pallibio's former office, Eddie noticed the green plastic bag coming loose at the top of the window on the door. He tore off a piece of duct tape from the roll and repaired the covering.

"Gotta pay attention to details," he stated. "And don't forget, if you both leave the room, lock the door from the outside."

They both responded with the silent look of 'we got it, get out of here'. Eddie closed the door, walked across the wooden floor of the office to the wide staircase, through the former machining area, and through the dark tunnel to the yellow house.

"He seems a little worried," observed Big Carl.

"Seems more like freakin' Hitler," Vince muttered in defiance toward his brother.

Once Eddie got to the kitchen, he walked out onto the back porch. He glanced around, no one was in sight. The neighborhood was its usual quiet self. Eddie entered the garage through the weathered side door. On a dusty, overloaded shelf, he grabbed a Phillips screwdriver and two Ohio license plates that Paul Pallibio had put in the trunk as part of the plan. He removed the SHARK plates and replaced them with the stolen ones.

"If anyone is looking for a Lexus with SHARK vanity plates," he thought. "They'll have a hard time finding it."

He placed the SHARK plates in a hole in the corner of the garage dirt floor. It was one of many that his dog, Rocky, had dug when he was alive. Eddie remembered how he had kept the German Shepherd locked in the garage when he and Vinnie were gone. Rocky had a bad habit of chewing most anything, and Vince especially didn't like his stuff chewed up. When he discovered Rocky chewing on his shoe, Vinnie took a belt to the poor dog. It was best for Eddie to get rid of the dog, so he did.

The older Burson pushed dirt over the plates. Satisfied that they wouldn't be discovered, he slowly opened the garage door, wary that this movement might be the one to make it fall off of its rusty hinge.

He backed the Lexus into the street and drove Paul Pallibio's car to the airport.

CHAPTER 18

Bill Mcnegay sat in the red leather chair in Jim Sweeney's office. He looked at his colleague sitting behind the massive cherry desk pondering the information they had on Paul Pallibio.

"I'm glad you're here, Bill," Sweeney stated to him. "I'm sorry we're not more organized, but this kind of hit us out of the blue."

"Usually happens that way," consoled the west coast agent. "At least I got some time with my daughter. Plus, I'm supposed to join the family at Dante O'Shea's big bash tonight. So it hasn't been a wasted trip."

"I wish we could've done more surveillance, but you know how the policies and politics are in the company," Sweeney stated. "Chickenshit rules. These guys are committing crimes and we have to follow the friggin' regulations."

"There hasn't been a crime yet," Bill reminded his friend.

"You know as well as I do that there will be one. And a big one at that," insisted the Cleveland agent.

"Innocent until proven guilty," was Bill Menegay's retort.

"Listen, Bill, Pallibio's deep in debt to known mobsters. He's in trouble with the IRS. He doesn't have a job, at least that we know of. And his back is against the wall. He's going to do something."

"Hey, I'm on your side, Jimmy. It's a tough situation. We know something is going down, we don't know what, when or where. I share your frustration, Jim. But there's little we can do except react when the time comes."

"He'll screw up somewhere along the line. They always do."

Bill Menegay nodded in agreement.

"Does your wife mind you meeting me today?" asked Special Agent Sweeney.

"Well, we were supposed to go shopping, so thanks for saving me from that," Bill replied with a smile. "Susan ended up going with Alise to help Lisa O'Shea decorate for their party tonight. I guess it's supposed to be a big surprise birthday party for Dante. It should be entertaining."

As part of his intense training as an agent, Bill Menegay learned to scrutinize the various guests at the social functions he attended. Of course, part of it was his job, as most of the events involved political figures he was to protect. It did make the parties a little more interesting. He had actually become quite adept at guessing a person's occupation just by observing their style of dress and mannerisms. Of course, in L.A. nobody was what they appeared, but that made it all the more challenging.

"What about your son-in-law?" queried Sweeney. "I thought for sure you'd go golfing with him."

"He's assigned to tying up Dante all day. It's part of Lisa O'Shea's scheme to pull off the surprise. Dante couldn't golf with that cast on his foot anyway, so Robbie is winging it. Hell, even with the cast on, Dante would probably still embarrass me on the golf course."

"Yea, he's a hell of an athlete. That ankle injury was a bad break, for him and the Musketeers. Well, like we say a lot in Cleveland, wait 'til next year!"

"Well, Jim, I think you've got a handle on everything here, right? I'm going to head out. You have my cell number in case anything breaks. I'll be at the party about 7:30, if I don't hear from you today, I'll check in tomorrow. We're planning to return to L.A. on Tuesday."

The two agents shook hands.

"Bill, thanks for your input. Have fun tonight."

Bill headed for the door.

"Take care, buddy," he muttered as he exited the Cleveland agent's office.

At the O'Shea residence, Lisa, Alise and Susan Menegay put the finishing touches to their decorating. They surveyed the living room with gleeful eyes. Blue and orange streamers stretched from the chandelier in the middle of the ceiling to all four walls. A large "Happy Birthday Dante!" sign covered most of an eight foot section of one wall. Another sign on the opposite wall simply stated, "GOTCHA BABE!!" Dozens of potted plants and flowers in vases added color to the altered room. Rented tables and chairs were strategically scattered throughout the living room, dining room, den and outside by the decked pool. Satisfied with what they saw, the three women sat in the living room and sipped a pre-party glass of Merlot. The caterers would be there at 5:30, in plenty of time to lay out the various appetizers, hors d'oeuvres, crackers and cheeses, chips and dips, and finger foods.

"I think we're ready, ladies," stated Lisa as she held her glass up to her helpers in salute. She smiled appreciatively at both of them.

In the basement closet, Robbie Dulik attempted for the hundredth time since he woke up to open his eyes. The duct tape made that impossible.

"Where am I? How'd I get here?" he wondered.

He remembered washing his hands and putting the towel back on the rack on the back of the bathroom door. When he opened the door, he was struck by a gorilla. He remembered a slight scuffle with the big ape, and that was it. Now he couldn't move his arms or legs. His eyes and mouth were useless to him. He could vaguely feel heat coming from something nearby, but had no clue as to his whereabouts, or how he had gotten there. Or how he could get help. He continually worked at whatever was binding him, resting every few moments from the tenuous work. His mind raced with all kinds of weird thoughts.

Eddie Burson drove the black Lexus to the Park 'N Fly parking lot a mile from the Cleveland airport. Upon entering the lot, he received his parking ticket from a machine and eased the luxury car down the first aisle. A sign at the end of the aisle stated that parking was available in the covered deck. He headed in that direction. On the second level, he found a suitable space located in a dimly lit area.

"If they're looking for a stolen car," he said to no one. "This ought to hamper them."

He locked the car and pocketed the keys. Pallibio had told him that he was going to abandon the car in Cleveland when this was all over. Eddie figured he'd keep the keys.

"I might be back someday," he surmised.

Deep down inside, he didn't believe it. He walked down the dark, littered stairs of the deck and over to row 185 in the back of the huge parking lot. There he found his rusty blue '89 Chevy Impala that he had parked earlier in the week in accordance with Pallibio's plan. Eddie drove out of the Park 'N Fly lot, and headed east on Interstate 90, back to the faded yellow house that he and Vince and Carl had rented from Paul Pallibio for the past two years.

And back to being a kidnaper.

CHAPTER 19

Eddie returned home at 3:30. He hurried through the long, damp tunnel and up the stairs. He jogged across the former office area. Approaching the door to the room, he could hear a stewardess asking someone if they wanted another refreshment.

"No, thank you, but how much longer until we get to Rome?" asked a shrill-voiced passenger. She sounded whiny.

"The captain will be making an announcement shortly, madam," was the stewardess's automatic reply. Two more hours would have been the correct answer.

Eddie opened the door. Vince and Carl were perched on the folding chairs taking turns tugging at the rope and providing turbulence for Dante's flight. The Musketeer player was still asleep, his head still on his chest, much like Eddie remembered seeing him two hours earlier. Eddie quietly entered the room, softly closing the door behind him. He noticed the card table was now unfolded and placed between Vinnie and Carl. On it he saw a Wendy's bag, empty sandwich wrappers, an empty Wendy's milkshake, a couple of empty beer cans and a black object partially hidden under a napkin. It was Vince's gun.

Eddie pursed his lips and motioned Vinnie to join him outside in the big office area.

"What the hell is the gun here for?" he demanded in hushed tones.

"Just in case," was his brother's smug reply.

"Just in case of what?" retorted Eddie.

"Just in case we need to scare him."

"Jesus, Vince, you know how I feel about those things," he reminded his brother.

As a seven year old, Eddie witnessed an accidental shooting. One that almost took the life of his then best friend. Little kids playing around with a gun his friend's father kept in his night stand drawer. Eddie hated guns from that moment on. And he feared them, too.

"Yea, I remember what a wuss you are around guns, big brother. But I know how to handle it. You don't have to touch it."

Vinnie glared at his older brother.

"That's not the point, Vin," Eddie quietly responded. "Why take chances? It's not like he's going to attack us when he wakes up. I just don't want it in there. Understand?"

"Listen, big brother," Vinnie's tone of voice was getting louder. "Me and Carl are getting sick of you giving all the damn orders. We can think for ourselves. You don't have to treat us like little kids."

"Up yours, little brother," Eddie replied. "Just remember who it is who's making you rich. When this is all over, you can kiss my ass. And I told you, no beer."

The two brothers stared at each other for a few moments. Eddie knew that Vince would be too stubborn to back down, so he chose to relent and keep peace among the three of them.

"Ok, fine, keep the friggin' thing, but make sure it's out of Dante's reach. Just in case."

Vince smiled the knowing smile that he had won one over his older brother.

"I knew you'd see it my way, peabrain." A brotherly parting shot.

"When did you give him the last injection?" asked Eddie.

"2:15, right on the nose."

"So he should be good until five or so, right?"

"Yea, should be."

"Well, it's twenty of four right now. If we do the car ride tapes 'til about 4:30, then we can move on with the plan."

"Sounds good," Vince agreed.

"Since you have everything under control, I'm gonna grab a sandwich," Eddie informed him. As an afterthought, "Is Carl doing ok?"

"He started talking awhile back about us not doing the right thing," Vince informed him. "I told him to shut his friggin' mouth. We weren't allowed to talk like that."

"But he's ok, right?"

"He'll be fine," Vince responded in an uncaring manner.

"Good. I'll be back in a half hour. And Vinnie, cut out the beer, ok?"

"Whatever you say, big brother."

Eddie retraced his steps back to the kitchen across the street. He was going to make a sandwich, but he really didn't feel that hungry.

Bad vibes usually made him feel that way.

CHAPTER 20

Paul Pallibio stirred in the comfortable recliner. Glancing at his Rolex, he realized that he had slept most of the afternoon.

"Fred'll be here at 7:00," he said out loud. No one was around to hear. "Better get a move on."

He walked into his bedroom. Most of his favorite clothing had already been packed. Tonight, he wanted to dress for success. He ambled toward his walk-in closet and chose a charcoal gray double breasted suit. A white shirt and patterned maroon tie completed his ensemble.

His mind wandered to the boys and their guest. He was dying to call Eddie and see how things were going, but he fought the urge. He thought it was possible that the kidnapping might not have been pulled off. He wouldn't know until tonight. At the O'Shea's.

In his original plan, he was going to have Eddie call him and give a yes or no signal over the phone. But after receiving the invitation to the party, he decided not to chance any contact with the boys. He would find out soon enough. If something had gone wrong, he would find that out tonight. Plus, he would not be implicated. As far as he was concerned, it seemed like the perfect plan.

He had an hour and a half to get ready. He would shower, shave and get dressed. Then call the police and tell them that he just discovered that his car, a black Lexus 986 had been stolen. He would tell them he witnessed the theft from his living room window. Took it right out of his driveway. No, officer, nothing is safe anymore, is it? Yes, officer, he had a description. Three white males in their early twenties. Two short ones with short hair, the other much bigger, wide and tall, like a gorilla.

Dante O'Shea slowly opened his eyes and stared at blackness. He intently listened to the sounds around him. He felt nauseous. And extremely sore. He vaguely recalled being belted in the mouth by Henry Pickett who was dressed in a gorilla outfit. And now, he seemed to be tied to a chair of some kind. He realized after a few moments that the blackness was because of a blindfold.

"How ya feelin', O'Shea?" It was Vince.

Dante tried to lift his head. He was too weak to even do that.

"Don't try to talk, O'Shea," ordered Vince in a fiendish voice. "We got you gagged so you don't scream."

Vince grabbed Dante by the hair and raised his head. Pain instantly shot through the ballplayer's skull.

"You're not a freakin' screamer, are you O'Shea?"

No reply. No movement.

"Get you off the court and you're just another wuss, right pretty boy?"

Dante sat rigidly in the chair. He tried to slide his head back a bit to relieve the pull on his hair. But to no avail. He remained mute. He did not want to upset his assailant. But he was getting mad. At the circumstances and at this punk who was taunting him.

Vince was alone in the room when Dante awoke. Eddie had decided that they would take turns guarding their prisoner for three hour shifts. He wanted Vince to be there in case Dante had any reaction to the Versed.

Vince grabbed his gun from the table and held it to Dante's head.

"I'm going to remove the gag now, superstar. If you mess with me, I'll blow your head away. 'Cause I don't give a shit. Understand. I don't give a shit."

Vince put the gun on the card table and hastily untied the knot holding the gag in his hostage's mouth. When the knot loosened, he picked up the gun and held it to Dante's right temple. He pulled the loosely hanging scarf from Dante's mouth. He was glad he thought to wear plastic gloves. No spit to contend with. And no fingerprints.

"Go ahead. Make my day."

Vince enjoyed his tough guy act. Especially now, with a defenseless hostage. No danger being a bad ass in this situation.

"You feelin' sick? You oughtta feel sick with all the drugs I pumped into you. Did you eat breakfast?"

Dante painfully nodded.

"Then your going to be sick, shithead. Don't you know you're not supposed to eat from midnight on when you get shot up with Versed? You are a sorry son of a bitch. Don't even think of pukin' when I'm in here or I'll make you eat it. I'd rather kill you than clean up your friggin' puke."

Dante felt sick to his stomach. The effect from the drugs, being tied up, listening to this punk mouth off, it all made him sick. He had a funny taste in his mouth and swallowed hard. He was convinced that this tough talking punk would kill him. And would probably enjoy it.

"You got any questions, stud? Sure you do. Like what're you doin' here, right? You stupid bastard, you just let us in your house, no questions, nuthin'. You sure are the dumb one, O'Shea."

"Funny," thought Dante. "Lisa told me the same thing for letting fans come to our house. Only she said it a little nicer. No, a lot nicer. Oh, God. Lisa."

Then he remembered the monkey and gorilla. Joey Riggs and Henry Pickett. He recalled letting them in, holding a cake, and the gorilla slugging him. He had been out since. Did Lisa come home while they were still there?

"My wife, sir, is she ok?"

Vince cackled a sickening laugh.

"Oh, she was just fine. You're a lucky man, O'Shea. That woman of yours was, well, never mind, a gentleman never tells."

The words stung Dante's ears like hot bee stings. He tried with all his might to pull free from the ropes that bound him.

"Don't like that, eh, hotshot? Too bad, she sure did. Said she hadn't had a man like me in years."

Dante sat in total frustration.

"When I get loose, I'm gonna kill you," he hoarsely proclaimed.

"Yea, right, stud," Vince coolly replied.

He really enjoyed all of this control. Not like at the Clinic where he was just a peon gopher. And to think, he'd get a million bucks on top of it.

"It doesn't get any better than this," he muttered.

And against his brother's advice, he guzzled another beer.

CHAPTER 21

It was a perfect May night for a party. The blue sky was fading into an orange glow from the setting sun. It was seventy-two degrees. Not too hot, not too cool.

The guests began arriving promptly at 7:30 P.M. They were greeted in the driveway by valets, decked out in white shirts and red bow ties. Their cars were driven away from the O'Shea residence and parked in an empty lot down the street.

Many of the guests complimented Lisa on her attention to detail. Right down to hiding the cars. They reassured her, Dante would suspect nothing.

At 7:55, Lisa rang a hand bell. It was a beautiful copper antique she had purchased in Phoenix while on a road trip with Dante. All of the one hundred and twenty guests hushed their various conversations to hear her speak.

"Dante and Robbie Dulik should be here pretty soon. We told Robbie no sooner than eight o'clock, but no later than ten after. In case you weren't aware, Robbie "kidnapped" my husband late this morning and has kept him away all day. Anyway, when they arrive, I'll give a signal, and I'd like everybody to scream "surprise, happy birthday". Then Mrs. Menegay, Susan, who's over there at the piano, will start playing the birthday song and we can all sing along. Everybody knows the words, right?"

A few people chuckled at her nervous humor.

"Oh, by the way, my husband's name is pronounced DON TAY, like Don, not DAN TAY, like Dan."

More chuckles.

"Oh, and one last thing," stated Lisa. "Thank you, thank you, thank you for coming tonight and joining in our celebration. It means a lot to me, and I'm sure Dante, too. If he doesn't kill me."

She smiled at the crowd.

"She's a nice lady," commented Fred Durzak to Paul Pallibio.

Paul nodded in agreement. A sickening knot lay in the pit of his stomach.

"You feelin' ok, buddy?" asked Fred.

"Yea, I'm alright, just a little indigestion," he lied.

He did not like what he had decided to do to this family. But it was far too late to turn back.

Halfway across the room, Bill Menegay listened to a boring banker ramble on about investing in physical therapy clinics.

"It'll become the next rage," he heard him say.

But Bill's attention was focused on the dark-haired man wearing the charcoal gray double breasted suit.

Eddie Burson walked into the room to relieve his brother. Vince was toting his gun and mumbling something in Dante's ear. Dante seemed quite upset, but quiet.

Eddie motioned Vince to step outside into the large office area.

"Is he ok, Vinnie?" asked his brother. "Any side effects from the shots?"

"He's all right," replied Vince. "He's a little pissed 'cause I told him we did his wife. But other than that, he's fine."

"Why'd you tell him that?" Eddie angrily asked.

"He just thinks he's a big shot and I had to put him in his place."

Eddie shook his head and peaked into the room to see if Dante was really all right.

"Vinnie, I sent Carl out to get some Italian food. You've been playing the tapes, haven't you?"

"Yea, sure. But this is stupid. I mean the guy has to figure out he ain't in Italy, for Chrissakes. I mean, really Eddie, did you really think putting some tapes on and rocking him and making him think he was on a plane really makes a difference?"

"It may buy us time, Vince. It may buy us time."

"Yeah, right," retorted the younger brother in his sarcastic way. "It'll buy us time."

"Go back to the house, Vin. When Carl gets back, send him over with the food. Make sure to put it on a plate. I don't want no American food wrappers and stuff. Got it?"

Vinnie just walked away.

"And Vinnie, no more friggin' beer. You hear me?"

Vinnie turned and gave his brother the bird.

"Mr. O'Shea, you awake," Eddie queried as he walked into the room.

Dante didn't verbalize an answer. He simply nodded.

"I got some food coming up here pretty soon," offered Eddie.

Dante again nodded.

"Is there anything I can get you?"

Dante listened to this voice. It sounded similar to the other, except for the tone. It was friendlier.

"Where am I?" Dante asked.

"You don't remember the plane ride?"

"No."

"You were in a plane for seven, I mean several hours," lied Eddie.

"He said seven. Seven hours from Cleveland," thought Dante. "Where would that put me?"

"Are we in the States?" he asked.

Dante felt this guy wanted to play a different game with him. A good head game. Good cop, bad cop. He definitely preferred playing twenty questions with this one rather than listen to that punk mouth off. Especially about Lisa.

"Not exactly," Eddie replied.

"How about Europe?"

"Right continent, Mr. O'Shea."

A little prodding and it would be simple making Dante think that this was Rome. But Eddie was also aware that he didn't want his hostage to know his whereabouts too early in the game. Better to keep him guessing for awhile.

"I don't know, man, we in France or something?"

Dante was getting impatient and tried to stifle the frustration in his voice.

"Listen, Mr. O'Shea. Just listen. You'll figure it out."

"Hey?" shouted Dante. "It doesn't matter where we are. Why am I here? What are you going to do with me?"

The veins in his neck started to protrude as Dante's anger and frustration became more pronounced.

"You'll find out when it's time, Mr. O'Shea. In due time."

Both men sat in silence. The basketball star and his kidnaper. Fifty minutes later, Big Carl entered the room with a large plate of lasagna. And a glass of water. He smiled at Eddie. Eddie smiled back.

As quickly and quietly as he came in, Big Carl Plath left.

CHAPTER 22

Lisa Callahan O'Shea looked at the diamond watch on her thin wrist. 8:15.

"Where are our husbands?" she asked her best friend.

"Robbie told me he would keep him occupied for the day," replied Alise. "He never told me where they were going."

"Do me a favor, would you, Alise?" inquired Lisa.

"What's that?"

"You know where Dante keeps the extra beer? You know, in the laundry room in that little closet?"

"Sure, I know where you're talking about," Alise answered. "But you don't need more beer now, I mean, before the boys come?"

"No, not right now. But after they come in, would you take one of the caterers and show him where it is. Tell them we're going to need to put more on ice. These folks do enjoy their beer. Wished I would've just let the caterers handle that, too."

"No problem," Alise replied with a smile.

Five minutes later, an excited employee of the International Courier Service rang the front doorbell of the O'Shea residence. He had heard a lot of commotion inside, but now all was quiet.

"Weird," he thought.

He had contemplated getting an autograph from his favorite player, but company policies prohibited such unprofessionalism. And he needed this job to get through college.

He rang the doorbell a second time. The door swung wide open by an unseen hand.

"SURPRISE!" shouted a hundred people. "HAPPY BIRTHDAY, DANTE!" they screamed. Susan Menegay, on cue, started playing 'Happy Birthday to You' on the baby grand. Some people started singing, then broke into laughter.

A very embarrassed Courier Service employee peered into the crowded living room.

"It's not my birthday, but thanks anyway," he tried to joke with a face as red as his hair. "I have a letter, special delivery, for Mrs. Dante O'Shea."

Lisa looked confused.

"Did you say, Mrs. O'Shea?"

"Yes, ma'am," the delivery boy politely replied. "The letter's from Rome."

Lisa accepted the letter from the redhead's hand.

"Please sign here, Ma'am," he quietly requested.

He wished he could have gotten Dante O'Shea to sign. He could always photocopy his signature.

"From Rome, you say?" Lisa asked.

"Yes, Ma'am."

"Maybe it's from the Pope," someone shouted from the crowd.

Several people laughed politely. Paul Pallibio inched his way closer to the door. Bill Menegay was not far behind.

Lisa took the large brown envelope and placed it on top of the piano.

"Aren't you going to open it?" Alise asked her.

"It's probably for Dante," surmised Lisa. "The post office called after you left this afternoon and told me they had two big bags of letters for Dante. So, I'm sure it's for him."

Paul Pallibio observed the conversation between the two women. He, of course, recognized the brown envelope. He certainly didn't plan on it not being opened.

"This could set the plan back for hours," he lamented to himself.

But he could see no way to convince Lisa O'Shea to open the envelope.

At 8:30, the guests were getting restless. The caterers kept ample food on the tables. But the refreshments were already running low. By now, Dante was supposed to be here and the crowd would start curtailing their drinking. This wasn't going to be an all night binge, so they figured a couple to three hours worth of beverages would suffice. The delay seemed to make the guests thirstier.

One of the caterers found Lisa standing beside the baby grand piano talking with Susan Menegay. He walked up to her and whispered in her ear. She nodded and pointed towards Alise Dulik.

The white-coated caterer ambled towards Alise, who was having an animated discussion with a loge-owning lawyer.

"I know there's all kinds of lawyers," she was saying to the handsome young attorney. "But I still think that some of them push society into lawsuits and divorces, simply by making it too easy, and being too eager to help people sue someone or divorce someone."

The young lawyer was politely agreeing with her, not aware that he was hitting on Robbie Dulik's wife.

The caterer politely tapped Alise on her right shoulder.

"Sorry to interrupt you, MRS. Dulik," he stated emphatically to save her from the amorous attorney. "But Mrs. O'Shea told me that you would show me where the, uh, the extra refreshments are kept. We're almost out."

Alise was relieved to have an excuse to leave the egotistical and inebriated attorney.

"Thanks," she muttered to the knowing caterer. "I'll show you where it's kept."

Lisa was nervously upset with Robbie and her husband. They were well over a half hour late. Robbie, at least, knew that the timing was important.

"My God," she thought. "I hope nothing has happened to them."

CHAPTER 23

In a tight basketball game, when the Musketeers were losing and time was running out, Dante would try to loosen up his teammates by saying something like, "we got them where we want them, guys". He tried to inflict his humor in any situation.

Eddie was feeding lasagna to his tied-up hostage. Not too successfully. The large noodles and sauce found its way down Dante's shirt and onto his lap.

"Sorry, Mr. O'Shea," Eddie apologized time after time.

"Couldn't have picked a better food to feed me," Dante half-heartedly joked.

"Would you like something else?" asked Eddie.

He was trying to be civil in an uncivilized situation.

"Pizza sounds good," replied Dante. "Any Pizza Huts around here? I'll buy and fly!"

"I'm a newcomer to this country, Mr. O'Shea. I haven't seen one yet."

"What brought you here, to this place, wherever we are?" queried Dante.

He was grasping for any information he could get to figure out where they had taken him.

"Why not just tell me?" he thought. "It's not like I'm free to roam."

"You brought me here, sir," was Eddie's reply.

"So you two guys kidnapped me and flew me to somewhere in Europe?"

"You got it."

"Why Europe?"

"It's where we have support. You know, in case you try to escape? We have a lot of backup here, Mr. O'Shea. Many supporters to our cause."

Eddie hoped his improvised lie would suffice.

"What's going to happen?"

"Well, if all goes according to our plan, your wife will be notified of your, uh, absence and, hopefully, will respond quickly so we don't have to take drastic measures."

"Such as?" Dante pushed.

"You really don't want to know, do you, Mr. O'Shea?"

The game continued. Dante probed. Eddie fed him tidbits of hints but wanted to keep him confused on his whereabouts. Mr. Pallibio had told him that if a hostage didn't know where he was, he was less likely to try to escape. And if there was no attempt to escape, there was a better likelihood that no one would accidentally get hurt and all would go smooth. Lack of location was power over the hostage. Of course, they also wanted Dante thinking he was far away from home. Part of the plan.

Dante tried another tactic. He wanted to keep this guy talking. He had traveled all over the world playing basketball tournaments in different countries. He had friends and contacts in almost every major city on earth. If he could determine where he was, exactly, when he escaped, and he knew he would, he would have a chance of getting back home, back to the U.S. of A., and Lisa.

"You mentioned my wife," stated Dante as calmly as he could. "Is she ok? She wasn't there when you, uh, you abducted me, right?"

"As far as I know, she's fine."

"Well, your partner said some nasty things that he and you did to her. That was a lie?"

"It was a lie. My partner gets a little carried away sometimes."

"So Lisa was safe," Dante thought. "At least this guy makes it sound that way. And it didn't sound like there was any love lost between him and his partner."

Like the moves of Daryl Varnell, Dante put that information into his memory for possible future use.

"I think I'm done eating," advised Dante to his captor. "It's stuffy in here. Any chance of opening a window or turning on a fan."

"No, sorry. We can't do that."

Dante leaned back and tried to get comfortable. The cast on his foot was itchy as hell. Yesterday, that had been the worst of his troubles. He tried to relax. He strained to listen to the outside noises. He could hear a whirring sound. Maybe an air conditioner somewhere. He heard street sounds. Cars going too fast on pavement. Horns honking. Occasionally, he heard voices. But they came and went too fast for him to pick up the language.

"Stay with it, old boy," he told himself. "The fat lady hasn't started to sing just yet."

CHAPTER 24

Alise Dulik led the gray-haired caterer down the basement steps and through Dante's impressive workout area. She apologized for Lisa for the mess in the laundry room. Alise pushed the white hamper out of the way.

"They keep the extra refreshments in there," she stated.

The caterer nodded and reached for the door.

"By the way, I want to thank you for saving me from that guy. That was very chivalrous of you."

"I see it all the time. Especially at weddings. Those kinds of guys think women are easy targets when the booze is flowing freely and love is in the air."

"Well, I did appreciate it. I'm going back up to the party. Don't want to miss the grand entrance, you know. Oh, do you want me to get you some help carrying those cases?"

The elderly caterer pulled open the door.

"No, that won't," he started to reply. Then abruptly stopped as he followed Alise's gaze.

"ROBBIE!" she screamed. "Robbie, oh my God, Robbie."

The caterer deftly moved out of the way.

Above all the commotion, conversation, and partying, Bill Menegay heard his daughter scream. He knew it was her as soon as he heard it.

"Lisa!" he yelled across the living room. "Where's Alise?"

"Downstairs," she mouthed to him. She pointed towards the ground.

He cupped his ear and shook his head. Lisa dropped her conversation with the same amorous lawyer who had been hitting on her friend. She rushed to Alise's father.

"What's wrong?" she asked.

"Where's Alise? I heard her scream."

"Follow me."

Lisa and Bill stormed through the crowded kitchen and down the steps. The caterer was just starting up the stairs.

"We need help!" he anxiously announced. "Over there."

He pointed in the direction of the laundry room.

Alise was trying to maneuver her husband out of the small closet. She felt his neck, frantically trying to find a pulse.

"Daddy! Lisa! Oh, God, help him!"

Bill Menegay moved quickly toward the closet. He put his finger under his son-in-law's nose and felt hot air expelling. Carefully, but quickly, he tore the tape from Robbie's mouth.

"Sorry, son. I know that didn't feel good. Can you hear me, Robbie?"

Robbie Dulik groaned.

Bill turned to Lisa and requested a pair of scissors. Lisa went to a cupboard above the dryer and retrieved a pair for him.

Like a surgeon, Bill carefully cut the silver tape that had mummified his daughter's husband.

"Don't try to talk, Robbie. I need you to be very still. If you can, scrunch your eyes shut. I'm going to remove the tape from there right now."

Bill gently pulled the tape, easing it off Robbie's eyes. With it he pulled off some of the Musketeers' eyebrows and eyelashes. But Robbie made no sound, nor movement. Red splotches appeared on his face where the tape had adhered. Bill continued cutting the tape off of his son-in-law. After a few moments, satisfied that Robbie was all right, Bill began to question him.

"What happened?"

"I was in the bathroom, I opened the door, and a gorilla hit me in the face."

His raspy voice echoed around the laundry room.

"A gorilla?" asked Bill incredulously.

"Not a real one. Someone dressed like one. You know, a costume."

"Where's Dante?" Lisa impatiently asked.

"The last I saw him, he was going to answer the front door. I had to go to the bathroom at the time. His pizza, from last night," he tried to explain.

"When did this happen?" asked the FBI agent and father-in-law.

"It was before noon, I got here around 11:00 or so."

"You mean you've been in here, like that," Alise pointed to the pile of tape. "For over eight hours."

"You're not going to bitch at me, are you, honey?" Robbie tried to joke.

Alise bent over and hugged her husband.

"Not for a long time."

The four of them and the caterer, who had shyly returned to the basement, made their way to the master bedroom. Quite a few of the guests saw the shaken Musketeer player. The party began buzzing with the news of what had been discovered downstairs. The caterer excused himself and told Lisa that he would take care of her guests. She thanked him and he returned to the basement closet to retrieve the beer.

Susan joined the foursome in the bedroom. Bill was on his cell phone calling Jim Sweeney's pager number. He dialed all the digits and hit the pound sign, then waited impatiently for a return call.

"Can I get you anything, Robbie?" asked his mother-in-law.

"Yea, a cold beer. And the son of a bitch who did this," he replied as he rubbed his black and blue chin.

CHAPTER 25

At 8:50 P.M., Carl Plath had had enough of Vince Burson. He sat on the worn, flowered couch in their small living room, trying to concentrate on the comedians entertaining the Comedy Central crowd on television. He half listened to his drunk friend brag about how he had scared the big star of the Musketeers.

"I'm going to go check on Eddie," he mumbled to the dozing Vince.

"Go on, peabrain," he slurred to Big Carl.

Vince reached for an almost full can of Busch beer and knocked it over. It added to the multiple stains on the orange shag carpet.

"Damn," he muttered. "Get me another beer."

"Get your own," countered Big Carl.

Carl didn't wait for a reply as he sauntered his huge frame through the kitchen, down the steps to the basement and towards the door leading to the tunnel.

Carl Plath was a big Cleveland Musketeer fan. Not only in size, but more so, in heart. He couldn't afford to attend the games, the exorbitant ticket prices prevented that. But any televised game, he watched on the big screen at the Warehouse Bar and Grille. Usually with Eddie and Vince.

As he walked through the tunnel and through the dark machine shop to the room, Carl's remorse for what he and his friends had done increased. Dante O'Shea was his hero. And his hero was being tortured by Vinnie, Eddie and even himself. He was full of despair as he made his way to Paul Pallibio's former office.

"All I can do is be nice to him and protect him from Vinnie," he thought.

He wanted desperately not to be here. But he was. And they were his friends.

Opening the door, he found Eddie lounging on the cot, and Dante apparently sleeping with his head on his chest. He was relieved to see the red scarf had been removed from Dante's mouth. It sat limply on the table by the tape recorder. Eddie was still playing the Italian tapes, keeping up the facade, according to the plan.

Eddie looked up and was surprised to see Carl. He motioned that he would meet him outside of the room and soon joined Big Carl on the opposite end of the large office area of the former machine shop.

"You're a little early," commented Eddie. "Is there a problem?"

"I just got tired of your brother," Carl admitted.

He did not look Eddie in the face.

"He's been drinking a lot, and, well, you know how he can be."

Eddie pursed his lips. He was angry and disappointed with his brother. He told Vince to lay off the beer, that they would have a lifetime to drink when this was all over. It had never occurred to him that Vince drank to overcome the fear he had. Not only about the kidnapping. But in facing life's problems.

"Is he asleep?" inquired Eddie.

"Almost."

"Maybe you and me ought to handle the rest of the night, Carl. You can watch him 'til midnight, and I'll take him the rest of the night."

"Ok," responded Big Carl. "You want me to go in there now?"

"Yea, why don't you," Eddie said. "He's asleep any way. I'll go have a few words with my brother."

"Good luck," offered Carl.

"Thanks," replied his friend.

Carl took big lumbering steps toward the room. The wooden floor squeaked and vibrated with each movement he made. He entered and stared for a few moments at his fallen hero.

"Poor guy," he thought. "He breaks his ankle in the game. Then this. He hasn't had a good week."

Carl Plath was a person full of compassion. He took a lot of ribbing about his size and his lack of intellect. Especially from Vince Burson. The thought of the younger Burson brother made him angry. He rarely exposed his anger to others. He just let his frustrations simmer.

Like a pot of boiling hot water. Ready to overflow.

CHAPTER 26

Bill Menegay stood up from the edge of the king sized waterbed in the O'Shea's master bedroom. His mind was whirring with questions to a puzzle he was now beginning to solve.

"I'll be right back," he announced to his wife, his daughter, her husband and Lisa O'Shea.

He walked down the hallway and into the living room full of confused guests.

"Do you think anything happened to him?" he heard a slightly overweight brunette ask the mustached man next to her. The man simply shrugged.

Bill worked his way through the murmuring guests until he stood in front of the baby grand piano. He briefly surveyed the top of the piano, spotting the brown envelope leaning against a vase of yellow, blossoming roses. He hastily grabbed it and put it into the inside pocket of his blue blazer. Turning around, he noticed a pale-faced gentleman striding toward the front door. It was Paul Pallibio. Bill Menegay wanted to somehow confront the former owner of Pallibio Machine, but had to confirm his suspicions before doing so. Maybe he could stall him.

"Leaving so soon?" he asked in a friendly tone. "The night's still young."

"He's not feeling so well," replied Fred Durzak for his friend. "Something he ate."

"I bet," thought Menegay to himself.

"Too bad," he said to the two men. "Dante should be here any moment. You'll miss the big event."

Paul Pallibio weakly smiled at the suntanned stranger and motioned to Fred that he wanted to leave. Bill Menegay wanted to know more about Pallibio's companion and was getting ready to engage the two in some more banter. But Alise was at his right elbow, trying to interrupt the interlude.

"You left your cell phone in the bedroom and it started ringing. I answered it for you, it's Jim Sweeney," Alise whispered in his ear.

Bill followed his daughter back into the bedroom.

"Menegay, here."

"Bill, Jim. What's up?"

"Hold on a second, Jim."

Bill retrieved the brown envelope from his pocket. He tore it open and silently read the note. In large letters, is stated:

DEAR MRS. O'SHEA,

DANTE IS SAFE AND COMFORTABLE. HE IS NOT IN THE COUNTRY. AND HE WON'T BE BACK UNLESS YOU FOLLOW OUR INSTRUCTIONS. IN EXCHANGE FOR HIS SAFE RETURN, WE REQUIRE TEN MILLION DOLLARS IN SMALL DENOMI- NATIONS, AND UNMARKED BILLS. YOU WILL BE CON- TACTED TOMORROW WITH FURTHER DETAILS.

"Oh, Christ, Jim," he said into the mouthpiece. "They've struck."

"Who? What?"

"They've kidnapped Dante O'Shea," Bill replied quietly.

But not quiet enough. When Lisa heard those words she exploded into tears. Alise and Susan reached over to her and the three women hugged and sobbed. Robbie stared at his father-in-law in disbelief.

"Who kidnapped him, Bill? Who is taking responsibility?" asked Special Agent Jim Sweeney.

"There's no indication on the ransom note," replied Bill Menegay in a professional tone. "The note was delivered about twenty minutes ago by courier. It appears to have originated in Rome."

"Do you think it's a terrorist plot?" Sweeney proposed.

"I don't know. Jim, I've got to do something here. I'll meet you at your office in an hour. Get on the phone and contact the bureau in Rome and fill them in. Also, start checking any flight to Italy that was made today. Include private charters on that one."

"Roger that, Bill." replied the Cleveland-based agent. "I'll see you in an hour."

Bill Menegay rushed out of the bedroom, ran down the hall, and pushed his way through the solemn crowd toward the front door. Rumor spread like wildfire around the O'Shea home. Something had happened to Dante O'Shea. Like most rumors, it became the worst case scenario very quickly.

"Dante's dead," one wealthy loge owner whispered to his crony. "Killed in a car accident. He was drinking."

Bill Menegay dashed out the front door and searched for one of the white-shirted valets. He found three of them sitting on folding chairs in front of the garage. They were each holding a bottle of Miller Genuine Draft.

"Did you see two guys leave her about ten minutes ago? One had dark hair and a double breasted suit, dark gray. The other was older and wore a red sports coat. Did you see them?"

"A lot of people have left, buddy," replied the under aged drinker. "We're lucky enough to find the right cars, let alone know what these people are wearing."

Bill looked at the other two attendants. Their drink induced giggles were their replies.

"Damn," Bill Menegay muttered to himself.

CHAPTER 27

"Pr-r-rosciotto," shouted a street vendor on the tape.

Dante heard the word very distinctly as he sat, bound to the wooden chair. His head still on his chest, he had feigned sleeping, trying to concentrate on the noises he occasionally heard. He still had not concluded where they had taken him.

Carl Plath sat on the folding chair behind Dante. Since relieving Eddie an hour earlier, he sat in boredom, occasionally studying the bound superstar who slept in front of him.

"Prosciutto," thought Dante. "I've heard of that somewhere."

Then the answer came to him out of nowhere. Grandma Miccike. His mom's mother. She occasionally cooked the Italian ham when his parents and he visited his grandparents. They lived on the outskirts of Meadville, Pennsylvania, on a little farm on Neason Hill, just north of the sprawling little town.

His latest guard had not spoken a word since entering the room. Dante sensed it was someone different, but wasn't sure.

"If it wasn't the friendly one," he surmised. "Then it must be the vulgar one. The punk."

He had deduced that there were two kidnapers involved, since he had remembered seeing only an ape and a gorilla.

"Is anybody there?" he asked the silence.

Carl jumped slightly at the question. He had been thinking about what a bad person he had become. Kidnapping a nice guy like Dante. His conscience was eating away at what little self esteem he had left. And it hadn't been much to start with.

"I know you're there," tried Dante again. "Can I get something to drink?"

Carl stood up. He had been instructed by Eddie to minimize his conversation.

"They're always ordering me around," he thought. "Screw 'em. I can think for myself."

"What would you like, Mr. O'Shea?" asked Carl. "We got some pop and I can get you water."

Dante did not recognize the voice. So there were three of them.

"I guess I'm not really thirsty," replied Dante. "I'm just sort of bored."

"Yea, me, too," offered Big Carl.

"I haven't met you yet, have I?" probed Dante.

"No, you met Vinnie and Ed," Carl cut himself short.

"Yea, Vinnie and Ed," Dante repeated. "Are you their friend?"

Dante didn't know why that was an important question to ask. He wanted to build a conversation and find out what he could before that loud-mouthed punk came back. He felt he didn't have much time.

"We've known each other since high school," Carl responded.

"When did you graduate?"

"In '89."

Carl did not let on that he was twenty years old at the time. He was talking to his hero. And Dante O'Shea seemed genuinely interested in him. Carl was quietly thrilled.

"You a Musketeer fan?"

"Oh, yea," replied Carl with enthusiasm.

"Did you see the playoff game?" asked Dante, referring to the final game against Chicago.

"Yea. I did," he responded dejectedly. "We kind of got screwed on that call."

"Well, I sure didn't like it," chided Dante. "But there's worse things in life."

"Mr. O'Shea, I—I—I want to apologize for hitting you," stammered Big Carl. "It wasn't my idea. They made me do it. It was part of the plan."

"What plan?"

"Their plan," he answered. "They made me do it. You understand, don't you? I didn't want to hurt you?"

Dante saw an opening. Like driving the lane for a layup, it required a quick decision and fast action.

"I understand," he replied. "Except for my jaw, no hard feelings."

Carl felt relieved and smiled at his hero's attempt at humor. He decided he liked Dante O'Shea. He liked him a lot.

"Maybe, somehow, he'll become my friend," he briefly fantasized to himself.

"What's your name? I already met Ed and Vinnie."

"Carl."

When Dante had heard the distinctive Italian word for ham, his mind calculated all that he had learned since his abduction. He had been kidnapped from his home around noon. He had been in a plane for seven hours, a car ride for maybe a half hour, and holed up somewhere ever since. The stuffy, humid weather and the various noises he heard helped him make his conclusion.

"Have you been in Rome a long time, Carl?"

Dante guessed it was Rome. He figured there weren't many direct flights from Cleveland to any other Italian city. Unless, of course, these guys had their own plane.

Carl was surprised at the question. He quickly decided that Eddie and Vince had given more information to Dante than they had let on to him. Probably part of the plan.

"No, not very long."

"It's a great city, Carl. If you get the chance to see the Vatican, and the Sistine Chapel, do so. It's really inspiring."

Dante now had his whereabouts. He remembered playing a charity game here last summer against an Italian professional team. One player stood out in his mind. Alfredo Sartori. Alfredo had scored eighteen points against Dante in that game. He was destined to go to America and play in the NBA. He had been drafted by Sacramento. He hoped Sartori was still in Rome.

"I'll try to get to them," promised Carl.

Dante was satisfied with this new information. He lay his head on his chest and planned what action he would take when the opportunity arrived. Like the disciplined basketball player he was, he would create an opportunity out of the situation.

CHAPTER 28

The O'Shea home became disturbingly quiet as the guests filtcrcd out of the Fairlawn residence. Fifteen minutes earlier, Lisa O'Shea, with tears streaming down her blushed cheeks, had bravely announced that Dante had been in a car accident. She knew no details, other than he was being transported to a hospital. His destination was unknown.

Very few of the party attendees believed her explanation of Dante's absence. But they were not going to confront her about the situation, delicate as it was. Except for the thin, balding, bespectacled reporter from the Akron Journal.

Ron Collins had been the Musketeer beat reporter for the past fifteen years. He knew the players, coaches, trainers, and owner as well as anyone in northeast Ohio. His insight into the NBA, as well as the Musketeer organization, was well regarded by readers and the Cleveland Musketeer members alike. Collins usually enjoyed an open door policy when it came to getting interviews.

"The Dante O'Shea birthday party took on a morbid overtone," Collins whispered into his miniature tape recorder. He intended to find out what that morbid overtone was all about.

One other guest remained. The forty-nine year old owner of the Musketeers. Bud Herrington had purchased the organization five years earlier for sixty-two million dollars. He made only one significant change in the operation. He spent from his vast millions, earned from designing and building shopping malls around the country, and invested in the free agency of the NBA. Prior to Herrington's ownership, the Musketeer organization didn't dabble too much into the free agency market. Asking prices were usually too exorbitant for the small market Musketeers. It was one of the imbalances of the NBA.

But Bud Herrington wanted to change that. His theory was simple: put a good quality team on the floor, win some games, and the fans would respond. And this year, that had happened. As the Musketeers became more successful on the court, attendance increased to the point that it was almost impossible to get a ticket during the last month of the season and during the playoffs.

Bud Herrington bought some very talented players for Coach Avery to work with. And the Musketeer head coach made his investments pay off. Last week's defeat to Chicago was the furthest any Musketeer team had ever gone. With one or two more free agent signings during the upcoming off season, Bud Herrington figured he would get the beloved championship he and the Cleveland fans wanted so badly.

Bill Menegay met briefly with the owner of the Musketeers.

"We have to play the game, sir," he flatly stated to Herrington. "It's a lot of money, but most of the time, it's recovered."

"I'm not worried about the money, Mr. Menegay," retorted the young owner. "The most important priority is Dante's safety. I'll give you anything you need. Dante's a good man, a good person. I don't want any chances taken. Do we understand each other?"

"His safety is our concern, too," stated the FBI agent. "We'll cover any avenue the abductors take. We'll get Dante back, sir. You have my word on it."

Lisa sat on the large waterbed in her bedroom trying very hard to organize her thoughts.

"I have to call Dante's parents," she stated numbly to her best friend. "They left Tuesday for a vacation in Virginia Beach. I've got their hotel number here, somewhere."

Alise and Susan stayed with and consoled the anguished wife of the Musketeer All-Star guard.

The caterers quietly cleaned up the various messes made by the party attendees. They tried to not appear to eavesdrop when they were near the hushed conversations that took place between those who remained at the O'Shea home. Ron Collins became a shadow.

Bill Menegay finished his conversation with the Cleveland owner. They had worked out the details concerning getting the cash and meeting the unknown requests of the kidnapers. Tomorrow's instructions would be dealt with as they became known.

Bill kissed his wife and daughter, and gave Lisa a reassuring hug as he left to meet Jim Sweeney at the Federal Building in downtown Cleveland. He had seen Lisa's look of despair on hundreds of family member faces from the many kidnapping cases he had worked through the years. Most of those cases involved estranged husbands stealing their children from their ex-wives. He never failed to marvel at the meanness displayed by his fellow human beings.

Paul Pallibio sat in Fred Durzak's Mercedes Benz and enjoyed the quiet ride back to his house. The midnight blue Mercedes pulled into Paul's driveway at 9:45 P.M.

"You want to come in for a nightcap?" offered Paul to his best friend.

"No, I think you need to get some rest, Pauly," Fred Durzak replied. "I'll see you tomorrow, ok?"

"I'm leaving in the morning for L.A.," Pallibio informed him.

"You are?" Fred responded with genuine surprise.

"Didn't I tell you?" countered his friend. "I'm going to visit my cousin for a few days."

"If you did, I forgot," answered Fred Durzak. "This sounds like short notice. When will you be back?"

"In time to tee off next Saturday," lied Paul Pallibio.

"Well, I guess I'll see you then," Fred mumbled.

"Hey, Freddie," added Paul. "Take care of yourself."

The unexpected statement confused Fred Durzak.

"Yea, you, too," he responded. "And when you get back, Pauly, I think we ought to discuss becoming partners in my shop. I'd like to retire someday."

"You're already retired," joked Paul.

Fred Durzak smiled at his friend. He eased the Mercedes into reverse and slowly backed down the driveway and started his short drive home.

Paul Pallibio went into his house, opened a cabinet door in the kitchen and pulled out a half full bottle of J & B Scotch.

He then proceeded to drink himself to sleep.

CHAPTER 29

The overcast skies promised rain later in the day for northeast Ohio. Lisa woke up around eight o'clock after a fitful night alone in the huge waterbed.

Alise and Susan sat at the kitchen counter, sipping coffee and indulging themselves with donuts. Alise had taken care to hide the Sunday edition of the Akron Journal. The front page report informed its readers that 'Dante O'Shea had mysteriously missed a birthday party in his honor last night'. The brief article stated that initial reports indicated that he was involved in a car accident, but no details were known. Ron Collins had a conscience after all.

Lisa joined her friends in the kitchen. She drank the black coffee offered her by Susan Menegay. The three women talked about everything except what was really on their minds. When the subject was finally broached, Alise and Susan reassured Lisa O'Shea that Bill Menegay was very good at what he did. If any one person could solve this case, and do it quickly, Bill was the man for the job.

Lisa informed her two friends that she wanted to have as normal a day as possible. She wanted to attend church. Then maybe visit the Wilson's next door. She would then deal with the rest of the day. She knew she would have to stay around the house, waiting for the instructions from the kidnapers, and allow the FBI and whoever else was involved, to do their jobs. It would not be an easy day.

The previous night, her parents had offered to drive up from Cincinnati, as did her in-laws from their vacation in Virginia Beach. She both wanted them there and didn't want them there. It would feel too much like a wake or something. But they had a right to be there, so she had made them all feel she would welcome their company and their support.

Lisa felt the need to pray. She wanted to vacate their home and go to church, even though she knew she shouldn't. Against the advice of Susan Menegay, Lisa quickly dressed and drove the fifteen minute ride to Saint Augustine Church in silence.

The church was located in Barberton. Across from Lake Anna. When Dante and Lisa had moved to Fairlawn, they had tried several of the area churches and finally settled on the hundred year old parish.

Father Byrider had been pastor at Saint Augustine's for thirty-five years. He wasn't good at names, Dante was known as Donnie, and Lisa somehow became Betty, but he was an affable priest and a good spiritual leader.

The rejuvenated parish had hundreds of young families active in its many projects. Young parents, who through the years had questioned their Catholic faith and had left the Church, now came back in droves, bringing with them their young families. What they had learned in their youth, they now wanted for their children. What made Saint Augustine Church different than most others was that it was open twenty-four hours a day. And there was always someone in the church. Commitments had been made by the parishioners to never leave the church empty. Day or night. That practice was in its fortieth year. And without any problems. God did take care of his flock.

Lisa arrived for the 9:30 Mass ten minutes early. She sat, as she and Dante had so often, in the fourth pew from the back. She remembered how the many parishioners had besieged Dante for autographs the first few times they had attended Mass there. Nothing seemed sacred to the avid sports fans of Cleveland. Dante signed his name on church bulletins and prayer books. But eventually, the novelty wore off and the O'Shea's were able to honor God without fanfare or unwanted attention.

Lisa knelt on the padded kneeler and buried her head into her hands.

"Oh, God, my Lord and my Master," she pleaded. "Please keep Dante safe from harm. Help those who took him and let them see the error of their ways."

Lisa remained kneeling. Out of the corner of her eye, she noticed the Robinson family processing down the aisle toward an empty pew in the front of the church. The proud husband and wife walked arm in arm down the aisle followed by their seven children, single file, likes ducklings following their mother. Lisa smiled at the youngest, a two year old girl, as she nearly fell over trying to duplicate the genuflection of her older siblings.

"I'm always asking You for favors, Lord," Lisa silently prayed. "I want a baby. Dante's baby."

She again buried her face into her hands.

As the priest processed down the center aisle of the church, preceded by four servers, the Liturgist holding the sacred scriptures high above her head, and four Eucharistic Ministers, the adult choir began to sing.

"Amazing grace! How sweet the sound. That saved and set me free. I once was lost, but now am found. Was blind, but now I see."

Lisa bravely fought back the tears that welled in her eyes. This was Dante's favorite song. She found comfort in the words. Much comfort. As if on cue, sunlight peaked through the overcast sky and shined through the red, green, blue, yellow and purple stained glass window that depicted the birth of Jesus. Lisa observed the brief sunlit moment.

"As the birth of Your Son has given us hope," she silently stated to the Father. "May that hope sustain me throughout this day and throughout this ordeal. Amen."

CHAPTER 30

In the living room of the faded yellow house on East Fortieth Street, Big Carl Plath awoke after a fitful few hours of sleep on the worn recliner. Vince was snoring on the couch. Carl quietly maneuvered out of the chair and crept into the bathroom to relieve himself.

Just as quietly, he snuck past the sleeping drunk and into the kitchen. As was his morning routine, he made a fresh pot of coffee. He glanced at the grease stained wall toward the clock. It was missing.

"Oh, yeah," Big Carl thought to himself. "Eddie took it to the room."

Fifteen minutes later, Carl carried three cups of steaming, black coffee through the tunnel, through the former machine shop, up the stairs, across the large office and to the sleeping Eddie and Dante O'Shea.

His entrance woke the two of them. He noticed that the room was silent. The tape players were both off. He thought about resetting them, but figured Eddie probably wanted it that way. Part of the plan.

The room was dark and musty. Little light filtered through the one inch crack at the bottom of the one open window. Dante stirred. He was stiff and uncomfortable, but welcomed the familiar smell of coffee. Carl placed the cups on the eight foot table along the wall. Eddie sat up on the cot where he had spent the night.

"Thanks," muttered Dante as Carl put the styrofoam cup to his lips.

Eddie nodded his appreciation. He thought how Big Carl had always been so thoughtful, and how he was always taking so much crap from him and Vinnie. Eddie silently vowed that he would be nicer to his large friend.

Carl motioned for Eddie to join him outside of the room. They walked slowly toward the opposite end of the office area, away from Paul Pallibio's former office where Dante sat, blindfolded, tied up and sore.

"What're we going to do today?" Carl whispered.

"According to the plan, we just sit tight. Mr. Pallibio's supposed to be sending the instructions to Dante's wife."

"About the drop off," he added.

"Can we move him around?" questioned Big Carl. "I mean, he's probably sore from everything and,"

He started to move towards the room.

Eddie stopped him.

"Carl, I know how you feel about him. He told me he thought you were a good guy. Just remember, our future is at stake here. We can't get too friendly. Tell you what, I'll ask him if he has to use the bathroom, we'll try to make him more comfortable, but we have got to be careful."

Carl smiled when Eddie told him what Dante had said about him.

"He doesn't like Vince too much," added Eddie. "In fact, I think he'd hurt Vinnie real bad if he could."

"Can't say I blame him," stated Carl.

"Well, it's probably better if we keep Vinnie away from him today," Eddie declared. "Is he still sleeping?"

"Yea, he's snoring like a bear."

"Let him sleep then," ordered Eddie. "You and me can take care of things."

Paul Pallibio woke to the dull buzzing of his alarm clock. As soon as he moved his body to shut off the annoying alarm, he knew he had consumed too much scotch the night before. His head throbbed.

He had almost three hours to get ready, before leaving Cleveland for what he figured would be the last time. He was to fly into Los Angeles, to LAX, arriving at three or so in the afternoon. He would then rent a car and drive to Manhattan Beach, four miles south of the airport, to the Residence Inn. There he would sit and enjoy the May heat of southern California. And kill time.

"And on Monday," he speculated. "I will be one rich bastard. Debt free."

He didn't want to consider the freedoms he would be losing.

Forty miles south, in Fairlawn, a small gathering assembled at the O'Shea residence. In the kitchen, Alise and Robbie sat at the counter, trying to decide if they should be there or not. Susan Menegay sat in a chair in the den off the kitchen and knitted. Her husband, Jim Sweeney and Special Agent Len Gill sat with Lisa in the spacious living room. They discussed the previous days, weeks and months, trying to help Lisa remember if there were any out-of-the-ordinary events that could have been now construed as a threat to her husband.

The doorbell rang, and the small group was joined by Bud Herrington, the owner of the Musketeers. In a large, black Samsonite suitcase, he carried the ransom money, as requested by the kidnaper and Bill Menegay twelve hours before. He looked tired.

"Good job, Mr. Herrington," Bill Menegay stated in his professional voice.

"The funds were available," the owner humbly mentioned. "I just had to get my banker to open the vault. He wasn't a happy camper, but he evidently cooperated."

"He won't talk, will he?" queried Special Agent Sweeney.

"No, of course not," replied the owner. "He understands the situation completely."

"So now what do we do?" It was Lisa.

As she asked the question, she noticed that she was chewing on her fingernail, a nervous habit she had broken years ago.

"Basically, we wait," Bill responded. "We have a lot of activities going on, well, not here evidently. We simply have to wait for their next move."

Lisa stared at the dark green carpeting that covered the living room floor.

At eleven thirty-five, a red minivan pulled up the long driveway. It was another vehicle from the International Courier Service Company. Lisa nearly jumped out of the front door and ran to the van, surprising the courier with her haste.

"Are you Mrs. O'Shea?" inquired the tall young man.

"I am."

"I have a special delivery for you. A letter from, let's see, Sydney, Australia."

"Sydney?" she responded in surprise.

"Let me double check."

"That's ok," declared Lisa. "Where do I sign?"

"Right by the 'x'," he instructed.

Lisa hurriedly scribbled her signature.

"Thanks!" she yelled to him as she hustled toward the house. The disappointed courier stood next to his van for a moment. He thought he'd get a hefty tip, this being the basketball superstar's house.

Lisa had never given it a second thought.

CHAPTER 31

The promised rain deluged the Cleveland area in the mid-afternoon. It beat down on the shingled roof of the old Pallibio Machine Shop, sounding like it might leak through at any moment. An occasional thunderclap accompanied the downpour. At least the spring shower relieved some of the humidity. Dante was grateful for that.

Eddie and Carl took turns watching Dante. They had allowed him to get up earlier and helped him limp into the bathroom in the corner of the large office area. Since there was no running water, his urine lay in the bottom of the toilet bowl and joined the other dank smells of the abandoned building.

When they re-tied him to the chair, Carl made sure the yellow nylon ropes weren't too tight. He kept the promise he had made to himself to help his hero to be as comfortable as possible.

Vince would occasionally pop his head into the room and shout some obscenity towards Dante. Eddie discouraged his staying, and Vinnie would promptly return to the yellow house and guzzle another beer. Dante knew it was Big Mouth each time. The combination of verbal abuse and the distinct odor of beer overpowered the musty smells in the room. Dante was drenched in sweat from sitting in the hot, humid room for the past twenty-two hours. He felt dirty and reeked like he had just finished an overtime game. And his captors' odor wasn't any better.

Dante engaged Eddie and Carl in small talk whenever they would cooperate. Carl said little, Eddie did the talking. Dante was bored stiff. He needed to find out more about their plans for him. Would they move him? Would they just let him go once the ransom money was paid? Would they take him back to the States? He needed to learn from their small talk so he could mentally prepare an escape.

As different as he and his kidnapers seemed to be, they all shared one common interest, the Cleveland Musketeers. Eddie and Carl asked him a lot of questions about what it was like to be an NBA player. He tried to be honest. But he was also careful not to glorify his job to the point where they became jealous. That would be a mistake. They talked about the players, different games, and how they would have used some of the players differently in game situations. Dante was impressed with their knowledge of the game. It gave some credence to his philosophy that the fans were not just observers; they liked to coach and guess who would do what in any given circumstance on the court. And they wanted to be a part of the game. Make a difference. Which is why the Cleveland crowds were considered the most vocal in the NBA.

"So, when's the next move?" Dante asked Eddie when they were alone.

He had decided that Eddie was the leader. Big Mouth seemingly was out of the picture. He was now being used as a gopher. Carl was friendly enough, but he seemed to be a follower.

"You know I can't tell you that, Mr. O'Shea," Eddie responded. "It won't be long now. It's not like the mid-East hostages. Couple of days at most. That's all."

"What if my wife doesn't pay the ransom?"

"She'll pay. If the roles were reversed, you'd pay, wouldn't you?"

"Guess so," Dante replied to the sound reasoning. "How much is the ransom?"

Dante felt a little strange talking about the kidnapping and ransom. It was kind of like he was talking over a business deal with Reebok.

"Winning is the ability to survive and adapt to the situation," he remembered one of his many coaches saying. "You survive, you adapt, you take action, you win."

Dante was determined to win this game.

Eddie replied to his question, "It's enough. A few million. But not so much that you're wife couldn't get it."

"My life for a few million dollars," Dante observed. "I guess I'll be the NBA's version of the six million dollar man."

"More or less," added Eddie.

They both chuckled to themselves.

Paul Pallibio arrived in Los Angeles thirty-five minutes later than scheduled.

"Sorry, folks. We flew into some gusty headwinds," the pilot explained to Continental's disgruntled customers.

Paul Pallibio exited the plane, one of the first passengers off since he flew in First Class, and headed toward the baggage claim area. His three leather suitcases were one of the first pieces of luggage from the flight. He grabbed them off the conveyor and proceeded toward the exit. He went through the ordeal of showing his flight ticket to the female guard at the claim area gate. She matched his luggage tickets with the stubs stapled inside of his ticket folder. Pallibio then proceeded through the automatic doors, across a crowded avenue of waiting cars, taxis, limousines and hotel buses, to a concrete island designated as the rental car shuttle bus pickup area.

Five minutes later he slumped in the back seat of the yellow and black Dollar Rent-A-Car Shuttle. Ten minutes after that, he found himself in front of the counter at the rental agency's building one mile east of the airport.

He left Dollar twenty minutes later in a new Mustang convertible. He journeyed south on Sepulveda Avenue towards Manhattan Beach. The four mile trip took him twenty-five minutes to complete.

"Love this traffic," he muttered to another traveler as he parked his rental.

"But the weather's nice," was the obvious response from the heavy set man. A brown ponytail with gray streaks rested halfway down his back.

"Horse's ass," chuckled Pallibio.

He strode into the gatehouse to the check-in desk. After completing the required paperwork, he paid cash for his room.

Pallibio retreated to the Mustang, and drove to the back of the lot where he had rented a studio suite. Paul Pallibio like the Residence Inns by Marriott. He stayed in them anytime he could when he traveled. The studio suites had a kitchen with all the conveniences, a small living room with a fireplace, a large comfortable bed, a desk and a large clean bathroom. The penthouse suites were even roomier. They included an upstairs bedroom and bath and an extra television set. Space was nice when traveling.

Outside of his room, in a little courtyard, Paul saw a barbecue grill and a Jacuzzi.

"Nice, but it isn't home," he thought.

But after tomorrow, what would be?

CHAPTER 32

Lisa O'Shea rushed into the living room of the sprawling ranch house she called home. With the excitement of a little girl on Christmas morning, she tore open the brown envelope she had just received from the courier.

She read the letter and slumped into a green and white high-backed chair next to the couch. Bill Menegay grabbed the ransom note from her limp hand. He read it for all to hear.

Dear Mrs. O'Shea,
Dante enjoyed his trips. He is still being well
treated. For now. That can change if our
instructions are not followed to the letter.
We assume by now that you have secured
our monetary request in small denominations.
If not, you had better hurry, for your husband's
sake. We also assume that you have involved
your husband's boss, Mr. Herrington. That is
good. Mr. Herrington is to put the cash into
a large golf bag. It will all fit. He is to put
the golf bag into a large black golf bag carrier.

He will know where to find one. He is to make
certain that the carrier bag is totally secure by
locking the top and bottom together. He will
be able to figure that out. Mr. Herrington is to
check the bag (and himself) on Continental
Flight 539 from Cleveland to Denver. It leaves
Monday morning at 6:35 A.M. (Cleveland time).
It will arrive in Denver at 7:46 A.M. He is to
unboard the plane and return to Cleveland on
United Flight 226. It departs Denver at 8:15 A.M.
The golf bag is to remain on the plane.
We do not wish to harm your husband. However,
for every instruction that is not followed to the letter,
we will have to take regrettable action. Your husband
is right handed. He needs his fingers. Don't make us
send them to you. Once our payment is received, your
husband will be allowed to walk away. We will graciously
provide him with tickets to return to the United States.

Bill hesitated, looking down at Lisa, before reading the rest of the
message. There was no name, no group claiming their sick victory in
kidnapping a basketball player. Only a postscript.

P.S. We have eyes all over the world. We are watching.

Lisa tried to stay under control. Tears welled up in her blue green
eyes, the moisture adding to their softness. The frustration, anxiety, and
fear were released with heavy sobs as she rocked back and forth in the
chair.

Alise hurried over to her friend and placed her hand on Lisa's
shoulder. Her caring touch added some assurance to Dante's wife.

Bill Menegay looked at the owner of the Musketeers.

"Are you willing to do as they instructed?" he quietly asked.

"Whatever it takes," Herrington replied without pause. "If it's all
right with you, I'm going to call my assistant and have her buy a golf
bag and carrier. I'll have it delivered here."

"Good. That's fine," agreed Special Agent Menegay. "Make sure she gets a black bag and carrier. Better get the biggest bag available, ten million dollars is a lot of paper."

"Tell me about it," Herrington replied as he motioned to the large Samsonite bag he had carried in.

These situations were made for Bill Menegay. His take charge leadership and ability to delegate orders made these types of circumstances easier for those involved to do what had to be done.

"Jim," he stated to Special Agent Sweeney. "Check out the flight to Denver. See if Flight 539 continues to any other destination. Also, put the word out that we want any information on any terrorist groups in Europe, Australia, and the Mid East. Find out if they have any active members in the U.S., especially in Cleveland and Denver."

He had a hunch as to who was behind the kidnapping. For the sake of Lisa, his daughter and Robbie, he wanted them to see that the FBI was taking action. His experience in these matters had taught him that action, any action, made the other victims of these terrible crimes feel less frustrated, and more hopeful. If his hunch was right, he also didn't want the others in the O'Shea residence that Sunday morning, to know that the kidnaper was in their home last night.

"Len," he stated. "Come with me."

The two agents walked through the kitchen and out the sliding doors to the deck. For the first time, Bill noticed the large Musketeer logo painted on the bottom of the swimming pool. With sword raised, the lone Musketeer was ready to fight. So was Bill Menegay.

"Lenny," he said in a low voice. "I want the tape of Pallibio's conversation with that kid."

"Eddie?" asked Agent Gill.

"Yea, Eddie. Can you edit the conversation and make separate recordings of each phrase?"

"It'll take a little time, but sure, no problem."

"I plan to be on the flight to Denver tomorrow morning," Bill flatly stated. "Wherever that flight ends up, that's where our man is going to be. I just know it."

"How do you figure?"

"They have to pick up the money sometime, right? Would you want the airlines handling a golf bag full of ten million dollars?"

"No, but why wouldn't they pick it up in Denver?"

"Well, number one, the note said that the bag was to remain on the plane, but Bud Herrington was to get off. Two, Denver is a major stopover for many flights to the west coast. And three, wherever that flight ends up will probably be more crowded than in Denver."

"So the person making the pick up will be less conspicuous," surmised Len Gill.

"That's right," Menegay nodded.

"Do you think O'Shea is where the pick up will be made?" Gill asked.

"I think he's somewhere in the country," replied Menegay. "These people have made too much effort in making us believe he isn't."

"You mean the letters coming from Italy and Australia?" inquired Agent Gill.

"That, and the fact that they'll give him a ticket back to the States. Not to mention how difficult it would be to move someone as high profile as Dante O'Shea from country to country without being noticed. It just doesn't add up. Do you have the dossier on Pallibio?"

"It's in my car."

"I want to see if he made any recent trips out of the country," Bill explained.

"Like to Italy or Australia."

"Exactly."

"Oh, yeah, Lenny, one last thing," the west coast agent continued. "I'm going to need some facial hair. A beard would be good. Pallibio met me last night at the party."

"Got it."

CHAPTER 33

"Hurry up and wait," lamented Vince Burson to Big Carl Plath. "Old Navy training. I hate to freakin' wait."

Big Carl just nodded in agreement as he had learned to do when Vince Burson complained.

"When we supposed to relieve Eddie, peabrain?" Vinnie asked in his usual way.

"Don't call me that," Carl retorted. "I'm getting tired of you calling me names."

In all the years they had known each other, Carl always took the verbal abuse from Vinnie. He was getting more and more aggitated with the younger Burson brother. He had never threatened Vinnie physically. Or, for that matter, never had he complained about how he felt. Eddie seemed to understand. But Vinnie, he was a different story. And his story was getting old.

"So answer me...peabrain," Vinnie demanded. "When we supposed to relieve him?"

"If you weren't drunk all the time, you'd know," Carl responded. "I'll go up in a few minutes."

"Screw you. Peabrain."

Paul Pallibio lay on a deck chair next to the rectangular pool by the gatehouse. He checked his watch. 5:30.

"Back home," he thought. "It's two thirty. I'll bet they're scrambling now."

His earlier remorse had departed. A calm anxiety replaced it.

At the O'Shea residence, they were scrambling. Alise kept herself and Lisa busy by cooking a meal for all of the people in the house. Most had not eaten since that morning. Choosing not to microwave a meal or make something that would cook in a hurry, Alise convinced Dante's wife to make spaghetti. They would cook enough to feed an army. That would take time. Time that Lisa needed to fill with some activity.

Robbie had left for the Dulik home in Copley. He had to borrow Dante's Beemer, since his car had been stolen out of the O'Shea driveway yesterday. He planned to get home and call some of his teammates who lived in the area and tell them about the situation. His father-in-law told him it would be ok to do so. As long as they didn't go public. Plus he had to file a police report on his stolen Jeep Cherokee.

Alise questioned him about the wisdom of telling his teammates.

"If nothing else," he told his wife. "They can pray."

Lisa's parents arrived shortly after three o'clock. They had driven from Cincinnati. Her father gave her a long, loving hug. She was not used to his affection. But it was appreciated.

Dante's parents soon followed. They had driven through most of the night from Virginia Beach. They were tired and, of course, deeply concerned. But for the sake of their daughter-in-law, they kept their conversation positive.

Bill Menegay commandeered the spare bedroom. He needed privacy and room to spread out the information he and his fellow agents had gathered on the case. The king sized bed became his desk. He kept the bedroom door closed.

As he sat on the edge of the bed, he pondered. He picked up the telephone, then set it down. He grabbed a legal pad and jotted notes on the yellow sheets.

"What do I know for sure?" he thought.

Under the heading PAUL PALLIBIO, he wrote: Huge gambling debts. IRS trouble. No apparent income. Looked sick at party.

"If he has a big gambling debt," he reasoned. "It's probably to someone who wants to be paid. On time."

Under a column titled MOTIVE, he jotted down 'needs money fast'.

"If the IRS is on to him," he continued thinking. "Then he needs enough money to pay them off, too."

Under MOTIVE, he added 'relocation funds'.

"I guess if I were him, I'd leave the country," he stated to no one.

Bill Menegay felt he was on the right track. But it was still a hunch. A hunch based on some circumstantial evidence in the form of need. And a hunch based on his experience with human nature. Once you got it, it's hard to give it up. The opposite of the concept that you never miss what you never had. A knock on the door interrupted his pensive theories. The door pushed open slightly. Lisa peeked in.

"Bill, I'm sorry to disturb you," she said in a low voice. "But, Mr. Wilson here, has some information that might help."

"Come in. Come in, Mr. Wilson."

The elderly O'Shea neighbor slowly advanced into the room.

"I'm Bill Menegay," the FBI agent offered his right hand as he made his declaration.

"Fred Wilson, sir," replied the nervous neighbor.

He firmly gripped Bill's hand and shook it.

"Go ahead, Fred, tell him what you saw," coaxed Lisa.

"Well," he started. "I was out in the yard yesterday weeding the garden at the end of the fence. You know, the one that separates our two yards?"

He looked at Lisa.

"The people before Lisa and Dante moved in didn't like our dog, we have a French Poodle, FiFi, they didn't like our dog taking a sh, er, relieving herself in their yard. They weren't the friendliest people. Treated us like old fogies. So I built the fence. Made it myself with two by fours and spindles. Showed them, I guess."

Bill remained patient.

"Tell him about the car, Fred."

"Yea, the car. Well, yesterday morning, it was around noon, or maybe a bit before because I remember I was getting hungry, but my Mimi, that's my wife, was out shopping with Lisa, and I figured I'd wait for her to get home so I could make us some sandwiches. Anyway, it was around lunch time."

"Well, I see this shiny black car come up the driveway and go right into the garage. At first I thought it was Lisa and Mimi, and I was starting to get up to go in the house, but then I thought to myself, that if it was them, then they would have waved at me, because I was right at the end of the fence and Mimi knew I was going to weed there. She certainly would've waved to me."

Bill nodded in agreement.

"Anyway, this black shiny car drives right into the garage. And when it drove by me, I thought I saw a gorilla or something big and hairy in the passenger's seat."

"Don't tell Mimi I thought she looked like a gorilla, ok?" he winked at his two listeners.

"Robbie was struck by a gorilla," thought Bill Menegay.

"So I kinda hid myself behind the fence and peeked around, you know, I spied on them. I'm not a peeping tom or anything like that, sir," he quickly added.

"You saw two people in the car?" Bill asked.

"Yea, the other one was an ape."

"An ape?"

"Yea, you know, a monkey."

"What'd they do, Mr. Wilson?" queried the agent.

"They went to the front door. They were carrying a white box, like the kind you get from a bakery."

"Go on."

"Well, they ring the doorbell and I see Mr. O'Shea, Dante, open the door and let them in."

"My trusting husband," thought Lisa. She immediately wished she hadn't had that thought.

"They didn't force their way into the house?" inquired Bill.

"No. They just walked in. I figured Dante knew them, so I went back to gardening."

"You saw nothing suspicious?"

"Well, no. Not really. In fact I forgot about the whole thing until this morning when Mimi told me what was going on. When I saw it wasn't Mimi and Lisa, I went in the house and fixed myself some lunch. Macaroni and cheese."

"What about the car? Do you know what kind of car it was? Or maybe the license number? Anything?"

"It was a nice car. A luxury kind, I think. After I ate lunch, I went outside to get Fifi. It was about twenty minutes after they came in, I would guess. Anyway, I saw the black car and the other car that was already there, a white Jeep, I think. I saw them leaving at the same time."

"Had you seen the Jeep pull in earlier?"

"No, I wasn't out in the yard yet."

"When the cars left, did you see the drivers?"

"Well, I couldn't see the black car, it was too far down the driveway. You see, when I came back out, I was in our back yard. But I did see a young man driving the Jeep."

"That was Robbie Dulik's Jeep," offered Lisa.

"Well, I know Robbie Dulik," Mr. Wilson stated. "And it wasn't him driving."

"Were there two people in the black car when it left?" Bill asked.

"I couldn't really tell," replied Fred.

"What about the driver of the Jeep? Did you get a good look at him?"

"Like I said," Fred reviewed his comments in his mind. "I think it was a young guy. He had dark hair. Not long, like those hippies. Kind of neat looking. And he was real big. I remember thinking that he should've gotten himself a bigger car. He was real big."

"Do you think he could have been the gorilla or monkey?"

"Well, come to think of it, I never did see the gorilla or monkey leave. Yes, sir, the big guy could've been the gorilla. In fact, I'm sure of it."

"And you never saw Dante get in either car with anyone, right?"

"No, sir. I suppose they could've put him in the black car, 'cause it was in the garage. They could've done it while I was in the house."

Bill Menegay made a note on the legal pad. 'Check with other neighbors' it said.

"Is there anything else, Mr. Wilson?" asked Bill. "Any little detail. Any unimportant thing? It might make a difference."

"Well, yes there was one other thing. In fact, that's what Lisa wanted me to tell you about before I got all sidetracked."

133

Mr. Wilson gave Lisa a knowing look. She remained patient with her elderly neighbor.

"The license plate on the black car. I noticed it when they drove into the garage. It was one of those vanity plates. It looked like S, H, A, N, K. SHANK. I remember thinking that that was an odd plate. Unless the guys a golfer. You know, he shanks his shots?"

He laughed at his own observation and conclusion.

"I was kind of curious, so I grabbed my binoculars. You know, I'm kind of the neighborhood watchdog, so I carry this small pair with me when I'm in the yard. Helps me make sure what I'm seeing, I'm seeing, if you know what I mean."

Bill again patiently nodded.

"So when I looked through my binoculars, I saw that it really said S, H, A, R, K. SHARK. You know, like the fish?"

Bill added this last piece of information to the pad.

"Thank you, Mr. Wilson, you've been most helpful. I'll process this information. I'm sure it's going to help us."

He smiled at the older man. Lisa escorted Fred Wilson to the living room.

"Thanks, Fred," she offered. "You've been a big help."

"That's what neighbors are for," he replied with a wink.

CHAPTER 34

Sunday evening, Special Agents Menegay, Sweeney, and Gill discussed what they knew about the kidnapping. They sat in Jim Sweeney's office in the Federal Building.

Bill Menegay informed his fellow agents all that he had surmised about the case. Especially about Paul Pallibio. He was convinced that Pallibio was the man. And, apparently, had two helpers.

"That makes sense," agreed Jim Sweeney. "If he was at the party on Saturday night, someone had to be guarding Dante. Unless he's already dead."

"No," stated Bill. "He didn't work alone. The way I see it, he masterminded the idea, then got someone else to do the dirty work. Remember, he once owned a business with many employees. He'd know how to manipulate somebody to get what he wanted. Offer them money. Lots of money. It could be a big incentive for most anyone."

"The root of all evil," quoted Len Gill.

The buzzing telephone interrupted their conversation. Sweeney answered it.

"This is Sweeney. Oh, hi Bill. Yea. Yea. You don't say. Is he a reliable source? Good. Black Lexus. That's S, H, A, R, K? Like the fish, right? Sunday morning? Oh, actually reported it Saturday night? Great, Bill. I owe you one. Yea, I know. I owe you many. Thanks, buddy."

Jim placed the phone onto its cradle and looked at his curious associates.

"That was Bill Fitzsimmons. He's the undercover cop I told you about, Bill. Very interesting information going on in the streets. He said that a reliable source told him that the guy who lost big time was, for sure, Paul Pallibio. He lost three hundred G's to, check this out, Benny Vetera."

The other two agents recognized that name. The FBI had nicknamed him 'the collection agency'. If you didn't pay your debts in one week to Benny, they had heard, his 'agency' came calling.

"And that's not all," continued Sweeney. "He heard that Pallibio dropped another hundred thousand to guys in Vegas."

"When did he lose it?" asked Len Gill.

"When the Musketeers lost in the semi-finals," said Sweeney. "Evidently, he tried to win enough to cover all of his debts, including our friends at the IRS."

"You mentioned a black Lexus," noted Bill.

"Yea, don't know why we didn't get this earlier, but Pallibio reported his car was stolen Saturday evening. Said three punks who'd been hanging around the neighborhood apparently took it. And, get this, two were medium build and height, the other, big. Like a gorilla is what Pallibio told the police in his report."

"What was Bill saying to you about sharks?" Len inquired.

"The license plates on Pallibio's Lexus say SHARK," replied Sweeney.

Bill Menegay smiled inwardly.

"The son of a bitch is setting up two, maybe three kids. The greedy scumbag," he stated out loud.

"Oh, by the way, Bill," added Agent Sweeney. "Flight 539 to Denver? It continues on as Flight 231. Its destination is Los Angeles."

"Fellas," said a smiling Bill Menegay as he stood up. "It's time to go catch some bad guys."

CHAPTER 35

Paul Pallibio sat near the oblong pool at the Residence Inn sipping a cup of coffee. He listened to the hundreds of cars driving eighty feet away on Sepulveda Avenue. He was glad he didn't have to fight the early morning rush hour traffic.

"Of course, out here," he surmised to himself. "Every hour is rush hour."

He finished his continental breakfast and returned to his studio suite in the back of the Residence Inn complex. He took ten one hundred dollar bills out of his wallet and placed them in a complimentary hotel envelope.

"A small deposit for now," he muttered to the room. "A bigger one later."

He smiled inwardly to himself. But that dreaded guilt feeling gnawed in his gut.

An hour later, at 9:15, he walked up the street to the branch office of the Orange County International Bank and Trust. There he opened an account under the name Pasquale Palmo. He provided the proper identification. He inquired if the bank was capable of wiring large sums of money to offshore banks. He was assured they could. They looked forward to his business.

Feeling one step closer to completing the plan, he walked back to the hotel. He located his rented Mustang and drove the red convertible four miles north to the Los Angeles International Airport.

"My golf bag should arrive at 9:52," he said to the world from the convertible. "Unless there're gusty headwinds."

Crawford Clark left his brown Ford Taurus and ambled to the Continental Airlines baggage claim area. There he found a suitable seat that afforded him the view of the luggage conveyor and the single gate guarded by a Mexican-American female. Her job was to insure that every passenger had the right luggage when they left the terminal.

Those who did not know Crawford Clark would have seen a dirty black man with a shaggy gray and black beard. He wore a fatigue hat, like the ones that had become popular after Desert Storm, and torn green, brown and tan army issued pants. Only the silver and black Oakland Raiders shirt and dirty Nike tennis shoes were not military.

"Help a 'Nam vet, please. Can you spare change for an ol' army vet?" was the convincing line he used on passers-by.

Those who did know Crawford Clark knew he was one of the hardest working undercover FBI agents in the country. He had a knack for fitting into any situation. Whether it was a Hollywood black tie affair or a bum needing a break on Vine Street, Clark could fit the role.

Clark settled into his seat on a marble ledge and leaned his back against the large plate glass window. He looked toward the Mexican-American guard and a young executive wearing his fashionable three piece suit. The young executive perused a Wall Street Journal while he waited for his luggage. Without any visible sign, they both let Crawford Clark know that they were ready for the stakeout.

As ordered by his boss, Bill Menegay, the night before, the black agent browsed the hurrying crowd as it scurried by him. He was watching for a dark-haired, slightly overweight Caucasian. No facial hair, no obvious identifying marks or scars. He would probably leave the area carrying a golf bag in a black golf bag carrier.

"With ten million big ones weighing him down," mused Clark. "Maybe he'll want me to carry it for him."

It wasn't a bad thought.

The arrival of the baggage from Flight 231 from Denver was announced in English, Spanish and French over the loudspeaker in the Continental claim area. Many passengers had already arrived and waited patiently for their suitcases and luggage to catch up with them.

There were the usual hugs and greetings as families reunited. A bearded gentleman, casually dressed, walked up to the black veteran and gave Crawford a buck.

"You can buy me coffee later," Bill Menegay whispered with a straight face.

He entered the baggage area and blended in with the rest of the impatient travelers.

The three piece suit agent looked in the direction of the large hall that was the entry way into the claim area. He folded his paper. It was his signal that he saw the bait.

Clark recognized the movement and scanned the crowd walking by him toward the conveyor in the claim area. Paul Pallibio walked by him, ignoring him like the others. He wore black pants, a white golf shirt with the colorful shark emblem, and a black baseball hat with the same emblem on the front.

"Regular Greg Norman," joked Crawford to himself.

Passengers grabbed their pieces of luggage from the circling conveyor. The crowd thinned out as they processed quickly by the gate security guard and scattered their different ways. The young executive grabbed a weathered blue suitcase and walked out.

Bill Menegay recognized the golf bag carrier he had helped to load the day before.

Paul Pallibio saw the bag. Twenty feet from him, the prize for his plan lazied its way toward him on the black-belted conveyor. He reached a sweaty hand into his pocket. He pulled out an airline ticket folder and a claim ticket he had removed from one of three bags he had carried in yesterday. He approached the bag, and pretended to survey it closely, using this process to attach the old claim ticket. He jerked the bag off the conveyor.

He had second thoughts about switching the claim tickets. A quick check revealed the same flight number. With the crowd pushing its way through the checkout gate, Paul concluded that the Mexican-American sweetie wouldn't bother to check his ticket that closely.

Pallibio half dragged the heavy golf bag to the end of the line. Bill Menegay fell in line two passengers behind him.

"Have a nice day," the pretty security guard told the passenger in front of him. Paul Pallibio inched the money-laden bag to the gate.

"How are you today, sir?" she asked in a friendly way.

"Fine. Just peachy," replied the nervous passenger.

"Good," she said as she gave the claim tickets a perfunctory look. "Have a nice day, sir."

Pallibio struggled with the bag as he proceeded toward the door.

"Got any spare change for a vet?" asked Clark.

Paul Pallibio kept on walking, then suddenly stopped. The bag was much heavier than he had anticipated. There were no porters around. And the luggage carts, provided for a dollar, would have easily tipped over from the awkward load. Paul didn't want to chance that. He did an abrupt about-face. The bag dropped to the floor.

"How about I give you a five spot for five minutes of work, my man?" Paul asked the black veteran.

He didn't expect a positive response.

"Sure, man, I do 'preciate the opportunity to work," Clark replied in his best ghetto accent.

"Just carry this to my car for me," ordered Pallibio. "Five bucks."

"No problem, Jack."

Crawford Clark followed Pallibio, carrying the heavy bag over his shoulder like an army duffel bag. Closely behind, but at a safe distance, they were followed by a young executive and a bearded man. The Mexican-American agent watched from a distance with a cellular phone in her hand. Her finger posed over the last digit needed to push to get instant help.

Clark and Pallibio approached the red Mustang convertible. Pallibio pushed a button on his keychain and the trunk popped open. Crawford Clark dropped the bag into the spacious trunk and, losing his balance, brushed against the unsuspecting kidnaper. Paul Pallibio had just been frisked. With another silent signal, Special Agent Clark advised his associates that Pallibio carried no weapon.

"Man, you use some heavy clubs," Clark joked.

"Yea, I'm a big hitter," replied Pallibio.

He chuckled at his own double meaning.

Paul Pallibio reached into his back pocket for his money clip. As he was doing so, the young executive agent slipped a camera out of his pocket.

"Hey, Pallibio. Paul Pallibio!" he shouted from ten feet away.

Instinctively, Paul turned to look at him.

"Smile, dirtbag." Click.

The camera caught Pallibio's surprised reaction.

"Well, my man, you be under arrest for the kidnapping of Dante O'Shea," Clark stated in his ghetto voice.

"Who? What? What's going on here?" blurted Pallibio.

"You have the right to remain silent. Anything you say, can, and will be used against you in a court of law. You have the right to a lawyer, 'cept you can't use the ten million in this bag to hire one," improvised Agent Clark.

He loved this part of the job. Catching the bad guy.

Bill Menegay slowly tore the beard from his face.

"Remember me, Pallibio. Dante O'Shea's surprise party? Of course not, you were too sick to talk to me."

"You guys are making a big mistake. I'm not Paul whoever you're calling me. I want a lawyer."

"Good choice," agreed Clark.

He handcuffed Pallibio's hands behind his back.

Two L.A. police cars screeched to a halt five feet away. The flashing lights scared Paul Pallibio.

"Where's O'Shea, Pallibio? Cooperation now will be meaningful to a judge later."

Paul Pallibio felt trapped. The sick feeling in his stomach, the guilt, the remorse, worked its way up his throat. He had a very nasty taste in his mouth. He knew it was over. His only leverage was Dante O'Shea's health. He had to negotiate to save his skin.

"If I don't make a phone call, he's dead," he flatly stated in a surprisingly calm voice.

"If he dies, so do you," Bill Menegay informed him. "Why don't you be a good Musketeer fan and tell us where their star player is?"

"What'll I get for the information?" inquired Pallibio.

"We'll make sure you don't get in a cell with Big Leroy, the biggest fag on cellblock A," chided Crawford Clark.

The realization of going to jail hit Paul Pallibio like a two by four to the gut. He lost all color. Then he passed out.

"Looks like he don't like my brothers too much," jived Agent Clark.

The other agents smiled at his observation.

"While he's out, look in his wallet," ordered Bill Menegay. "My guess is he has a number written down somewhere that he has to call to have Dante released. If we can find it, and he doesn't want to cooperate, we're a little more prepared."

He thought of the tapes that Lenny Gill had edited for him on Sunday afternoon. It was somewhat risky, but Bill Menegay often relied on his hunches. Almost always, they were correct.

The FBI agents laid the collapsed kidnaper onto the back seat of a squad car. Crawford Clark handed Bill Menegay the wallet.

"Looks like he carries a lot of cash," observed Agent Clark. "Don't like to leave home without it."

The organized billfold turned up just what Special Agent Menegay wanted. On the back of an old Pallibio Machine business card, a ten digit number had been scrawled.

Pallibio started to wake up. He sat upright with the help of one of the officers.

"Last chance, Pallibio," stated Bill Menegay. "Where's Dante O'Shea?"

"Dante who?"

CHAPTER 36

Dante tried to adjust himself in the chair, pushing against the nylon ropes to get a little more room. A little more comfort.

Carl Plath sat on the edge of the cot looking at the All-Star Musketeer guard. He had been feeling more down, more depressed as each long hour dragged on.

Eddie kept Vince out of the room and out of Carl's way. His big friend was extremely upset with his brother. Eddie Burson was surprised that Big Carl hadn't already attempted to beat his brother senseless.

"Lay off the beer, Vinnie, ok?" Eddie ordered and asked his brother. "We should be getting the call from Pallibio any time. I need you sober. Ok?"

"Bug off," was the reply he didn't want to hear.

Vinnie slouched lower onto the living room couch, then changed his mind.

"I'm taking your car, I'll be right back," he told his brother.

"Where you going? I need you here," Eddie informed him.

"Just to the store, I wanna buy some fish."

Eddie was a little confused about his brother's decision and his timing, but didn't fight it.

"Have you heard anything, Carl?" asked Dante.

It was his attempt to open a conversation. Carl had been watching him for what seemed like an hour. He was uncommonly quiet.

"No, we should be getting a call today," Carl replied in a dreary tone.

"You sound kind of down," Dante stated. "You're not letting Big Mouth get to you, are you?"

It seemed odd to Dante that he should even care about these guys. He remembered reading about how captives would sometimes begin to identify with their captors. Almost feeling sorry for their kidnapers, hostages assumed a big brother or sister role, consoling and comforting their guards.

Carl thought for a long moment.

"If Vinnie comes in here and gives you any kind of grief, I'll knock him into the next county."

"Well, just keep cool, Carl," advised his hero. "Just like in a ball game, you got to keep your cool. The refs always see the second elbow or the second shove. They never see what prompted the retaliation."

"Yea, I guess you're right," Big Carl replied.

But he felt bad for other reasons, too. Like kidnapping his favorite NBA player. And hitting him, too. He just wanted to go to work and run his big machining center. Tomorrow would be the first time he would miss work since he started the job two years ago. He felt bad about disappointing his boss.

At 1:48 in the afternoon, the phone rang at the home of the Burson brothers and their friend, Carl Plath. Eddie almost knocked the phone off of the table in his effort to grab it. Vinnie was in the kitchen putting away the little groceries he had bought.

"Burson," he excitedly mumbled into the receiver.

"Eddie, Pallibio here," Pallibio's voice said.

"Is everything ok, Mr. Pallibio?" Eddie nervously asked.

Lenny Gill sat at the other end of the phone conversation in Jim Sweeney's office. He held the phone to the speaker of the tape player and pushed the play button.

"Everything's a go," stated Paul Pallibio's voice.

Lenny had edited the word 'right' from the original conversation the two conspirators had one week ago. He had six tape recorders, each labeled with different bits of conversation. He could only hope that Eddie couldn't tell the difference between Pallibio's real voice and the Memorex tape.

"So, we should let him go, right?" inquired Eddie.

There was a three second pause.

"You still there, Mr. Pallibio?" We should let him go, right?"

There was no good reply to that question. Special Agent Gill took a chance.

"Everything's a go," stated the taped voice. A brief pause.

"You guys are going to be rich, Eddie, understand, RICH!"

Eddie paused for a few seconds.

"I guess he means we let him go," he thought to himself.

"See you in L.A., Mr. Pallibio."

He heard a click on the other end of the line. End of conversation. Eddie thought he had sounded strange.

"Probably partying already," he muttered to his brother.

Across the street and on the second floor of the old Pallibio Machine Shop, Carl looked around the room. He noticed the gun, Vinnie's gun, sitting on the table next to the quiet tape recorders.

"Eddie had told him several times to get rid of that thing," Carl thought. "I'll get rid of it before that drunk son of a bitch gets carried away and hurts somebody."

"Carl?" groaned Dante. "These ropes are biting into my arms. Could you just loosen them a little bit?"

Carl looked down at his basketball hero. The remorse and bad feelings were now ever present. Bending to one knee, he loosened the rope on Dante's left arm, giving it enough slack so Dante could comfortably slide his arm up and down the padding on the chair. It still kept Dante captive, but it did provide him some relief.

Carl started to do the same with Dante's right arm. He heard a noise downstairs. It was somebody running through the shop.

"No," he thought. "That's two people running."

He could track their location by the sound of pounding feet on the wooden floor below. A few seconds later, it came up the steps.

"Must be Vince and Eddie," he stated to Dante. "Maybe they got the call."

Remembering the gun, he hustled to the table and grabbed the thirty-eight special. Before Vince got to the room, he was going to hide it.

Carl left his unfinished tying job, the rope loosely wrapped around Dante's right arm. He opened the office door to look for a quick stashing spot.

Too late. Vince was halfway across the old office area and saw the gun, his gun, in Carl's large hand.

"Where you goin' with that, shithead?" he sternly inquired.

"It shouldn't be here," replied Big Carl. "We don't need it."

"You big sissy," admonished Vinnie. "Give it to me."

"You're the last guy I want holding this," Carl responded.

"Listen, Carl, give me my gun, or I'll kick your big, lard ass!"

It was the last straw. Carl took one giant step towards Vinnie and grabbed him with his left hand. He lifted Vince Burson one foot off the ground. He held the gun to Vinnie's head with his right.

"NO MORE!" he shouted. "No more of your, your crap. I've had it with you."

"Put me down, you big, freakin' ape!" Vinnie shouted back.

"Carl, let him go!" ordered Eddie.

Big Carl threw the younger Burson to the ground. Vinnie landed hard at the feet of his brother.

"You've really pissed me off this time," yelled Vinnie. "I gonna kill you."

He stood up and took one menacing step toward the red-faced giant.

Carl pointed the gun at Vince Burson's head.

"Not one more word," he muttered between gritted teeth.

"UP YOURS!" Vinnie shouted at him.

The gun exploded. The unexpected kick jerked Carl's arm upward. He missed his intended target by four inches at close range. Vinnie instinctively ducked. His brother didn't. The bullet lodged in the forehead of the eldest Burson.

Eddie Burson died before his body slumped to the wooden floor.

"LOOK WHAT YOU'VE DONE, YOU FRIGGIN' IDIOT," Vinnie screamed at him. He stared at his dead brother. He didn't know what to do.

The second shot nearly made Vince Burson's heart stop. He again ducked, not sure what Carl was doing behind him. In a crouched position, he turned around to face Big Carl.

The big hulk of a man staggered for a brief moment, then fell to the floor with a loud thump. The hand holding the gun to his mouth reflexed away from his face and harmlessly released its death grip on Vinnie's gun. It clanged harmlessly onto the floor.

Vinnie Burson vomited. He sagged to the floor. He stared at his brother, then his friend. His mind raced with a thousand thoughts.

He knew that whatever he did next would affect him for the rest of his life.

CHAPTER 37

The decision was made by Bill Menegay in Los Angeles. And seconded by Jim Sweeney in Cleveland. After they had found the number in Paul Pallibio's wallet, it was a matter of one call to the Ohio Bell Telephone Company to find the name and address of the billing party. One Mr. Edward Burson who lived on 122 East Fortieth Street in Cleveland, Ohio.

When Bill Menegay heard the East Fortieth Street address, a bell rung in his head. He looked at the reverse side of the business card that Paul Pallibio had relinquished when he had passed out.

Pallibio Machine Company. 125 East Fortieth Street.

He was positive he knew where Dante O'Shea was being held captive! It was then that he called Special Agent Jim Sweeney in Cleveland.

"If we go in with sirens blaring and using force," he reasoned to his friend in Cleveland. "Eddie and his friends may panic, run and take Dante with them."

"Or," added Agent Sweeney into the mouthpiece of his office phone. "They may try to fight their way out. We don't want Dante hurt either way."

"Do you think they bought the taped conversation?" Menegay inquired.

"I can't say for sure," replied his counterpart. "But if they did, we bought some time. And we may even get lucky and they'll just let Dante go. Assuming that was Pallibio's plan, that is."

"I agree," replied his west coast friend. "Worse case scenario is that they don't buy the taped conversation and panic. On the other side of the coin, maybe they'll just say 'the hell with it' and let him go."

Neither agent believed that would happen. Thus their decision was made.

Jim Sweeney and Len Gill rode in the same unmarked agency car. They drove directly to the former Pallibio Machine Shop. Neither said much. They collected their thoughts, mentally preparing for what would greet them.

Four black and whites from the Cleveland Police Force joined them on Saint Clair Avenue, two blocks from the shop. From there, they advanced on foot. A better chance to go unnoticed.

Sweeney and Gill walked to the yellow house first. They knocked persistently on the front door. For three long minutes. No answer.

They calmly walked to the garage. An old Chevy Impala sat lifeless in the dilapidated building. A brief search resulted in nothing, except the car had been recently driven.

"Must be across the street," Special Agent Gill concluded.

Sweeney agreed.

They joined the eight police officers at the front door of the shop.

"Everything is locked up," reported the only female in the group.

"Well, how hard can it be to break into an abandoned building?" queried Sweeney to no one in particular.

That's when they heard the shots. Two shots. About thirty seconds apart. The ten officers scattered. They took cover behind trees, parked cars, and against the wall of the building.

There was silence. For a very long two minutes. Nothing but silence.

CHAPTER 38

Dante had easily heard the arguing not thirty feet away in the other room. Carl had loosened the rope on his arms, the right arm was much looser than the left. Dante frantically struggled to get free. Using his forearms as leverage, he pulled against the yellow nylon rope, stretching it until it scorched his arm with pain. But it worked.

He maneuvered his right arm and worked it free from the yellow bondage. He tore off his blindfold. He adjusted to the darkness in the room. The door was open, Carl had left it that way. He worked on the binding rope on his left arm.

That's when he heard the shot. Dante worked the rope on his left arm, desperately reaching whatever knot he could with his right fingers. Pulling. Pushing. His fingers bled from the effort.

Then the second shot. He heard the ominous thud of a human body hitting the wooden floor.

"Who's out there?" he wondered.

He wanted to shout Carl's name. Eddie's name. He hoped Big Mouth wouldn't walk through that door.

Frantically, he worked the rope. He pulled and stretched the nylon. With a loud, painful groan he pulled his left arm free.

In fast and frenzied movements, he worked himself completely free from the wooden chair that had held him prisoner for almost forty-eight hours. He stood up and almost fell down. A quick rush of lightheadedness engulfed his brain. He had completely forgotten about the heavy cast on his foot. He stood again, more carefully. He listened. For the longest time. He tried to still his pounding heart.

He heard movement outside of the door. It sounded like footsteps coming his way. Sneakers squeaking on the wooden floor. Suddenly the noise stopped.

Dante sensed it was time to make a move. Just like he did in his last game against Chicago. Then he had broken his ankle. Now, he hoped the outcome would be better.

He slowly ambled toward the open door. Quietly. He peered out into what appeared to be an old office area.

Vince Burson peered right back. Ten feet away, Dante saw one of his antagonists and froze.

"Which one is it?" he thought.

He said nothing. Neither did Vinnie.

The sound of a window breaking broke the standoff. The noise downstairs got louder. A pry bar breaking wood, a chain being slung aside. Muddled voices speaking in whispered tones.

Vinnie stared at the Musketeer player, then turn and ran. He almost tripped over his dead brother's body. Down the stairs he flew. The police were at the far end of the shop. He could see them trying to crawl in through the window they had broken. He raced for the tunnel. Quickly, quietly. It was his only chance.

Dante did not know what to do. He turned back toward the room and stared at the only light he could see.

It was a window. Slightly cracked open.

He limped through Paul Pallibio's former office. He reached the window and bent over, peeking through the small opening. Sunlight. It's daytime in Italy.

Dante tried to slide the heavy window upwards. The green plastic bag and foam covering hindered his progress.

He stood still. Listening. He heard more noise. Another window breaking, more wood being pried loose. Then he heard running. He heard no sirens. No sign that whoever was running downstairs was friendly. He didn't know what to expect and he was afraid.

"This is Italy," he thought. "It could be a terrorist group coming to steal me away for their own ransom."

He just didn't know. But he did know that outside of that window, he could get help. He could find his friend, Alfredo Sartori. Yes, he must get out of here and find Alfredo.

Dante turned his attention toward the window. He saw the hindrance and ripped the green plastic material down. He clawed at the foam, ripping at it like a madman. He placed both hands under the window, resting the back of his hands on the sill.

Like a weightlifter in competition, he jerked the heavy window upward, pushing harder and harder.

The window moved grudgingly. Then in one fluid motion, it slid up the track. Dust sprayed across Dante's face. He now had a two foot opening. Dante poked his head out of the window. Below him, about twenty feet, was a pile of rubbish. Wooden boards, tires, pieces of metal, rags, paper.

Dante again listened. If it was help, they would have called his name. Or at least shouted 'police'. Or 'policia', whatever it was in Italian. But he heard nothing. It was more trouble coming. He just knew it.

Dante lifted his cast foot onto the window sill and through the opening. He balanced himself, trying to force his tall frame through the too small opening. Half sitting, half crouching, he dangled his broken foot outside over the edge of the sill. He maneuvered his other leg until both of his legs dangled out of the window. Bending over to his side as far as he possibly could, he forced his upper body through the opening. Precariously balanced on the sill, Dante positioned his legs against the brick wall. He would use them for leverage as he made his leap. Like a crouching tiger, he prepared to jump. He tried to aim toward the papers and rags.

He heard the footsteps getting louder. They were coming to get him, but he was not going to let that happen. He leaned over and forced his head to turn toward the door. He saw several faces approaching, but none looked friendly to him. It was too dark to recognize their clothing.

Agent Sweeney was the first to the door of the kidnaper's former office. He saw Dante perilously balanced in the window before him.

"Dante!" he shouted. "FBI! We're here to save you!"

Dante O'Shea never heard the words. It would have been better if he had.

CHAPTER 39

The pounding on the door startled Vinnie Burson, even though he was waiting for it. He slowly advanced to the front door, peering out at the suited gentleman standing on the deteriorated front porch.

Slowly, he opened the creaking wooden door.

"I'm Special Agent Gill, FBI," stated Lenny Gill.

He flashed his shield at the young man.

"Do you live here?"

It seemed an odd question to Vince.

"Of course I live here, you idiot," he thought.

"Yes, sir," he replied.

"May I see your driver's license?"

"What's this about?"

"Just cooperate, son, and I'll ask the questions."

Vinnie slowly pulled his wallet from his rear pocket and found his driver's license. Hesitantly, he slipped it through a hole in the screen door, pushing it toward the FBI agent.

Len Gill studied it for a long moment.

"Mr. Burson, I would like you to come with me."

"Where? Why? I didn't do anything wrong."

"I just have a few questions to ask you. Routine stuff. Please come this way."

Special Agent Gill smiled at the nervous youth. He turned to walk down the unpainted, worn porch steps.

"Can I turn off the tv and change my clothes?"

"I'd rather you just come with me. Now."

The smile had disappeared.

Agent James Sweeney waited in the car while his partner did his job. He was visibly shaken.

CHAPTER 40

Doctor Ernest Kavalecz, one of the Cleveland Musketeer team physicians, walked into the large waiting area at the Cleveland Clinic. Families sat in small groups, idly chatting, consoling each other as their loved ones went through the process of admission.

Doctor Kavalecz sauntered toward the gang of men and women sitting quietly on the uncomfortable couches and chairs in the corner of the waiting area. He recognized some of them, they were Musketeer players. He did not know most of the women. He did recognize Lisa O'Shea.

Mustering all of the bedside manner he had obtained through years of practicing medicine, the Musketeer doctor approached Lisa O'Shea. She was standing.

"Mrs. O'Shea," he started. "I'm sorry that you are going through this. Dante is alive. But he is in very critical condition."

Tears welled up in Lisa's eyes. Trying very hard to be strong, she held them back.

"How's my husband doing? Is he going to live? Can I see him?"

"Mrs. O'Shea, may I call you Lisa?"

She nodded.

"Lisa, Dante has some very serious injuries. We are still conducting tests to see the extent of all his injuries."

"What kind of tests?"

"We've done several x-rays, and we're setting him up to do a Cat Scan."

"What do you know so far, Doctor?"

"Lisa, please sit down."

She obeyed.

Doctor Kavalecz sat next to her and gently grasped both of her hands and placed them in his.

"Lisa, I don't pull any punches. I believe you have the right to know everything going on with your husband. Do you agree?"

Lisa nodded. The tears escaped from her eyes. She unclasped the doctor's hold and grabbed a tissue offered her by Alise Dulik.

"Dante's injuries are extensive. He has broken both of his legs. He broke at least three ribs. He broke his left wrist and right arm."

Lisa numbly nodded in acknowledgment of the news.

"There's more," continued the team physician. "Lisa, Dante jumped out of a second story window onto a pile of trash. That's what we were told. It appears that he hit his head on some cement blocks. There may be brain damage, Lisa. To what extent, we don't know."

He hesitated to let this terrible news sink in.

"As I said before, we are conducting more tests. He is not out of danger by any means, Lisa. And,"

Lisa interrupted.

"Will he live? Will he play ball again?"

Doctor Ernest Kavalecz took a deep breath. This was so hard.

"Lisa, we are going to do everything we can to get your husband back to as normal a life as possible. Will he live? I can't answer that. Will he play ball again? I doubt it."

It was harsh. It was reality. It was honest. And Doctor Kavalecz wished he was not so honest. Sugar coating would have been easier.

"What can I do to help?"

"Right now, Lisa. Pray. Pray for Dante. Pray for his doctors and nurses. Pray. And rest. He will need your strength, Lisa."

The words seemed so hollow. So meaningless. So medical. But Lisa O'Shea knew in her heart that Doctor Kavalecz was right. She had to be strong. She had to pull on her inner strength, her faith in God, to help her husband.

Through the tears, she managed to smile at the doctor. "Thank you, Doctor Kavalecz. We will do our best."

"So will I," he replied.

CHAPTER 41

Jim Sweeney sat at his desk, his head buried in his hands. His partner, Lenny Gill, tired to console him.

"I may have helped him fall," stated the weary agent.

"No, Jimmy, you tried to help him not fall. I was there. He was on his way out the window when we got there. You did all you could to try to grab him. You didn't have a chance."

Jim Sweeney looked at Len Gill. He wanted to believe what he heard.

"Lenny, I had him, then he just…fell out of my grasp. I keep seeing him falling and then hitting the ground, laying on top of all that rubbish, like a mutilated doll. It was horrible. I don't know how he's still alive. I feel terrible."

"Jim, quit beating yourself up. You, me, we all did the best we could. There was nothing more we could do."

The phone rang. Both agents jumped at the sound.

Agent Gill grabbed the phone before his partner did.

"Jim, this is Bill Menegay."

"Bill, Jim's here, this is Len Gill. Can I help you?"

"Oh, Lenny. I heard what happened. Is Jimmy ok?"

Lenny looked at his friend and partner. He turned in his chair, away from Jim Sweeney. Looking for a little privacy.

"He's taking it hard, Bill," Len whispered.

There was silence from the west coast agent.

"Len, what can you tell me about the Burson kid?" Bill Menegay finally asked.

"He's claiming he had nothing to do with it."

"What do you think, Len?"

"I think he's lying. He was with them. But he does have an alibi."

"What's that?"

"He's telling us that he went fishing. Was gone since Friday."

"Does it stick?"

"We have no witnesses stating otherwise, Bill. He says he left for Pymatuning Lake, in Pennsylvania, on Friday. He spent the whole weekend there, fishing and camping. Says he came home early Sunday afternoon, the house was empty. Just had sat down to watch tv and take a nap when we came to the house."

"How'd he get to the lake? Anybody go with him?"

"Says he drove his brother's car. No, nobody went with him. We checked Cleveland Clinic where he works, they said he talked about going fishing all week. Took Friday off so he could get an early start."

"Didn't you or Jim tell me the car was in the garage when you first went there?"

"Yea. The engine was warm. It appeared to have been recently driven. I asked him why he didn't answer the door the first time we showed up. He said he was putting his fishing gear away and taking a shower. Didn't hear us knocking."

"Did the search of the house or the old machine shop turn up anything?"

"Well, we've fingerprinted everything. The room they had Dante in. The tunnel to the house. The car. We found several prints from Eddie Burson and Carl Plath, but nothing on Vinnie Burson, other than in the car he said he drove. We did find a pair of nylon surgical gloves in the living room of the house, but the Burson kid said he used them to unhook the fish he caught. He didn't like touching fish."

"Did the gloves smell like fish?"

"No, but we did find a few fish in the freezer. Maybe he used the gloves when he was in the room where they kept Dante, but it's a dead end right now. We were thinking of doing some finger print lifting at the O'Shea house, maybe the Burson kid was involved with the actual kidnapping."

"Well, it's kind of late for that," stated Bill Menegay. "Anyway, they had such a crowd of people in that house for Dante's party, you'd never get a good print. And Dante's neighbor, was it Mr. Wilson? He said they were dressed up in monkey and gorilla costumes, they probably wouldn't have left prints anyway. I'm sure of it."

Len Gill agreed.

"What about Pallibio?" asked the Cleveland agent.

"He's not talking. He hasn't said a word since he requested a lawyer. His attorney is flying in from Cleveland tomorrow."

"Well, I hope he does talk, and implicates the Burson kid," Len Gill remarked.

"That would make life easier."

"Yea, it sure would," agreed his west coast counterpart. "Tell Jimmy to take it easy. We'll get to the bottom of this."

Len Gill hung up the phone and looked at his friend.

Agent Jim Sweeney ignored his doctor and the sign on the wall behind his desk. He lit up another cigarette.

CHAPTER 42

"DANTE O'SHEA KIDNAPPED!" stated the headlines of the Akron Journal. Under the large print, a second line told readers, "Escape Attempt May Prove Fatal to the Musketeer All-Star".

Ron Collins had kept his word. He did not leak out any of the truth as he had promised the FBI, Mr. Herrington, and Lisa O'Shea. But now it was national news and he had the breaking story.

His article explained how Dante had been duped by two men he apparently thought were teammates who showed up at his door on his birthday. They were dressed up like a gorilla and a monkey. In the process of abducting Dante O'Shea, they had beaten Dante's friend and teammate, Robbie Dulik. He was expected to have a full recovery.

Lisa O'Shea had received ransom note telegrams from Rome, Italy and Sidney, Australia, leading the authorities to think that Dante was being held prisoner in one of those two countries. Special Agent Bill Menegay, coincidentally Robbie Dulik's father-in-law, was called in from Los Angeles to help with the kidnapping investigation. He worked with several Cleveland Federal Agents to help find Dante O'Shea.

Although there were several indications that Dante was not being held in the United States, Agent Menegay was able to determine that he was actually being held captive on the east side of Cleveland the whole time.

The article went on to explain that Dante was apparently abducted by two young men, Mr. Edward Burson and Mr. Carl Plath, both had resided on East Fortieth Street in Cleveland. Dante was held hostage in the former Pallibio Machine Shop, located directly across the street from the residence of the alleged abductors. Both alleged abductors were found dead at the machine shop, from an apparent murder-suicide.

A third person, Mr. Vincent Burson, brother of the late Edward Burson, was questioned and released. Authorities have stated that they believe he had no role in the kidnapping of Dante O'Shea.

One other person was alleged to be involved. Mr. Paul Pallibio, the former owner of Pallibio Machine Shop, and the owner of the house rented by the late Edward Burson, the late Carl Plath, and Vincent Burson. He was arrested in Los Angeles on the charge of kidnapping. He remains in jail in Los Angeles pending a preliminary hearing to have him extradited to Ohio to face the same charge.

Ron Collins concluded his article by telling the northeast Ohio readers that Dante O'Shea is currently in the Intensive Care Unit at the Cleveland Clinic. He was listed in critical condition. The extent of his many injuries was not yet known, tests were still ongoing.

Northeast Ohio was rocked by the news. In their way, they wanted to help their fallen hero. Cleveland Musketeer jerseys, shirts, sweaters, hats, jackets, pennants sold like hot cakes. It was their tribute to Dante O'Shea. It was how they showed they cared.

The people loved Dante, he was one of their own, he grew up in the area, and they wanted him back.

So did his wife.

CHAPTER 43

Doctor Ernest Kavalecz grew up in Barberton, Ohio. Just south of Akron. He was a gifted athlete. Before he was known as Doctor Kavalecz, he was called Ernie K. He was a three sport star in high school, and had planned to play his favorite sport, baseball, as a professional before bad ankles ended his promising career. He chose to get into sports medicine and eventually became a doctor. He loved working with the professional athletes. They trusted his judgment. And his honesty.

Lisa O'Shea sat on the side of the hospital bed staring at her husband. Both legs had heavy casts on them. His right arm was in a cast. His left wrist was in a cast. Bandages mummified the top of his head. His eyes were black and swollen. His face was blue, purple and yellow. A tube protruded from his chest, providing relief to a collapsed lung. His already broken ankle had been fit with a new cast.

"Oh, Dante," she lamented. "Don't give up. Come back to me."

His response was silence.

Doctor Kavalecz whisked into the room, it was his last stop of a very busy day.

His entry startled Lisa.

"Sorry," he apologized. "I didn't mean to scare you."

"It's ok," she weakly replied.

"Lisa, we have more test results," the kind doctor stated. "I wish it was good news."

Lisa O'Shea's shoulders drooped. She didn't want to hear anymore.

"It appears that Dante has increased intracranial pressure. What this means is that his head is swelling, expanding inwardly, and causing pressure on his brain."

"What does that mean, doctor?" she asked.

"It means that Dante may go into a coma. We are watching for the signs."

"Like what?"

"Well," he continued. "If one eye is dilated more than the other, that would give us an indication. If Dante cannot be aroused by outside stimuli, that's another."

"What, what can we expect if he goes into a coma?" Lisa nervously inquired.

"Well, in one sense, if he does become apoplectic, his body will have a better chance of healing itself. He won't be moving around. That's the good news."

"What else?" she demanded.

"Lisa, there could be paralysis. And," he didn't want to be this truthful. "And, he might not come out of it."

"Those are worse case scenarios, Lisa," he added.

"If he's in a coma, can he hear me?"

"If it happens, and I'm again not saying it will, but if so, just keep talking to him, hold his hand, rub his arm, try to be calm and natural. He may hear you, he may not, we don't know everything yet about where a person's mind may go in a comatose state, but I recommend you just try to be as normal as possible when you are with him."

Dante's wife leaned back in the chair. She let her arms dangle over each side. Her control had ebbed. She was drained. The sobbing started slowly, then rocked her body convulsively as she let the emotions out. Doctor Kavalecz dropped to one knee and stared into Lisa's swollen blue green eyes.

"I know this is hard," he said softly to her. "Your husband is a fighter. You're a fighter. I know we can beat this. I know we can. And we will. You have to believe me, Lisa. You have to believe."

Lisa cast her eyes downward and stared at a black design on the white tiled floor. She wished she could believe. She really did.

In the middle of the night, her husband slid into a coma.

CHAPTER 44

"Well, Big Time," started Crawford Clark. "You're famous now."

He thrust a copy of the front page of USA Today at the former owner of Pallibio Machine Shop.

"You didn't make the headlines," continued Agent Clark. "But you made the front page."

Paul Pallibio didn't bother to look.

"So, is today the day we talk?" asked Clark.

There was no reply.

"Suit yourself, Paulie baby," the agent stated with a sneer. "We got you, and you know it. Why don't you make it easy on yourself? Why don't you cooperate?"

Paul Pallibio looked up and stared deeply into the brown eyes of the FBI agent.

Crawford Clark stared back. There was no emotion in the eyes he saw. Pallibio was a beaten man. He didn't show sorrow, regret, nothing. Just emptiness. It was as if he didn't exist anymore.

Crawford Clark decided to try another tactic. All the evidence was there, Pallibio was aware of that. And the agent knew he knew. The only missing information was 'the who?'. Who else was involved? The motive was apparent. Paul Pallibio was deep in debt and he needed a big hit to right his sinking financial ship. The how was slowly coming together. The article in the Akron Journal, copied by hundreds of papers across the world, had pieced together the known details on how the crime was committed.

Who was he protecting with his silence? Was Benny Vetera, the Chicago gambler involved? Was Pallibio afraid of him?

What about the other Burson kid? Vince Burson. Was he an accomplice? Were there others behind the scene that Pallibio was protecting?

Crawford Clark settled down on the bed across from Paul Pallibio. He would wait him out. So he sat. He said nothing. Did nothing. Just waited. For two hours he sat across from the kidnaper and watched him. Emotionless. Unmoving. Uncaring. He just stared. Then he had to pee.

Not that Paul Pallibio cared, but Crawford Clark told him that he would be right back. He left the cell and ambled towards the restroom a couple hundred feet away.

Paul Pallibio picked up the newspaper and read the article. Then he saw his picture on page two. He was wearing his shark shirt and had a big smile on his face.

He placed the paper next to his pillow on his bunk. And he placed his head in his soft hands. Tears streamed down his cheeks. He made another decision.

He removed the belt from his trousers. He moved the only chair in the cell to the center of the room. On top of the chair he placed the pillow from his bunk and the pillow from the second bed in the small cell. He added a couple of books his attorney had brought him. He looped his long belt over one of the several bars that served as the ceiling. He balanced himself on top of the books. Stretching as far as he could, he wrapped the belt around his neck. It barely made a noose. But it was enough.

As Crawford Clark walked down the corridor of cells, Paul Pallibio finally spoke.

"I'm sorry, Dad," he whispered. "I'm sorry for disappointing you and being a rotten son. I'm sorry I became the man I did."

The books crashed to the floor. The pillows quietly hit the ground. The chair clattered onto its back.

And Paul Pallibio spoke no more.

CHAPTER 45

Vinnie Burson sat at the kitchen table that he had shared many times with his brother and friend. A small pyramid of empty beer cans stood in their remembrance. He picked up the newspaper and read the article once again.

The small column, highlighted within a black box on the sports page, gave the latest update on "The Dante O'Shea Case". Each day, the paper told the interested Cleveland readers, any breaking news about the kidnapping and about Dante's condition.

Today's article stated two new facts. One of the alleged kidnapers, Paul Pallibio, former owner of the Pallibio Machine Shop in Cleveland, had apparently committed suicide. Authorities had found his body hanging in his cell at the L.A.P.D. downtown precinct. An unnamed source reported that they had made no progress in their interrogation of Pallibio. He had spoken only to his attorney, who wanted anonymity, and would not divulge any of the conversation with the FBI or local authorities. The source indicated that the authorities were looking into subpoenaing him.

The other bit of information made Vinnie Burson smile. It was reported that Dante O'Shea had slipped into a coma. The article then stated some possible long term effects of his condition, and finally stated that Dante was still in critical condition in the Intensive Care Unit at the Cleveland Clinic.

Vinnie reviewed in his mind what he had told the authorities. He had gone fishing early Friday morning and returned Sunday afternoon. They bought that alibi. Having unwrapped fish in the freezer was a good touch.

When asked about his brother and Carl, he had told them that the two of them weren't getting along. Carl Plath had been on Eddie about not having a regular job like Carl did. He was upset with Eddie because he wasn't holding up his end on money matters. And Eddie was getting more and more aggravated with Carl for continually bringing it up. He told the FBI agents that Carl had threatened Eddie and said he would kill him.

When he was asked if he felt Carl was capable of murder, he told them that Carl had a bad temper. Ask around, he stated to them, and you'll find out that he was always in fights. Of course, he didn't indicate to his interrogators that it was he that usually initiated the altercations, and Carl was just defending him.

And when Eddie got the gun, yes, he did suspect it was stolen, he told him he should get rid of it because it could only lead to trouble. But Eddie feared Big Carl, so he kept it for defensive purposes. Just in case.

Did he know anything about the kidnapping? Not at all, he told them. Eddie and Carl hung out without him an awful lot, so he wasn't privy to their plans.

Did he like his job at the Cleveland Clinic? Absolutely, he told them. He loved to be able to help people. Especially the patients.

Did he know about the tunnel over to Pallibio Machine? It scared him, he told them. He was claustrophobic and he didn't like being near it. He told the agents that he had told Eddie to ask their landlord, Mr. Pallibio, to fill it in, but Eddie never did it.

What about the surgical gloves they found in the living room? They told him it didn't smell like fish and was quite clean for the use he said he made of it. He didn't tell them that he started wearing it after kidnapping Dante O'Shea. The possibility of leaving fingerprints at Dante's house had terrified him, so he wore his gloves the whole weekend. Bad oversight on his part to leave them lying around. What he did tell them is that he had washed his hands after unloading the fish into the freezer, and had simply forgotten to take the gloves off. When he realized they were still on his hands, he removed them and must have tossed them on the table in the living room where they evidently had gotten knocked off. They seemed to buy his explanation.

Vinnie knew that he was very lucky. The bullet intended for him got his brother, then Carl did himself in. And when he read that Mr. Pallibio had committed suicide, it was even better.

"Everyone involved is dead except me," he thought. "And Dante O'Shea."

The only other potential problem was the attorney.

"If Mr. Pallibio had spilled his guts," he reasoned. "I could be in trouble. But nobody really knows who was totally involved. Nobody was here, not Mr. Pallibio, not the attorney."

He would continue with his story and with his life.

"And if anybody causes me grief," he said to the kitchen walls. "Shame on them."

He then formulated in his mind another plan.

"You should always have a Plan B," he said out loud.

And then he laughed. It was a menacing sound.

CHAPTER 46

Bill Menegay balanced the telephone on his right shoulder. He shifted the papers in the O'Shea file in front of him. Jim Sweeney was intently waiting for his answer.

"Jimmy," started the west coast agent. "I think it's an open and shut case."

Sweeney started to say something, but didn't.

"Listen, Jim. All the facts are in. Pallibio masterminded the plan. He hired Eddie Burson and Carl Plath to do the dirty work. The monkey and gorilla outfits found in Pallibio's Lexus at your airport were almost perfect fits."

"He had motive," continued Bill Menegay. "He was caught red-handed with the loot. He had flown to Italy days before the kidnapping and apparently made the tapes you found at the machine shop. The tape recorder had his prints on it. The room where they kept Dante was full of Burson's and Plath's prints.

"We had a witness at the O'Shea residence, Mr. Wilson, saying he saw the monkey and gorilla, evidently Burson and Plath, go into the house. And my son-in-law was attacked by the gorilla, again, the Plath kid. And they're all dead. Case closed. Justice has been served."

Jim Sweeney had no response. It all made sense. But something in his gut said there was more to it.

His questions to Carl Plath's employer indicated that Carl was a big, slow kid who took great pride in his work and in the fact that he could operate a CNC Machining Center. His coworkers told him that Carl was a very nice guy. He would do most anything for his friends. They liked him a lot.

He was told by patrons of the Warehouse Bar and Grille that Eddie was a regular. They all liked him. He was an easy going guy with a good sense of humor. Every one of the people he interviewed were genuinely surprised that Eddie could be involved with the kidnapping of Dante O'Shea.

Vinnie Burson, on the other hand, was not as well liked. He was a troublemaker and was very vulgar. That's what the waitresses at the Warehouse had told him. If any one of the three was suspicious, it would be Vinnie.

He had told his findings and feelings to the west coast agent. He respected Bill Menegay and he really wanted to believe what Bill had stated. But something wasn't right.

"Well, Bill," he articulated into the phone. "If you are convinced it's over, then it must be. We brought you in because of your expertise. I respect your point of view. Thanks, again, for all of the help you gave us. Tell your people in L.A. we appreciate their assistance."

"Thank you, Jim, and you're quite welcome. Tell you what, Jim," countered Bill Menegay. "If your Musketeers make it to the finals next year, which will undoubtedly be against my L.A. team, we'll invite you out for a game, ok?"

"It's a deal," replied the Cleveland agent.

Agent Jim Sweeney hung up the phone. He then picked it up and called the Cleveland Police Department Headquarters.

"This is Special Agent Jim Sweeney, FBI," he stated to the sergeant. "May I speak to Captain Oldakowski?"

"Uh, he's out right now, Mr. Sweeney," stated the desk sergeant.

"Can I leave him a message?"

"Sure, I can do that for you," replied the twenty year force veteran.

"Tell him to cancel the protection for Dante O'Shea at the Clinic. The case is closed," Jim Sweeney informed him.

"Gotcha."

"Thanks."

Agent Sweeney put the phone on its holder. He took a deep breath. The gut feeling didn't go away.

CHAPTER 47

Dante O'Shea dribbled through the maze of Michigan defenders. Ohio State was losing by one point, eight seconds showed on the clock when he grabbed the rebound and started his attack toward the basket on the other end of the court.

He dribbled the ball around a backpedaling Wolverine and started his jump as the seconds ticked down. Three, two, one, he released the ball. It ascended toward the basket, then disappeared. The buzzer sounded. Michigan won.

"What's going on?" he thought. He was very frustrated.

He looked around the gymnasium which seconds before had been filled with boisterous Buckeye fans. Nobody was there.

He wandered outside of the building and saw a tall wall of sand. It was in the middle of nowhere he recognized. Up on top, he saw his mom and dad and Lisa. They waved to him to come to them.

"I'm coming," he shouted.

But they didn't seem to hear. They kept calling his name and telling him to come back.

"I'm coming, I'm coming," he yelled louder.

But they ignored his shouts. The frustration grew.

All of the sudden he felt very different. He floated above the wall of sand. He could look down and see his parents. And Lisa. She was holding a baby.

"Finally!" he screamed to her. "We have a baby!"

But she didn't seem to hear. She showed no reaction.

He continued ascending skyward. He felt ok about it. Not scared. Not even wondering what was going on. He just felt peaceful. Everything was real, yet was so unreal. It was an odd feeling, but he'd go with it.

The Being was like nothing he had ever seen before. He didn't feel like he was really seeing it. It was more like experiencing it. It was bright, but not the brightness that hurts your eyes. It was the most beautiful thing he had ever experienced. He was drawn to it. He didn't care about anything except the peace and love it showered upon him. He felt like it was a part of him and he was a part of it.

Somewhere in his mind he remembered a teacher explaining how God was in each one of us.

"God is like a big water tower," the teacher told the class. "A water tower holds millions of gallons of water. Each gallon of water is made up of tiny drops. You and I are the tiny drops. And when we are born into this world, we begin our spiritual journey, that's all this life really is. A spiritual journey. And we travel down all the pipes that lead away from the water tower, all going our separate ways. And we live our lives, striving to be good enough to get back to that water tower again."

"You see," the teacher continued. "We all start our spiritual journey, our life on earth, with God. And He wants us to come back to Him and be a part of Him again. And when we are good, all of that goodness comes together and makes God even more powerful."

Dante remembered asking, "What about purgatory? Aren't we supposed to go to purgatory to cleanse our sins?"

"When you return to God, you may feel unworthy of His love and peace, then you can decide if you should go to purgatory for a while and cleanse yourself."

It was a concept Dante couldn't totally comprehend. Until now.

He wanted to ask a thousand questions. The Being answered his first thought.

"I am who you think I am," it said without uttering a word. The answer came to Dante as clearly as if it had been whispered directly in his ear.

"I saw a baby with Lisa," thought Dante.

"And you will return to your baby. It is not time for you. You have more to do."

Dante missed his wife and family and friends, yet wanted to stay in this feeling of total reality filled with unimaginable love and peace. He couldn't have both.

Suddenly, he inhaled a familiar smell and opened his eyes. He had been in a coma for one week.

CHAPTER 48

Robbie Dulik was the first to see the movement.

"Dante?" he whispered. "Dante?"

Lisa looked up from the book she was reading. It was about parenting. She glanced at her husband, then bolted out of the chair.

"Dante!" she screamed. "Oh, Dante, I…"

She started to cry.

Robbie removed the basketball he had put by Dante's head. It was the familiar smell that Dante had awakened to.

"I kind of thought," Robbie started to explain. "Well, I thought it might help."

Dante blinked his eyes several times. He tried to talk but was hindered by a tube shoved down his throat.

"Get the nurse!" ordered Lisa.

Alise Dulik had already been heading toward the door to do just that.

"Oh, Dante," Lisa cried. "I thought I had lost you. Oh, my husband, I love you so much."

She leaned over the bed rail and brushed her cheek against Dante's face. If he had been able to smile, he would have. He was able to cry. And he did.

Moments later, the head nurse, Barb Sullivan, entered the room. She joined in the excitement and the tears. Dante was her hero, too. She was thrilled to be a part of his recovery.

Nurse Sullivan, 'Babs' to her co-workers, noticed that Dante seemed alert. She took his right hand into hers.

"I'm going to ask you a few questions," she kindly stated.

Dante's eyes focused in on her. With a tube down his throat, he didn't know how he could reply.

"Dante," she began. "We have a nasogastric tube in your nose. That's what you feel in your throat. That's how you've been eating for awhile."

Dante heard it, but didn't comprehend everything she explained. He blinked his eyes.

"Squeeze my hand," Babs ordered.

Dante complied.

"Ok, good. I'm going to ask you a few questions. Squeeze my hand, once for yes, twice for no. Ok?"

Dante squeezed her hand once.

"Do you know where you are?"

Two squeezes.

"Do you remember what happened?"

Two squeezes.

"Do you recognize your visitors?"

Dante darted his eyes around the room. He squeezed once. Very hard.

"Dante," Babs told him. "You've been injured and are in the Cleveland Clinic. You've been in a coma for a week. Do you understand?"

Confusion showed in the Musketeer player's eyes. He looked at his wife. Then Robbie and Alise. He wasn't sure why he was there. But his aching body told him he was in the right place. He squeezed the nurse's hand once. He understood.

"Dante," Babs continued. "I'm going to consult with the doctor. Then I'll be back and take that tube out. You'd like that, wouldn't you?"

Dante's mind was now elsewhere. Back to that peaceful place. Was it a dream? He didn't know. But he was at peace with it all. And he was back.

Babs got one more squeeze.

CHAPTER 49

The Cleveland Indians weren't doing too good in this game. Their nemesis, the New York Yankees were pounding them, eight to nothing. It was the bottom of the seventh inning.

Tommy Benner was at the plate when the game was halted for an announcement.

"Ladies and gentlemen," the loudspeakers blared. "May I have your attention, please?"

The crowd became eerily silent. The home plate umpire backed off his stance behind home plate and looked up into the area of the press box. He had a major question mark look on his face.

"Ladies and gentlemen," continued the announcer. "I am pleased, very pleased, to inform you."

He stopped. For a brief moment, the announcer said nothing. The announcement he had to make choked him up. In a happy way.

"I am very pleased to announce that Dante O'Shea is out of his coma and is doing much better."

The baseball palace called Jacobs Field erupted. The crowd stood, many of them near tears, and cheered and cheered and cheered. For ten minutes, they hooted and screamed and barked and high fived. It equaled the pandemonium of a few years ago when the Indians had won their fifth Divisional Title in a row.

Their Dante O'Shea would live. Life would be good again.

On East Fortieth Street, in the yellow house that badly needed repair and painting, Vince Burson watched on his tv. Even though Tommy Benner followed the announcement with a home run. And even though his team rallied from eight runs down to win the game in the bottom of the ninth on Tommy's second home run of the inning, Vinnie Burson was not happy.

He reluctantly decided to put Plan B into action.

CHAPTER 50

"I know, I know," Dante stated to his therapist. "A waterfall starts with a single drop of water."

"No pain, no gain," added the burly physical therapist.

Dante just rolled his eyes.

Two months had passed since his release from the Cleveland Clinic. His therapy had begun only a week ago. It took that long for his broken arm, wrist, and ribs to heal and all of his abrasions to clear up. His legs and knees presented a different problem. They would take a bit longer.

Doctor Ernest Kavalecz waltzed into the therapy room located on the first level of the Cleveland Clinic.

"How's our prize pupil?" he asked.

The therapist looked down at Dante. He wanted to know this answer, too.

"Well, Doc," Dante started. "Other than a few aches and pains, I feel pretty good. Only a couple of months until practice begins."

Doctor Kavalecz pursed his lips.

"Dante," he said in a low voice. "We need to talk a bit."

The physical therapist understood the statement well enough to know that he was excluded. He wandered over to another patient and kept a respectful distance from the Musketeer team doctor and his patient.

Doctor Kavalecz sat on a padded bench near the weight machine that Dante had been utilizing. This was not going to be an easy conversation. Just the thought of it opened some old wounds for the doctor. He had been there on the receiving end himself. He knew about the disappointment and disbelief he would soon encounter from Dante O'Shea.

"Dante, you know that there's been extensive damage, not only to your body, but, well, you had major head trauma, too," he stated. "And besides all that, I'm worried about your heart."

"There's nothing wrong with my heart, Doc," Dante interjected.

"I don't mean the organ, Dante, I mean your heart, your feelings."

"What are we talking about, Doc?"

"You had a lot of injuries, two broken legs, your arm, your wrist, your ribs, and the ACL on your left knee. You've come a long way just to get to this point."

"Well, I know I ain't a hundred percent," Dante emphatically stated. "But I'll get there. We got two or three months to heal me up. You can do it, right?"

He had already accepted the fact that he'd miss half the season. His game plan was to make it back after the All Star game, join his team, and, of course, win the NBA Title.

"Dante, you've always known me as a straight shooter, right?"

It was the same speech he had given Dante's wife on that dreadful night in May.

"Yea, you're a straight shooter, Doc. But are you saying I don't have enough heart to come back. Because if you are, you're wrong."

"No, Dante, I'm not questioning your heart or your stamina, or, or your manhood, nothing like that. What I'm going to tell you, I will tell you as your doctor and as your friend. I'll tell you because I know from experience that we can only do so much, and then the body says no more."

"What are we talking about here, Doc?" Dante asked again.

Dante was getting confused with the conversation.

"I think you ought to consider retiring, Dante," the doctor blurted out.

"What? Me, retire? No way," Dante half shouted back. "Where are you getting these ideas, Doc?"

"Dante, here's how it is, ok? You are a great basketball player, a great athlete. You've never been seriously injured in your whole career, right?"

"Well, I broke a wrist in high school, but that was nothing."

"My point is this, Dante, you are not going to be able to play the way you once did. There are too many indications that you will have lingering problems and they will affect you."

"I've played hurt a lot, Doc, you know that."

"Not like this, Dante. Your wrist and your arm will heal. They'll be fine. But your legs, Dante. We didn't even know about the anterior cruciate ligament damage, your ACL, until after you were out of the hospital. You know that's a major injury. It has shortened many careers."

Dante didn't like what he was hearing.

"You broke both legs. Badly. Not simple fractures. You splintered the fibula on your right leg. It will take a very long time to heal, to say the least. I just don't want you getting your hopes up, because it may never happen, Dante."

"How are you going to handle it," continued the doctor. "When you can't run as fast as you did, or jump as high, or pivot as quickly, in other words, do all the things that set you apart from your competitors? It will wear on you, Dante, physically and mentally. You'll find yourself wanting to do a move you've made a thousand times, then you'll have a nagging doubt that you're not capable of doing it. I know, Dante, I've been there."

Dante's face reddened.

"That's you, Doc, not me. Just because you quit, doesn't mean I will."

Doctor Kavalecz grimaced at those words. He decided to try another approach.

"Dante, what does your therapist have you working on today?"

"Same as every day I've been here. My upper body."

"Why?" asked the doctor.

"Well," Dante answered. "With these casts on, I can't very well work on my legs now can I?"

"How long do you think it will take before you CAN work on your legs?"

"Hey, you're the doctor, you tell me."

"I am telling you, Dante. I'm trying to tell you. Dante, you're going to have to learn to do many of the things that came naturally to you all over again. It will be a very slow and hard process. And once you learn to,"

Dante cut him off.

"You're saying I can't do it?"

Dante stared at Doctor Kavalecz. His face was getting redder. Anger and disbelief were sinking in.

"What you can do in the future is up to you, Dante. However, I want you to know that the quality of playing that has earned you your reputation will probably never be there again. I'm sorry to be so blunt. But I feel you have a right to know. And the right to prepare for life after basketball."

Dante leaned forward on the lifting machine. His eyes burrowed in on the face of the team doctor.

"Get out of here, Doctor Kavalecz, JUST GET OUT!" he shouted.

"Willie!" he bellowed to his therapist. "Get over here. We've got work to do!"

Doctor Kavalecz slowly stood up.

"Dante, if anyone can come back from all of this, it's you. I truly believe it. I will help you any way I can, you know that."

He stared directly into Dante's eyes. His compassion and empathy were apparent to the basketball star.

"I do care," he added.

Dante looked away from the doctor and stared at his legs.

"I know, Doc," he whispered. "I know you care."

He turned his body toward Willie.

"Willie," he ordered. "Put more weight on here. We've got a lot of work to do. And don't even think of wimping out on me. Got it?"

His therapist slowly nodded. And smiled. So did Doctor K.

CHAPTER 51

"Excuse me," he mumbled as he almost collided with the Musketeer doctor.

Vince Burson firmly grabbed the meaningless file in his hand and proceeded through the door to the physical therapy room. It wasn't too crowded, and he easily discovered the whereabouts of Dante O'Shea. He worked his way closer to the patient and his therapist.

"Yeah, Willie," he heard Dante say. "I'm getting my memory back. Now I'll be able to remember how badly you treat me."

They both laughed.

Willie saw him standing ten feet away. Without giving any thought as to who Vinnie Burson was, in relationship to the kidnapers of his patient, Willie shrugged Vinnie's presence off as just another Dante O'Shea admirer trying to get close enough to his hero to say hello or mumble some encouragement. Although these visits were being controlled, it still happened frequently.

"Yeah," Dante continued. "Lisa and I are going to visit the Feds today. Guess they want some details about my kidnapping."

He grimaced.

"Well, if it will help their case," Willie commented.

"To be honest," Dante stated. "The whole thing is like a bad dream. I seem to remember bits and pieces, but it's not all back yet. It's kinda like it really didn't happen."

"You've made big strides," Willie chimed in. "Heck, I remember when you couldn't remember my name. Kept calling me everything but Willie."

They laughed again.

Vinnie got a sick feeling in his stomach. Then left the room.

The session lasted two hours. As had become her habit, Lisa O'Shea showed up about twenty minutes before the end of the workout and did some reading. She was engrossed in an article. It was yet another parenting magazine.

Lisa stopped reading and looked at her husband. She admired her husband's work ethic. Doctor Kavalecz had intimated to her that Dante's recovery would be difficult at best. He even mentioned to her that Dante might be forced into retirement. She hoped that would not be the case. Not playing ball would kill her husband. Sometimes, she felt he was hard enough to live with when he was healthy. She watched the sweat pour off of her husband's face. He smiled at her. She smiled back, then resumed reading the article on artificial insemination.

"At least that part of Dante still works," she smiled to herself.

On the second floor of the Cleveland Coliseum, Coach Avery talked with his coaching staff.

"Well, you all know the situation," he stated to his coaches. "Dante won't be playing most of this year, so we're going to have to formulate a battle plan to offset his offense and defense."

Not an easy task.

They had each given the situation much thought prior to this meeting. But what they were not informed about was Coach Avery's decision regarding Dante O'Shea. His idea was overwhelmingly approved by Bud Herrington, the Musketeer owner and his boss.

Coach Avery looked at his assistants.

"We're going to carry Dante O'Shea on the active roster," he said.

"That means we will only have eleven active players," one of the assistants pointed out.

"I know what it means," Coach Avery interrupted. "But this is more about what Dante has done for this organization and for this community. It's the right thing to do. He needs it. And to be quite honest, I want him on the bench with us. I guarantee his presence and insight will help this team."

"Can't we put him on injured reserve? He can still be on the bench," advised another assistant.

"We could, but we won't," the head coach stated. "Listen, right now put yourselves in Dante's shoes. Think about how he must feel. He may never play basketball again. He's working hard right now in therapy to overcome all the odds against him. He needs our support, and he's going to get it. It may only be symbolic, but it's what I want to do. And I might add, it's what the boss wants, too."

The assistant coaches all nodded or voiced agreement. Then they went to work. Discussing and planning strategies on how to best utilize the various skills of their players. Practice would begin in eight weeks.

They would be prepared.

CHAPTER 52

Dante sat in the office of Jim Sweeney and racked his brain for an answer. What else, if anything, did he remember about his kidnapping? It was his second visit with the FBI since getting out of the hospital. His first visit was confusing to him. The doctors at the Clinic had told him he might have some recall loss from the head trauma he had suffered. And he did. But little by little the recollections of the ordeal were working their way back into his memory. He had read the newspaper articles that Lisa had kept, but it all seemed hazy, like a dream, like it had really happened to someone else. He couldn't seem to put the names and faces together. It was very frustrating.

"I remember Robbie was having coffee with me, then he had to go to the bathroom. The doorbell had rung and when I opened the door, it was two guys dressed like a gorilla and a monkey. I thought it was Henry Pickett and Joey Riggs, our trainer. But I guess I was wrong."

"It was only the two of them, as far as you could see, right?" asked Agent Gill.

"Yeah, like I said, just the two guys, or whatever. So I let them in, they handed me a box or something, and next thing I knew, I was blindfolded and on a plane to Italy. Or so I thought."

"What made you think you were on a plane to Italy?"

"Well, there was a lot of airplane noise, you know, the stuff you hear when you're flying. The engines, conversations, announcements from the cockpit. And, oh yeah, there was a lot of turbulence. It seemed we were really rocking up there."

"You now know that it was all rigged, right?" queried Jim Sweeney. "The rocking was a chair and the noise was tapes. Agent Gill explained that to you when we met last time."

"Yeah, right. But I'm just telling you what I thought was happening. I kind of feel stupid for being fooled like that."

"Well, you were also under heavy sedation, Dante," Len Gill reminded him.

"So, when you thought you were in Italy," Jim Sweeney stated. "You told us that you got to know the abductors a bit. Let's review that again."

"Well, they kind of spoke freely to me, not at first, but after quite a few hours, I guess. One of the guys was really mouthy, he worried me a bit."

"What do you mean?" asked Sweeney.

"Well, he talked about stuff he, or they, did to Lisa, which I now know was a lie. And he was pretty threatening to me."

"In what way?"

"He told me that if I caused any trouble, he would kill me?"

"Did you think he really would?" asked Jim Sweeney.

"I thought he might be capable, I don't know. Hard to judge things like that when you can't see who's saying it."

"You said there were others, how many do you think there were?" Jim Sweeney asked.

It was the question that had been haunting him since the case was officially closed. In fact, this meeting was officially off the record. Jim Sweeney just wanted to make sure. And up until now, Dante O'Shea had not remembered enough to put the agent's mind at ease.

"I remember there was a guy who seemed really sad about everything, he's the one that loosened my ropes, before everything went down."

It was starting to come back. Like a switch turning on a light bulb, Dante's mind illumined with more details.

"Yea, his name was Carl. He was real, ah, remorseful. It was like he was suckered into doing it. He didn't really want to be a part of it. In fact, he admitted that he was the one who hit me at my front door. He was really sorry about that."

"Carl Plath was his name, Dante," Gill advised him. "Real big kid. And from what we were told, he was a good guy. Except for this, of course."

"I think the mouthy one's name was Vince, or Vinnie, something like that," Dante continued. "He was bad news."

"Vincent Burson," muttered Jim Sweeney.

"The third one was Eddie. He was the leader from what I could tell. I know that he was killed by Carl, so the paper said. The two of them were the ones who took care of me. It was like they were protecting me from the Vinnie kid. The paper said that it appeared that Carl killed Eddie. I don't understand why he would have done that. But then again, I don't understand why they would've kidnapped me either."

"Do you think Eddie and Vinnie are the same person?" Len Gill asked. "You know, like a Jekyll and Hyde syndrome?"

"I don't know," Dante slowly answered. "I suppose that's possible."

"You know," Dante continued. "Eddie seemed to be in control and real polite. He called me Mister O'Shea all the time. The Vinnie character was way too different. I don't know for sure."

"So, going back to when you escaped, Dante," Agent Sweeney started. "You worked yourself free; then what happened? What can you recall?"

Dante gave the agent a look. He felt like Sweeney was questioning his mental ability. He let it go.

"I remember getting my arms loose, but that was after I heard the gunfire, I think. Then I stood up, and I totally forgot about my ankle being in a cast, and I almost fell down. I remember I was real lightheaded."

"Did you go right for the window?" Lenny Gill asked.

"I think I did, that's kind of hazy," Dante replied.

"Do you remember any other commotion, I mean other than the shots being fired?" Jim Sweeney inquired.

"I remember the door to the room was open. I think Carl had gone out of the room and,"

He stopped talking. Dante closed his eyes and concentrated. The agents said nothing.

"And, I…saw…one…of…them," he finished.

"You did!" exclaimed Jim Sweeney.

His heart pounded. The gut feeling was going to be right, he just knew it.

"Yeah, that's right, I remember now. I went to the door and I looked out. It was a big office or something like that. And one of them stood, maybe ten or fifteen feet away and just stared at me."

"Did he say or do anything?" Agent Sweeney excitedly asked.

"No, he just looked at me. Then he turned and ran."

"Did you get a good look at him?" Len Gill queried.

"Well, kind of, I guess I did. He was a short guy, short hair. Just average looking, I guess."

Jim Sweeney turned to his partner. A small smile formed on his lips.

"Len, if this happened after the shooting, then there had to be a third person. Carl and Eddie were already dead."

Len Gill nodded in agreement.

"Dante, the next part of what happened, I, uh, I need to kind of clarify in my mind," stated Jim Sweeney. "When we came up the stairs, we saw the two bodies on the floor, and we saw you ready to jump out of the window. What do you remember about that?"

"Well, after the kid ran, I heard all kinds of noise from somewhere in the building," Dante explained. "You have to realize, I thought I was in Italy. I thought it was someone else coming to get me, you know, some terrorist group or something, I don't know."

"So I forced the window open as far as I could, and I put my foot out first, the one with the cast, and I was positioning myself to jump away from the building. I remember seeing a bunch of trash below, but there were rags and what looked like a better landing area further from the building. Maybe about ten feet."

"I was getting ready to jump, and I heard some shouting behind me, in the room, and then everything happened so fast, I remember thinking, I think these are the good guys, but then I lost my balance and fell out of the window."

"Do you remember anyone trying to help you, someone trying to grab you?"

Agent Sweeney needed to hear this answer.

"I remember looking back, and realizing that I didn't have to jump, it was you guys, or the Italian police, somebody there to help me. I remember a hand reaching toward me, but it was too late, I had already started to fall. Whoever it was didn't have a chance to grab me."

"It was me, Dante," admitted Jim Sweeney. "And I am glad to hear that I didn't cause your fall."

"No, no way, sir," Dante stated. "I was falling before you were near the window. Maybe if you had arms like Henry Pickett, I mean, that man's got some long arms, then you would've had a chance. But no, I simply fell."

Jim Sweeney sighed a good sigh.

"Thank you, Dante," he said. "I'm sorry this happened to you, I really am. We'll get the other Burson kid now. Then the case will be truly over."

Lisa O'Shea maneuvered behind her husband's wheelchair and pushed him out the FBI agent's office door.

A shiver ran down her spine.

CHAPTER 53

Vinnie Burson told his supervisor that he wasn't feeling well. She looked him over and told him he looked a little peaked.

"Go home and get some rest," she told him.

Vinnie did go right home. As had become his routine, he scoured the neighborhood for strange cars, or cars with city or state plates on them. He saw none.

He parked his brother's car in the garage and hustled through the back door into the kitchen. He opened the utensil drawer and didn't find a knife to his liking. Then he remembered Eddie's hunting supplies.

Running two steps at a time, he entered his brother's bedroom. Nothing had changed since Eddie's death. Dirty clothes carpeted the wooden floor. The bed remained unmade. He flung the closet door open and scoured through Eddie's hunting box. He found what he wanted. A ten inch hunting knife.

"That'll do," he thought.

Then he heard the knock. More like pounding on the old wooden door. He knew who it was. He stayed in his brother's room and waited. The knocking stopped. He positioned himself near the window and peered outside through the dirty, sheer curtain. They were in the garage. Even though it was still light out, they shined their huge flashlights around the interior of the dumpy building. He knew they would now wait around. He left his brother's bedroom and headed for the stairs. They would not be able to see him on the staircase from any window in the house. If they were looking. He slowly descended the stairs, then crawled on his belly to the kitchen.

They were at the back door. He could hear them. Between him and them was the refrigerator. That's where he stood. Unseen by them. The basement door was on the other side of the fridge, next to the back door. He heard them walk off the back porch. He listened intently. He could hear them walking on the driveway. What little gravel there was sounded very crunchy under their FBI shoes.

He crouched low, eyeing the back door window. No one was there. He reached the basement door and headed toward the tunnel. The one he told them he hated because he was claustrophobic.

Hc worked his way through the dark tunnel. Nothing had changed since he last was here. He was going to go up to the room and think things out, but then saw that the windows the FBI had broken out were still not fixed. Who cared about broken windows in an abandoned building?

Vinnie stuck his head out of the opening. Forty feet away and across the street, he saw a car parked in his driveway. Two men were sitting in it. That much he could tell.

He squeezed through the ample opening and ran along the side of the old machine shop to the back of the building where all the rubbish lay. He thought he saw blood on some of the boards, but really didn't care.

He jumped a fence and scrambled through a yard. A dog barked. He then starting searching for transportation. He found it two blocks away. In front of a convenience store. The car was running. The owner evidently in too big of a hurry to care.

Vinnie jumped into the driver's seat, put the car in reverse, slowly backed up, then screeched out of the parking lot and headed for Interstate 77.

Plan B was now in effect.

CHAPTER 54

"Dante," Lisa stated. "I'm worried."

"About?"

"Well, if there were three kids involved, we know they only got two. Or their dead, I mean. There's another one out there. Aren't you a little concerned?"

She maneuvered his wheelchair out of the door of the Federal Building and headed toward a ramp. Several people witnessed the young lady gently pushing the young man. They knew who he was. Some even stopped to yell hello to Dante O'Shea. They'd later tell their family and friends they saw the basketball hero and he looked pretty good.

"I have confidence that he won't be running around for long," Dante replied. "Believe me, the FBI is already working on it. Anyway, if he thought he got away with it, why would he try something now?"

She wished she didn't have that fearful feeling.

"No use taking it any further," Lisa thought. "He'll just tell me to suck it up and everything will be all right".

She both liked and disliked his way of dealing with issues. But at least Dante did deal with issues. She couldn't say the same about herself. The thought that she was hiding something from her husband started to bother her. Again.

"Let's not go right home," Dante suggested. "Why don't we go get a bite to eat somewhere? You don't mind not cooking tonight, do you?"

Lisa knew what to expect. They'd go into a restaurant and Dante would succumb to his need to please the fans. They'd ask for autographs or want to talk with him about this or that, and he would, as usual, comply.

It was another of his habits she understood, yet detested. She would, of course, oblige.

"Good idea," she stated half-heartedly.

He never gave her lack of enthusiasm another thought.

Fred Wilson had just taken Fifi back into the house.

"Where's your toy, Fifi?" he asked the poodle.

The dog looked at him, and as if replying, scurried to the back door. Fred Wilson followed, then remembered he had just been playing retrieve with his dog outside.

"I'll go get it," he told his pet. "You stay here."

The elderly O'Shea neighbor walked around his back yard, searching for the rubber bone. He finally found it near the fence separating his property from the young O'Shea couple's driveway.

He slowly bent over to pick up Fifi's toy. That's when he saw a young man saunter up his neighbor's drive and walk right into the open garage. The visitor didn't see him. Fred picked up the rubber bone, put it in his pocket, and moseyed down toward the front yard so he could get a better look at his neighbor's visitor. He wasn't being nosy. He was the self-proclaimed neighborhood watchdog. He was doing his job.

Vince Burson quickly deduced that Dante O'Shea and his wife weren't home. He knew where they had been. His visit by the FBI had endorsed that. There was no car in the garage, and it appeared that the house was empty. There was no noise from within.

He hadn't really thought this out so well, but he was here and he would adapt.

Vinnie looked around the garage, then decided to try the door to the house. He remembered it led to the kitchen. It was locked. He approached a door at the back of the garage and peered out the curtained window at the vast backyard.

He unlocked the door and found himself on a brick patio. The deck and pool were to his left. He sauntered up three wooden steps to the huge deck and gazed at the sliding doors that led into the kitchen. He tried the sliding door. It moved a bit, but did not open.

He walked toward the pool and surveyed the back of the residence. Many windows, but none were open. He heard an air conditioner chattering on the roof.

Vince Burson wanted the element of surprise. But he also did not want any indication of a break-in. The house probably had an alarm anyway. He returned to the garage.

Fred Wilson could see the young man roaming around his neighbor's garage. Not real clearly, but he knew the kid was in there. He waited by the fence.

Vince spotted a large, yellow rubber raft leaning against the wall at the back of the spacious two car garage. It could easily conceal his small frame. He would hide there. And wait.

Fred Wilson heard Fifi barking.

"I'm coming!" he yelled. "Don't wake up mommy."

Mimi was taking her beauty nap. When she awoke, Fred would tell her about the O'Shea visitor.

If he remembered.

CHAPTER 55

Lisa O'Shea wheeled her husband out to their BMW. She opened the passenger side door and helped her husband maneuver into the seat. She collapsed the wheelchair and placed it in the trunk. It was a procedure she had done now at least a hundred times.

"That was a good meal," Dante exclaimed. "Worth the drive."

As usual, Angello's was crowded. But the owner found a table quickly for Dante and his wife. And it was out of the way. Lisa appreciated that.

"Wish I could get his pizza recipe," Dante continued. "It's almost as good as mine."

Lisa smiled at her husband. She put the Beemer into gear and started the forty-five minute drive home.

Mimi Wilson was finishing the dishes while her husband perused the paper. It was the second time that day he read it. It was a habit Mimi didn't mind.

"Dante and Lisa had a visitor today," her husband stated.

"Oh, yeah?"

"Well, I saw him go into their garage, and he didn't come out," Fred continued. "Guess he might've had a key. Curious thing though, he didn't drive here, he walked."

"That is curious," stated his wife.

The conversation ceased as Fred turned to the classifieds.

"You know, sweetie," he suddenly stated. "I ought to sell that old gun of mine. We don't need it. It's just collecting dust. I bet I could get a pretty dollar for it. There're a lot of collectors looking for things like that in these classifieds."

"You do that, Fred."

It was a suggestion he had made numerous times. When Fred abruptly put the paper down and stood up, she wondered what he was up to now.

"I'm going to go find it," he stated.

"Ok," she shrugged.

The dark green BMW cruised up the driveway toward the garage. Lisa slowly drove the car into its parking place. She hit the trunk button on the car door and got out of the car. As she approached the back of the car, the yellow rubber raft suddenly fell to the ground. She jumped.

"Stay right there and do what I say," Vince Burson ordered in a low voice.

He waved his brother's hunting knife menacingly at her.

"Get away from the car and close the garage door."

Lisa obeyed.

Dante looked on from the passenger seat. His first inclination was to honk the car horn to get attention. Then he thought of quickly dialing 9-1-1 on his cell phone. He did neither.

As Lisa pulled the large door toward the ground, Vinnie opened the car door and faced his former hero.

"So we meet again," he simply stated to the frustrated basketball star.

"I need my wheelchair," Dante advised.

"Just shut up," he was told.

"Get over here," Vinnie yelled to Lisa.

Vinnie looked beyond Dante into the car.

"Give me the phone," he stated.

He grabbed it and threw it near the fallen raft.

"Put your hands on the dash and don't move," he told Dante. "Or I'll slice her."

"You," he said as he motioned with the knife toward Lisa. "Get his wheelchair. NOW."

Shaking with fright, Lisa lifted the chair from the trunk. She carried it toward the passenger side of the car.

"Get him in it," Vinnie ordered.

Dante badly wanted to overtake this punk. Memories of Vinnie's threats stormed his brain. So did his comments about Lisa. But he decided to do nothing. Yet.

Vinnie wielded the knife switching it from hand to hand as Lisa and Dante obliged his last command.

"We have to go through the front door," Dante told him. "Unless you plan to carry me up those stairs."

He nodded toward the steps leading to the kitchen door.

"Ok, ok, just wait," Vinnie impatiently stated.

Dante sat in his chair. Lisa stood behind him. They both stared at the kidnaper.

"I ought to do you both right here," Vinnie declared.

Lisa started to cry.

"Shut up!" he yelled.

Dante reached for his wife's hand. She was too distraught to notice.

"Funny, there's no answer," Mimi told her husband. "I saw them drive up a few minutes ago, and their garage door is shut, so they must be in the house."

"And you call me nosy," Fred said with a smile.

"Well, Lisa always pushes Dante in the wheelchair to the front door, and I can see from here that the garage door is shut, I'll try again."

"Go ahead," her husband responded.

He laid his gun on the table and limped to the refrigerator.

"Want some juice?" he asked.

Mimi was too busy dialing again to answer.

The three of them heard the phone ring from inside the garage. It was the second call in two minutes.

"Here's what we're going to do," stated Vinnie. "I'm going to open the garage door, you are going to push him out and I am going to follow right behind you to the door. If you make any noise or try anything, I will cut you. Bad."

Lisa nervously wheeled Dante into the hallway just inside the front door. Vinnie recognized it all.

"In there," he motioned to Lisa.

She pushed her husband into the living room.

"Ok, here's what's going to happen," Vinnie stated. "I am going to rob you, and, oh, yeah, give me your car keys. I'll need to borrow your car for a while. Believe me, you won't be missing it."

"So that's your big plan," Dante said.

There was a hint of sarcasm in his voice.

"You're going to kill us and make it look like a robbery?" That's original."

"Just shut up," was the kidnaper's reply.

He turned toward Lisa.

"Since superhero here can't do anything, you and me are going to gather some of your valuables. We're going to go get me something to put stuff in. I know you won't get stupid on me. I'll kill you. And then him."

He waved the knife at her for effect. Then he walked over to a table in the corner of the living room and yanked the phone away from its wall jack.

"You stay put," he ordered Dante.

With a knife jabbing precariously close to her back, Lisa led Vince Burson toward the kitchen. She stopped in front of the sink.

"A garbage bag do?" she nervously asked.

She was again near tears and trembling with more fear than she had ever known.

"That'll be fine, little woman," Vinnie retorted.

He was beginning to have fun with this. Like the fun he had at Dante's expense a couple of months ago.

The door bell chimed. Lisa jumped at the sound. Vinnie stood still.

"Ignore it," he whispered.

It rang again.

Dante started to wheel himself toward the door. Then stopped. He couldn't take the chance.

Whoever it was, gave up. The few tense moments passed. Vinnie following Lisa from room to room gathering whatever appealed to him. The bag was getting full.

Mimi returned to her house.

"Something's wrong, Fred," she told him. "Now the garage door is half open, and they don't answer their front door."

"Maybe they don't want to be disturbed," he suggested.

Mimi picked up the phone and again dialed her neighbor's number. This time there was no ringing. Nothing.

"I'm worried, Fred."

"Oh, ok," he muttered. "I'll get the key and go check things out. You stay here. I'm sure it's nothing."

As good neighbors sometimes do, the Wilsons and O'Shea's watched each other's home. Since Dante and Lisa traveled so much, it was helpful for Mimi and Fred to keep a key to the O'Shea house at their home. And Dante and Lisa did the same. With elderly neighbors, it wasn't a bad idea.

Fred Wilson started out his back door. Fifi wanted to join him. He ordered her to stay put. As an afterthought, he sauntered back into his kitchen and grabbed the gun he had been cleaning on the kitchen table.

"What are you going to do with that?" Mimi asked.

"Catch a bad guy," her husband retorted.

He made a face at her. She just shook her head.

CHAPTER 56

Agents Sweeney and Gill sat in the driveway of the Burson residence on East Fortieth Street. They awaited a piece of paper that would legally allow them to enter the old yellow house. It would be forthcoming at any time. So they were told. It had been almost an hour.

"The car had just been driven, he left work early, evidently came home, and I'll bet he's in there waiting for us to leave," Sweeney told his partner.

"Let's get some back up, Jim," Gill advised. "He may be in there arming himself for God knows what."

"You call, I'm going to try again."

Jim Sweeney approached the front door, and as he had done every fifteen minutes, pounded on the wooden frame. As usual, no answer. No movement inside. At least from what he could see.

"Jimmy, come here!" shouted his partner. "Back ups coming, but something else is going on."

"What?" Sweeney yelled as he hustled to the car.

"The office got a call from Dante O'Shea's neighbor, a Mrs. Wilson. She said she's worried that something's wrong with the O'Shea's. Said she's tried calling them and even knocked on their front door, but there's no answer. But their car is there and she thinks something's wrong."

Special Agent Sweeney absorbed this information. He thought it over and made a decision.

"I know how we can get into this house," he stated. "Follow me."

Agents Sweeney and Gill ran across the street to the machine shop. Their entry from two months before was still available. The two agents climbed through the broken out windows and quickly found the tunnel entrance.

With guns drawn, they traversed the ninety foot tunnel and cautiously advanced into the basement of the house they had been patiently waiting to enter. Jim Sweeney guardedly ascended the wooden stairs and found himself in the kitchen. Len Gill soon joined him.

They listened intently and heard nothing. Searching room by room, they soon discovered that Vinnie Burson was indeed not home. Sirens broke the silence as the back up units charged down East Fortieth Street.

Fred Wilson nonchalantly pushed the key into the lock of the kitchen door. He opened the door slowly. He feared disturbing his neighbors, especially if they were doing what he had earlier thought.

He quietly entered the kitchen and started toward the living room. Even though it was getting dark outside, no lights were on. He noticed that. Something told him that maybe Mimi was right. He would be careful.

"Ok, that's enough," stated Vince Burson.

He set the second bag of stolen goods on the winged chair in the living room. His next move would be critical. It's something he knew he had to do.

"You know," he said to Dante. "I really didn't want to be involved with this. It was all Pallibio's idea. I stayed out of the way. I really did. I let Eddie and Carl do the work and I just stayed away. And then that idiot kills my brother and then himself. And then you see me. No matter what I tell the cops, they're gonna put me away."

"I could tell them that you weren't involved," Dante told him. "I mean, I didn't really see you. It could've been your brother, and it could've been before he was shot. I could tell them that."

"Dante's memory has been playing tricks on him," added Lisa. "Believe me, they'd believe his story."

"No, it's too late for that," Vinnie reasoned out loud. "Let's just get this over with."

"It's not too late," Dante pleaded. "We can work it out. You want money? I got plenty. I'll set you up and never talk about it again. To anyone."

The doubt and remorse ended for Vinnie Burson.

"Get over there," he told Lisa. "By the piano."

He watched as Lisa again obeyed. She began to cry.

"I don't want to die," she wailed. "I don't want to die."

"Shut up," Vinnie ordered.

She cried louder. Her body quivered. Dante had enough.

"That it!" he shouted. "No more. I've had it with you."

The meanness returned to Vinnie Burson.

"What you going to do to me, superstar? Kick my butt?"

Dante slowly wheeled himself toward his protagonist. Vinnie instinctively backed up. He flashed his knife toward Dante's chin, but it didn't stop the Musketeer player. He eased his wheelchair forward until his bandaged legs pushed against Vinnie's thighs. Vinnie raised his brother's knife.

"Now what, Daaante?" Vinnie singsonged the question to him.

He felt the cold touch on his neck. It was metal. And it felt round. Like a small circle.

"Go ahead, kid, make my day," whispered Fred Wilson in a barely audible voice.

Vinnie Burson did nothing and the pressure on his neck was increased. Fred Wilson repeated his request in a strong, more audible voice.

The knife fell to the ground. Vincent Burson gave it up.

Later, over a cup of coffee, Fred would share his story with the FBI. And he would tell them what he had told the Burson kid after the cops had arrived.

"It wasn't even loaded."

CHAPTER 57

"You can do it, Dante," Willie told him. "I know you can."

Dante supported his upright body by leaning against the chest of his therapist. Beads of sweat worked their way from his forehead into his eyes. Willie wiped them away.

"Thanks," Dante grunted.

Four months after his fall, Dante began the process of learning to walk again. It would be an uphill battle. His legs were weak from non-use. There was little he could do to keep the atrophy from setting in. His upper body strength was very close to what it had been. As part of his workout, Willie would let Dante shoot baskets from his wheelchair. Dante loved the feel and the smell of a basketball. It was just a ball to many, but to the Musketeer player, just holding it made him feel good.

He worked hard. He painfully pushed himself to get it all back. He would do whatever he had to in order to play his game again. He pushed Willie to push him. And his therapist resolved to bring Dante back.

Doctor Kavalecz entered the therapy room as he had done many times during Dante's recuperation.

"How's our star pupil?" he asked.

Dante said nothing. He balanced himself on the silver metal bars and looked straight ahead. Determination burned in his green eyes.

Dante lifted his right foot. It moved two inches off the ground. He pushed and pushed to make it go forward. It finally did.

He braced himself and willed his left foot to do the same. Little by little, Dante made his way down the parallel bars, sweat pouring from his battered body, determination, like a beacon of light, shining from his eyes.

Doctor Kavalecz broke the silence.

"Good news, Dante. The MRI showed that your ACL is healing ahead of schedule. See, there is a silver lining in that black cloud. All that sitting around has helped your healing process."

"Great," Dante mumbled. He gasped for air.

"Let's take a break, bud," Willie told his patient.

"Let's do it again," retorted Dante.

And the process was repeated. Over and over and over again.

Vince Burson slouched on the bed in his cell. He listened to the counselor, not really caring what was said.

"Vince," continued the bearded advisor. "Tell me about your family."

"You got it all there, man, in your file. Just read it."

"I know I do, but it's just words on paper. I want to hear it from you."

Vinnie looked at the counselor, then beyond the tall man, staring at the wall behind him.

"Family," he thought. "What family?"

After several minutes, he decided to open up.

"There was me and Eddie," he began. "My dad took off when I was four, I don't know where he is, nor do I care. Mom raised me and Eddie until she died. I was sixteen."

"How did she die, Vince?"

"Drug overdose."

"So it was just you and Eddie after that? No relatives took you in?"

"Nobody wanted to, I guess. Eddie was in high school. He played football, and was pretty good. I think he could've got a scholarship to Kent State, but he knocked up some girl and married her. I quit school and joined the Navy. Then I came back and worked at the Clinic."

"Me and Eddie decided to rent a house, since it was just him and me. We needed more money, so we got Carl to join us. That was my family."

"Vinnie, I want to help you," stated the prison counselor. "Do you want help?"

Vince Burson looked at the man. What did he really want? Help me so he could tell his cronies what a great therapist he is? He didn't believe he needed any help. But if playing this game would get him out of this hell hole quicker, he might as well play it. Twenty years to life is a long time. He decided at that moment to play the game.

"Yeah, I want help," he whispered to the counselor.

Lisa O'Shea sat in the leather chair across from Doctor Francis. Tears streamed down her eyes.

"I don't know what's wrong with me," she confided.

The doctor handed her a tissue.

"I appear to have it all," Lisa continued. "But something is missing. I love Dante, but even before his 'accident', something between us wasn't right. He seems to be in his own world, and I feel like, like an attachment. I'm the wife of the great Dante O'Shea. I have all the comforts anyone needs. I've traveled all over the world. But, sometimes, Doctor, I don't know who I am. Or worse yet, why I'm here."

"What do you feel you need to do to feel better about yourself?" Doctor Francis asked.

Lisa didn't respond very quickly. She looked down at her lap. Wiped another tear from her eyes. She knew what she had to do. But she had doubts about doing it.

"Find my identity. Be my own person." Lisa replied. "I think if I had a baby, it would be great. I've always wanted to be a mom."

"That's nice," replied the doctor. "But you realize that it won't solve the problems you have with Dante. It's true that a baby can bring a family together, but it can also drive a wedge between the two of you. How does Dante feel about kids?"

"Oh, he wants a son real bad," Lisa said with some excitement. "He's real good with kids."

"Well," the therapist concluded. "That just might be your answer."

Lisa wholeheartedly agreed. She wanted to tell the therapist more, but she felt that some things were left better unsaid.

CHAPTER 58

The winter months brought the usual gloomy weather to Northeast Ohio. It was always nice to have snow on the ground around the holidays. It made for a Bing Crosbyish dreamy white Christmas and for fond memories of Christmases past. Families sitting by the fireplace, the smell of pine from the tree in the living room, the excitement of opening gifts, the music of the season.

Winter in the Cleveland Musketeer family wasn't all that glorious. The Cleveland team had worked their way from a disappointing ten game losing streak at the start of the season, to a record that just barely kept their playoff hopes alive. They needed a jolt. An awakening. They needed to turn it around. Robbie Dulik decided to provide that spark. He called a team meeting. No coaches.

The players filed into the practice gym, grumbling, none too happy to be where they were called on their day off. Fifteen minutes after the appointed time of the meeting, the last of the eleven active players finally arrived.

Robbie Dulik looked at his teammates. They looked tired. Defeated. The veterans, who last season had helped the younger players evolve in the NBA, possessed the attitude of 'been there, done that', 'wait til next year'. Not exactly leadership qualities. Missing Dante was the general excuse by all the players for their dismal season. Robbie would not accept it.

"I want to show you guys something," he started.

Staring at the big screen television that Robbie had rolled into the practice gym, one of the players asked if Robbie was going to inspire them by making them watch 'Hoosiers'. Although none would readily admit it, they had all watched the legendary story of the Indiana basketball team that beat all the odds and won the State Championship. None of them would ever admit that they actually had tears in their eyes when little Hickory High beat the heavily favored team from Indianapolis.

"No, it's not Hoosiers," Robbie interjected among the moans from the players.

He pressed the play button on a remote control and the screen became alive with the image of Dante O'Shea. He was looking at each player from the television, like one of those portraits where no matter where you are, the eyes follow you. He was sitting in his wheelchair.

"Hey guys," he started. "I miss you. All of you."

A tear formed in Henry Pickett's eyes.

"I need a favor from you," Dante continued.

Then he stopped. Willie appeared behind the wheelchair and pushed Dante to the parallel bars. The physical therapist helped Dante get up, and positioned him on the end of the bars. Dante took a small, painful step forward.

"I need a favor," Dante repeated.

He took another step forward. It took him half a minute to do it.

"I am not giving up," Dante stated. "I am coming back."

Five steps and two minutes later, sweat drenched the workout outfit of the Musketeer star. He stopped walking.

"As you can see," Dante told them. "I need a little more work to get back into shape. I'll be honest with you guys. This ain't easy. Sometimes I think of giving up. But I won't."

He had the full attention of each player.

"That favor I asked for?" he continued. "I need for you not to give up either. That's it."

Robbie turned off the television. Several players tried to disguise the wiping of tears from their eyes.

"So why hasn't he come to see us personally?" one player asked.

Robbie remained mute. He looked toward the door.

"I am here," their teammate simply stated.

Pushing a walker, he struggled toward his teammates. Not one player hid his emotion. The clapping started with Henry Pickett. A rhythmic sound.

"Dante," he chanted. "Dante. Dante. DANTE."

His teammates joined the chant. The eleven Cleveland players clapped and chanted as the Musketeer star picked up his pace. In seconds, he was surrounded by the men he loved. Hugs, high fives, and a lot of emotion greeted him.

"I'm here," he simply stated again.

CHAPTER 59

The Cleveland Musketeers did awake. After the All Star break, the annual halfway mark of the season, they reeled off thirteen victories in a row. They were now in a position to control their destiny and make the playoffs.

Dante graduated from the walker to a cane. His rehabilitation continued its course. And he continued to work toward his goal.

During one session, he seemed to get discouraged. Willie recognized it.

"Let me tell you about a little girl named Kathryn," the therapist started.

Dante needed a break, so he stopped and listened.

"Kathryn is the daughter of a friend of mine," Willie continued. "She was a pretty good athlete. And she was very smart. When she was in seventh grade, she played basketball. Halfway through the season, she broke her arm. Her left arm. Her shooting arm."

"Her team was undefeated at that point, but when she got injured, they lost every game. The thing is, Kathryn kept coming to practice. She insisted on being there. She couldn't really practice with the team, so she would practice by herself on the sideline. She learned to dribble with her right hand. And she learned to shoot right handed, too."

Dante wiped perspiration from his face.

"The last game of the season, Kathryn was allowed to play. The cast was off and she had that one game to get back into playing shape. Well, her team lost that game, but they still had enough wins to make the tournament."

"I'll never forget that tournament game," Willie said. "The team they played would get ahead, and Kathryn's team, the Irish, would always tie it. But they could never take the lead. They were down by three points and there was something like ten seconds to play, the other team had the ball."

"I remember the coach was yelling for someone to commit a foul. You know, to stop the clock, get the other team on the foul line, give his team a chance to try to pull it out. So that's what they did. They committed the foul."

"Good coaching," Dante stated.

"Yeah, so it happens that the girl's on the foul line and she misses both free throws. The Irish got the rebound off the second shot and dribbled up court and called a timeout. There was like five seconds to go."

"So the coach draws up this play, and he tells Kahliah, who played center on the team, that she's to try to pass the ball to Kathryn at half court. He told Kathryn that if the other team comes after her, she's to pass it back to Kahliah, who was told to run inbounds as soon as she made the pass and get ready behind the three point line."

"A desperation three pointer to tie the game, right?" Dante asked.

"Yeah, something like that. So, anyway, Kahliah throws the ball to Kathryn and nobody comes out on her at half court. So she takes two dribbles in from half court and launches the ball as the buzzer sounded. She banked it in and tied the game."

"That's pretty cool, especially for a seventh grade girl," Dante surmised.

"Thing is, Dante, she shot the ball with her right hand, not her left. She had practiced so much when she was not able to play, that it just came to her to shoot it with her opposite hand. In other words, she didn't give up. She took the curve thrown at her with her injury and ended up hitting a home run!"

Willie was way too excited about telling this story.

"Any chance that Kathryn is your daughter?" Dante queried.

"Well, yeah," Willie sheepishly replied.

"Any chance you were the coach?"

Willie nodded.

"Thought so," Dante smiled. "So, Coach. How'd the game end?"

"Oh, we won," beamed Willie. "In triple overtime. Kathryn made eight points including the winning foul shots."

"There was no time on the clock when she made them both," he proudly added.

It was a good story. And Dante again became more determined to work harder and get back to his team.

His team that was finding themselves just in time for the playoffs.

CHAPTER 60

As had become his custom, Dante limped, cane in hand, into the Musketeer locker room. Nervous excitement dominated the room.

"I can't believe we're this close," Robbie whispered to him.

"As long as we're here, let's finish it out," Dante replied.

The expert basketball analysts called it chemistry. The bonding of players with a common goal. Whatever it was, the Musketeers had it. Even without their best player, the Cleveland team clawed and fought themselves into this game. The seventh and final game of the NBA World Championship.

Outside the locker room, twenty minutes before the game, the chanting started.

"Let's go, MUSKS!" shouted twenty-three thousand voices. "LET'S GO, MUSKS!"

The vocal enthusiasm of the crowd worked its way through the walls of the Musketeer locker room.

Robbie Dulik looked at his friend, his inspiration.

"Wish you could play this one, Dante," he told him.

"I'm there with you, Robbie. You just keep leading this team like you have been. Just play your game."

Coach Avery tried to settle his players down.

"It's been a rough series," he told them. "I've got to tell you guys, I am so proud of you. You have come very far this season. Win or lose, I admire each and every one of you."

With his feelings out in the open, Coach Avery approached and hugged each player. He whispered heartfelt affections in each player's ear.

The players sat and stood with nervous anxiety to get out there. To go to battle. It was time to review the game plan.

"Well, as usual, we're short-handed," Coach Avery stated to his team. "They call it the Cleveland jinx, I guess. You all know that only eight of you are healthy enough to play, but we are all going out there in spirit."

"Watch your fouls," he warned them. "We can't take the chance of losing any players to fouling out. The math is easy. We have three healthy substitutes. So play aggressive, but play under control."

"Does anyone want to say anything?" he asked them.

The players looked around the room. Nothing more had to be said.

"Go get 'em!" Dante yelled.

They stormed out of the locker room. Dante limped behind.

CHAPTER 61

Bill Menegay sat with his friends, Jimmy Sweeney and Lenny Gill. To the left of the west coast agent sat his wife Susan. She was engaged in an animated conversation with Lisa O'Shea. His daughter, Alise Dulik, looked even more excited than when they had arrived at the Cleveland Coliseum. They sat three rows behind the Musketeer bench.

Bill Menegay would not cheer for his team from Los Angeles. Not this night. Not with his son-in-law playing for the opposition.

"I am so happy for you," Alise told her friend.

The crowd noise drowned out her other comments. Lisa just nodded and focused her attention to the court.

The eight Musketeer players huddled around their coach. The game was close to beginning. The cheering of the crowd roared like a freight train throughout the Coliseum.

Dante took his position at the end of the Cleveland bench. For this game, he used his significant influence and received permission for Willie to join him. His physical therapist was thrilled. Dante loosened his tie and shed his sports jacket. He lay his cane on the floor under the bench.

The tip off was controlled by the west coast team. The L.A. point guard, Preston Price, dribbled nonchalantly up the court, stopped at the top of the key, and drilled a three point shot. L.A. took an early lead, 3 to 0.

The Musketeers worked the ball into Henry Pickett. With his back to the basket, he pivoted and launched a perfect hook shot towards the hoop. It swished through the nylon net. L.A. led, 3 to 2.

The first quarter of the game was a seesaw battle. Los Angeles never trailed. When the buzzer sounded, ending the first twelve minutes of the NBA Championship Game, Cleveland was down by a basket, 27 to 25.

"Man, they're calling everything," Henry told his coach.

"I know. I know," agreed Coach Avery.

He looked at the stat sheet handed to him a moment earlier by his assistant. Two Musketeer players already had three fouls.

"Play aggressive," he implored his team. "But, please, play under control. Yeah, the refs are calling a tight game. So be aware of that. No ticky-tack fouls. Play smart."

Dante helplessly looked on. He so wanted to contribute. On the court.

Cleveland played the second quarter poorly. Afraid of being too aggressive on defense, they allowed Los Angeles to control the offensive boards. L.A. took advantage of the opportunity and poured in thirty-two points in the period. Fourteen were the result of offensive rebounds and the easy baskets that followed. The Cleveland crowd was quieted by their team's lack of quality play. The scoreboard high above the center of the court told the story, L.A. 59, Cleveland 43.

The locker room was too quiet at half time. Players sat and contemplated defeat. The veteran head coach of the Musketeers would not allow that attitude to take over.

"Ok, men," he yelled. "You either go out and give it your all. Or just stay here. If you don't want to give one hundred percent, I'd rather not have you on the floor."

Robbie looked at his head coach.

"I think we're too worried about fouling out, Coach," he stated. "I mean, we're underhanded already. I think we have to go all out, and foul out if that's how it goes, but at least go out trying. And trying hard."

It was an understatement. They all knew that. But it needed vocalized.

"No fear" became their second half motto.

Midway through the third quarter, Cleveland cut the Los Angeles lead in half, 67 to 59. Robbie was determined to lead by example. He was taught by the best to do just that. His mentor sat at the end of the bench, arms folded, and watched the action. He had a look of determination on his face. A look that said, "it ain't over til the fat lady sings".

Robbie played harder.

When Henry Pickett rebounded Robbie's missed three pointer and thundered it with a slam through the hoop, the Cleveland crowd became hopeful again. The dunk had cut the lead to four points. One minute remained in the third period. The ensuing play dashed that hope.

Preston Price dribbled the ball to the left side of the basket. His pass inside to Elvis O'Connor was soft and high. The L.A. center jumped to catch the pass, two Cleveland defenders jumped with him. Whether it was the jinx rearing its ugly head in Cleveland once again, or just a freak accident, both players landed awkwardly after missing their defensive attempt to steal the pass. One landed in a heap under the basket. The other lay prone on the floor five feet away. Both were injured. And both were helped off the floor by their teammates and by Joey Riggs, the Cleveland trainer.

Bobby Hale just shook his head.

"Well, folks," he told his radio audience. "Here we go again. It appears that neither player will be back, they're both on their way to the locker room. Now we're down to six. And Robbie Dulik has five fouls. One more and he'll be gone, too."

The period ended with no additional scoring. Los Angeles held on to a slim four point lead. But they also had twelve healthy players.

It didn't look good for the home team.

CHAPTER 62

"Come with me, Willie," Dante demanded.

His physical therapist replied with a questionable look on his face. Dante reached for his cane, stood up, and slowly hobbled toward the tunnel leading to the Musketeer locker room. Willie ambled behind him. Hardly anybody in the capacity crowd noticed the Musketeer leave the floor.

"Well, we're still in it," Bobby Hale told his listeners. "L.A. still leads by four, 86 to 82. There's 9:52 left in the game. The Musketeers have done an admirable job of hanging in there, folks. Let's see how they finish."

Movement on the L.A. bench indicated more bodies were joining the action. The Los Angeles coach would wear out the opposition. It was a simple game plan. He continued to put fresh players on the floor.

The Cleveland fans wanted to do something. Each time the Musketeers scored, there was loud cheering. But it wasn't constant. It wasn't inspirational.

"Put more on," Dante told Willie.

"Man, you look like a mummy now," stated his therapist.

"I need all the support I can get," Dante advised him.

"You sure you want to do this, Dante?"

"Got to, Willie. The team needs me."

"You haven't played in a year. I mean, what do you think you're going to be able to do out there? I don't mean to be negative, but it isn't your time yet, Dante, you're not physically ready to play ball."

"We'll see," was the Musketeer's answer.

Bobby Hale saw it first. Little by little, so did the crowd.

The radio announcer spoke into his mike, "Folks, you're not going to believe this."

The roar of the crowd caused him to shout his next sentence.

"What you're hearing, folks, is the reaction to Dante O'Shea. He is dressed in uniform! I can't believe he's going to play. By gosh, he's still using a cane. They won't allow that on the floor."

The "Dante" chant started in several areas of the Coliseum. Like steam beginning to escape from a tea pot, it started slowly, then became a loud shrill. Soon the whole place was rocking with the shouting of one name.

"DAN…TE," they cheered in unison.

"DAN…TE!" twenty-three thousand voices cried.

Coach Avery watched his star player advance, ever so slowly, toward the bench. Legs wrapped so tightly in white tape, Dante walked like Frankenstein, each step painful, each step small. The orange number twenty-five on his blue jersey already showed signs of perspiration as he worked his way toward his teammates. The Musketeer coach called a timeout.

After the commercial break, Bobby Hale reviewed the situation with his radio audience.

"Well, folks, there's 2:52 remaining in this game. The Musketeers have two timeouts remaining. Los Angeles is up by six, 102 to 96. The Musks are down to five players, I think. I know Dante O'Shea is dressed, but I truly doubt he could play. It's Cleveland's ball. They'll inbound at half court."

Coach Avery had drawn up a very basic play. Most coaches knew this one, but it was rarely used. Robbie inbounded the ball to Henry Pickett at the top of the key. Henry turned and faced the basket, then pivoted his body back toward Robbie, who hesitated briefly before stepping inbounds after his pass.

Robbie caught the chest pass, made one quick dribble, then

launched a three pointer from the left side of the court. Nothing but net. The Musketeers again cut the L.A. lead in half, 102 to 99. Two minutes and forty seconds showed on the clock.

"DEFENSE," shouted the crowd. "DEEEEFENSE."

The rejuvenated Musketeers responded. They played their man-to-man defense to perfection. Every pass was challenged. Every dribble was stopped. The shot clock showed two seconds when Preston Price launched a desperation shot over the outstretched fingers of Robbie Dulik. It missed everything.

"Air ball! Air ball!" came the crowd's automatic response.

Robbie dribbled the ball up the court. The L.A. defenders double teamed him at half court. His pass to a teammate on the right side was intercepted. L.A. started their patented fast break after the steal. Elvis O'Connor ended it with a slam dunk. Their lead increased to five, 104 to 99. Less than two minutes remained in the game.

This time, Robbie Dulik's teammates helped him as he approached the huge Musketeer logo at half court. As a defender advanced toward him, Robbie lofted a pass to the right wing. His teammate returned the pass, which Robbie quickly caught and threw to the left wing. Again, the ball came back to Robbie. He was at the top of the key. Henry Pickett worked his way open under the basket. Robbie bounced a pass beyond the reach of two L.A. defenders to the Musketeer power forward. Henry caught the ball, and extended his six eleven frame towards the basket. It became an easy lay up. Cleveland was again down by three. A minute forty remained in the game.

The two teams traded baskets during their next possessions. As the clock ticked closer and closer to the thirty second mark, Dante O'Shea stood up. He used Willie's shoulder to balance himself. Raising his cane, he twirled it over his head. The boisterous crowd got louder. An L.A. foul gave Robbie the opportunity to cut into the Los Angeles three point lead.

Robbie Dulik stood at the foul line. He bounced the ball five times. He rolled it in his hands. He took a deep breath. He shot the ball. Swish!

The scoreboard high above the Musketeer logo at half court read: Los Angeles 106, Cleveland 104.

Robbie's second shot followed the first. Nothing but net. Twenty-eight seconds remained: L.A. 106, Cleveland 105.

"Folks," shouted Bobby Hale. "This is a real battle. The Musks by right shouldn't be in the position to win. But they are. L.A. has called timeout."

Dante joined the huddle as his tired teammates came to the bench. Coach Avery looked at him, a respectful smile showed on his lips.

"Coach," Dante stated. "They'll work it inside to O'Connor. That's their tendency. I watched enough film on them to know it'll happen."

"Dante's probably right," the coach agreed. "Look for the inside pass. If O'Connor gets the ball, Henry, you stay between him and the basket. Robbie, drop off Price and double team. Let's try to tie up the ball. Keep close to your guys, men. Let's make them work for this shot."

Their hands joined together in the huddle.

"Defense!" they said as one.

The crowd's chant echoed their sentiments.

CHAPTER 63

Twenty-two seconds remained in the game when Preston Price received a return pass from his teammate at the top of the key. He back-dribbled toward half court, staying three feet on his side of the line. Robbie charged toward him. The two players squared off. Valuable time ticked off the clock.

With ten seconds left in the game, and six seconds on the shot clock, Preston Price made his move. He did a clever crossover dribble and easily maneuvered around Robbie. His pass to Elvis O'Connor was caught in the paint, six feet from the basket. Henry Pickett was the only defense between Elvis and the hoop. Robbie hustled from beyond the three point line toward the L.A. center.

As the shot clock expired, Elvis O'Connor attempted his shot. Robbie grabbed his arm from behind. The shrill whistle of veteran referee Earl Seifert pierced the Coliseum air.

"Foul. Number 22." he stated.

Robbie knew it, but was still disappointed. He dejectedly walked over toward the Musketeer bench. He had fouled out of the game.

"Time out," Henry told the ref.

"We've paid all the bills, so we'll stay right here," Bobby Hale told his listeners.

"When we return to action, Elvis O'Connor will be shooting two for L.A. Elvis is a seventy eight percent free throw shooter. L.A. still clings to a one point lead. Six seconds left in the fourth quarter."

Coach Avery looked at his players. He had a decision to make. Out of the eight players who started the game, two sat on the bench with crutches by their sides. And two more had fouled out. Four players. Six seconds. A one point deficit. And O'Connor at the foul line for L.A.

"Put me in," Dante told him. "I can at least get in the way."

"You know I can't do that, Dante," the coach replied.

"I'm here. I'm dressed. Put me in," Dante demanded.

Whether it was the determination in his player's eyes or the total frustration of getting this close and then having the usual bad luck of Cleveland sports catch up with him, the head coach of the Cleveland Musketeers relented.

"Report in," he told his star player.

Dante instinctively grabbed his cane. He took two steps toward the scorer's table. Then he looked at the crowd. Three rows behind the Musketeer bench, he spotted his wife.

"Here, catch!" he yelled to her.

Like a vaudeville performer, he tossed the cane toward his partner. Lisa caught it before it hit Alise Dulik in the head. Lisa shook her head. She knew Dante had to do this. He would never give up. She smiled at her husband.

Dante led his team onto the floor. He took a position at the other end of the court, at the foul line. Out of harm's way.

Elvis O'Connor bounced the ball twice, grabbed it with his large hands, and heaved it toward the basket. It hit the front of the rim, then the backboard, and bounced in. Los Angeles now led by two points. The crowd groaned, then quickly became very vocal.

"Miss it! Air ball! Choke!" they shouted at the L.A. center.

Elvis O'Connor repeated his routine and again elevated the ball toward the basket. It was not a pretty shot. Hitting the front of the rim, the ball this time caromed right into the anticipating hands of Henry Pickett.

Instinctively, he turned and threw the ball in the direction of Dante O'Shea. As soon as he released it, he wondered why he did it. What could Dante do, even if he caught it?

The ball took one large bounce just beyond half court and headed toward Dante's waiting hands. Preston Price hustled down the court at the same time. Attempting to knock the ball away, he instead collided with the Musketeer guard.

Dante collapsed to the ground. The crowd became eerily silent. There was little movement from their hero.

Preston Price knelt down beside his opponent. He was joined by most everyone on the court.

"I'm sorry, Dante," he stated. "Let me help you up."

Dante looked up at the L.A. guard. A smile formed on his lips.

"I know, Pres. Welcome back, right?" he stated.

Coach Avery called his last timeout. Three seconds remained in the game. The Musketeers were down by two points. Dante O'Shea would be shooting two free throws.

The Cleveland players did not go to the bench. Instead, the bench joined the team at the foul line.

"Coach, I've got an idea," Dante stated.

The crowd knew the situation. The Musketeers needed both of Dante's free throws to tie the game. Then overtime. Maybe. But how would they fare with four very tired players and one mummified superstar? They wanted to hope. The chant started.

"Dan...te!" they screamed. "DAN...TE!"

It was soon replaced by a rhythmic clap.

"Let's Go MUSKS!" they shouted.

Dante had little leg strength. His taped legs would not even bend. His shot would have to be all arm strength. He appreciated the times that Willie had taken him to the basketball court at the Clinic and allowed him to shoot from his wheelchair.

It had been over a year since Dante attempted a shot in an NBA game. He knew the rust would amass around him as he attempted his shot. And he knew he needed every ounce of strength to get the ball to the hoop. Especially with no help from his bandaged legs.

He dribbled the ball five times. He rolled it in his hands. It was the same routine his friend Robbie had adapted from him. He took a deep breath. With his eye on the target, he released his shot.

It fell one foot short of the rim.

A collective groan emanated from the crowd. The L.A. players relaxed as they stood at their various positions around the basket. With three seconds left, Dante would make this basket, the Musketeers would quickly foul, and this game would drag on to its predictable end. That's what they all thought. It's what Dante hoped they would think.

Eyeing his competition, Dante again went through his routine. The L.A. players seemed too relaxed. He made eye contact with Henry. He took a deep breath. Then a second deep breath. He grasped the ball in his right hand.

A hundred thoughts went through his head. Last year's game. His fall. The pain during his recuperation. Dr. K's comments. Even more determined, he took a third very deep breath. His shoulders relaxed. This was it.

Dante let the ball fly. It floated in a high arch toward the basket. As planned, it didn't go in. The round sphere hit the front of the rim. On the right side. The same side that Henry Pickett now stood. Ready to pounce.

As soon as he had released the ball, Dante O'Shea turned his back to the basket. He hobbled toward the three point line, eight feet back from the foul line. Dante took one step beyond the line, then painfully turned around to face the action. Observers may have thought that he was trying to get out of the way. They would have been wrong.

While Dante worked his way behind the line, Henry Pickett jumped as high as he possibly could. The ball was coming right at him. The crowd, the L.A. players, everyone expected Henry to catch the ball and put it back in the basket for two points. That would have tied the game.

He didn't grab for the ball. He swatted at it instead. Like a spike shot in a not-too-friendly volleyball game, Henry hit the basketball squarely with his right hand and directed it toward his teammate. The one anxiously waiting behind the three point line.

Dante caught the spike. The force of the ball knocked him slightly off-balance. Like he had done a thousand times in his wheelchair, Dante launched a two-handed shot toward the basket.

As the ball arched its way toward the basket, Earl Seifert raised one hand indicating a three point attempt. An instant later, he raised the other, as if signifying a field goal in football. It was good!

Dante fell to the ground.

"I don't believe it!" Bobby Hale yelled into his microphone. "THE MUSKETEERS HAVE WON THE GAME! I don't believe it. The Cleveland Musketeers are the NBA Champions."

His listeners didn't have a clue as to what had just happened.

Twenty-three thousand fans inside of the Cleveland Coliseum did. Nothing could describe the absolute thrill that filled the heart of every Musketeer fan. The frenzied crowd tried to storm the court.

The scoreboard high atop center court said it all: Cleveland 108, Los Angeles 107.

Henry Pickett was the first to reach his teammate. He picked Dante up off the floor and hugged him. Willie worked his way through the celebration and helped Henry hoist their friend onto their shoulders. Robbie Dulik soon joined them.

"This is it, Robbie!" Dante shouted above the noise. "Drink it in, this is what it's all about!"

"I LOVE IT!" Robbie hollered back.

Willie and Henry lowered the Cleveland hero to the floor. Lisa O'Shea joined the boisterous celebration.

"Lisa!" Dante yelled to his wife. "Lisa! You gotta love it. It doesn't get any better than this!"

Mrs. Dante O'Shea looked at her husband. Her face beamed. It was the joy of the moment. The pride for her husband. And the news she was about to lay on him.

"Yes, it does, Dante!" she screamed back.

The Musketeer hero had a questioning look on his face. His wife grinned at him.

"I'm preg," she started to say.

Dante was one of the first to see it. But his bandaged, beat up body wouldn't let him react in time.

CHAPTER 64

The Cleveland Coliseum was a monstrous structure built in the cornfields of Richfield, Ohio. Out in the middle of nowhere, it looked very out of place. It had been the home of the Cleveland Musketeers for over thirty-five years. The antiquated scoreboard was held in place by four cables. Three weeks before the playoff games, during the last building safety inspection, one of the three inspectors suggested that the cables be replaced. The connectors to the girders looked a little worn, he had told the maintenance supervisor. That information was passed on to management who made the decision to wait until the season was over to make any repairs. Bad decision.

The swaying scoreboard at mid court, high above the swaggering Musketeer logo, was hardly noticed. The crowd was way too excited about the victory to care.

Lisa O'Shea never had a chance. The unfinished sentence was greeted by her husband with a horrible, pain-filled look on his face. It wasn't the reaction she expected.

The huge scoreboard descended quickly on the small crowd at half court. They had little warning. It was over in a few seconds.

Dante had seen the movement and tried to reach for his wife. But she was two steps away, two steps he could not quickly make with his taped up legs. How ironic he felt life was at that very moment. From the joy of winning to the ultimate defeat, all in a moment.

The force of the crashing scoreboard sent Dante falling backwards toward the basket where he had made the winning shot. From the ground, looking up, he could see the steel girders where the scoreboard had been.

"LISA!" Dante screamed.

Then he passed out.

CHAPTER 65

"LISA," Dante called out.

"I'm here, Dante," she replied. There was some excitement in her voice.

"You're alive?"

"Oh, yes," he heard her say.

His eyes popped open. Wide open. He looked around. His mind raced. Confusion reigned in his head. He stared at the white tiled ceiling, the dim lights helping him to focus in. The room was strange to him. Yet it was very familiar.

Dante turned his head slowly toward the voice. Her voice. He did not know what to expect. He didn't know what he would see.

"You're alive?" he muttered again.

The gushing smile, like a giddy schoolgirl's, greeted his gaze. It hid the hollowed eyes, red from days of crying, dark from sleepless nights.

"Oh, Dante," she cried. Lisa O'Shea leaned over the bed railing and burrowed her head in his chest. Her sobbing confused the Musketeer player.

"Lisa, I thought I lost you," he whispered. "I thought I lost you after the roof collapsed. How did you escape? I saw the scoreboard come down on you."

Lisa slowly raised her head. She had been warned that when he awoke, he might have trouble deciphering reality from his comatose dreams. She would help him through it. She had to.

"Dante, do you know where you are?"

"Evidently in a hospital, Lisa." There was some aggravation in his voice.

"Do you know how long you've been here?"

Dante thought hard. The game had just ended; he remembered celebrating, then the roof caving in. He remembered lying on the ground, below the basket, looking up. It couldn't have been more than a few hours. Or was it?

"No," he replied. His response was quiet. Thoughtful.

"Do you remember the accident, Dante?" his wife asked.

"You mean my escape? That was no accident. I didn't know it was the FBI coming. I just kind of fell out of the window."

Lisa O'Shea had no clue what her husband was talking about. She dismissed his reply.

"No, I mean the car accident, Dante. Do you remember anything about it?"

Dante slowly shook his head. No.

"Dante, you've been out, I mean, in and out of a coma for almost four days. Do you remember driving to the Coliseum before the game with Chicago?"

Dante's confused look was his response.

"Do you remember that you wanted to go to the gym early, so you told me you'd meet me after the game?"

He shook his head. No. No. No. What was she talking about? He stopped her questions.

"Here's what I remember, ok? I got hurt in that game, twisted my ankle, no broke it, then I got kidnapped, and got taken to Italy, but it was really some abandoned building near downtown and then I escaped, but I got hurt real bad, then I came back and made the winning shot just last night, I think, then the scoreboard came tumbling down on you and Robbie and Henry."

He stopped talking. His wife was listening, almost amused at his memories, his recollection of his past year.

"Sweetie," she implored. "Slow down. You've been through a lot. Let's work together here, ok? I'll tell you what I know; you tell me what you remember. Ok, sweetheart?"

Dante closed his eyes. What was real? Was this real? Were his memories real? What was going on in his head? Was he dead? Was Lisa dead? A few silent moments elapsed. Lisa spoke again.

"Dante," she continued. "Here's what I know."

Dante re-opened his eyes and focused with all his mental strength on every word his wife now proclaimed. Her explanation would be his truth. His reality. If it was all a dream, he would figure it out. And he would try to find its purpose.

"The night of the accident, you left the house and drove to the Coliseum. From what the police and a witness have told me, you were driving on Akron-Peninsula Road and came around a curve and had to dodge a biker in the middle of the road. You swerved and lost control of the car, Dante. You hit a tree. Do you remember any of this?"

Dante mouthed the word 'no' and shook his head side-to-side.

"The air bag saved you from more serious injury, but you did hit your head very hard on the roof of the car. They air flighted you to here, Saint Thomas Hospital. Dante, you've been in and out of a coma ever since."

A quick question entered Dante's mind.

"Did the Musks win the Eastern Conference Finals? Did we beat Chicago?"

Lisa knew the importance of the game to her husband. Her mind raced with thoughts of his dream to be the best player the Cleveland franchise ever had. She knew that Dante wanted to help bring a championship to his hometown. But his playing time was almost nonexistent in his first year as a pro. Robbie was the star. Dante would have to bide his time.

"Dante," she stated. "The Musks lost the game."

"It was very close," she added. "In fact, we thought we had it won,"

"Don't tell me," he interrupted. "A winning shot was called off."

Lisa looked at her husband.

"How did you know that?" she queried.

"I'm not sure," he honestly replied. "Did Robbie shoot it?"

The mention of Robbie's name made Lisa look down.

"What's wrong, Lisa?"

"I didn't want to tell you this right away, not after all you've been through," his wife replied.

"What?" he asked again.

Lisa looked tenderly into her husband's eyes.

"Robbie's missing. He may have been kidnapped."

CHAPTER 66

Special Agent Jim Sweeney had received the phone call from Mrs. Dante O'Shea. She seemed very concerned about Robbie Dulik's disappearance and stated that her husband wanted to discuss the case with the FBI. Sweeney looked at his partner, Len Gill, and shrugged his shoulders.

"I don't know, Len, probably a waste of time," he bluntly stated.

"Well, Jim, it's not like we have a lot of leads," Agent Gill replied. "Isn't Dante O'Shea that kid from Ohio State?"

"Yeah, he is. Hometown boy doesn't make good," Sweeney surmised. "He was supposed to be the second coming, if I remember the draft day prognosticator's predictions. Fell a little short of expectations I'd say."

"There's always next year," chimed his partner. The Cleveland battle cry.

Dante O'Shea was finishing his second meal since awakening from his coma. The two FBI Agents patiently waited for him to finish his orange juice.

"This is really weird," he stated to them. "I feel like I know you guys, yet we just met."

Their silent reply didn't encourage him.

"I don't know where to begin, and I don't know if this is anything, but something bizarre has happened to me and I don't want to ignore it."

"Your wife mentioned that you might have information on Robbie's location," Agent Sweeney stated.

"Sir," Dante hoarsely replied. "What I want to tell you about is so clear to me, it's like it really happened…to me, that is. But my wife tells me I've been here, in a coma, for the past few days, so it had to be a dream."

"What happened, Mr. O'Shea?" Agent Gill asked.

"I dreamed I was the one who was kidnapped," Dante rasped out. "It was shortly after the Chicago game. And the kidnapers were three kids who rented a house near downtown Cleveland. And the mastermind was a guy who owned a machine shop. But I think it was closed down or something. Anyway, the kidnapers went to great lengths to make it appear that I was taken out of the country; that I was in Italy. When I was being rescued, or actually had escaped, I found out I had actually been in Cleveland the whole time."

The two agents looked at each other.

"That's an interesting, uh, dream, Mr. O'Shea," Jim Sweeney told him. "But what makes you think there might be a similarity between your dream and what's happening with Robbie Dulik?"

Dante looked at the agent, then his partner. He stared beyond them at his wife. He hadn't even told her what he was about to say. The detail that made it make sense.

"Sir," Dante weakly stated. "I awoke from a coma just a few hours ago. I haven't read a paper, or talked to anyone about our game with Chicago. Other than Lisa telling me that we lost, and how we lost, Robbie's shot being called off and all. And I know this seems very farfetched, but I bet I can give you a vivid description of the last few minutes of that game, and how Earl Seifert called off the last shot, five minutes after the game was over. Am I right?"

They nodded. The name of Earl Seifert was being bandied about in Cleveland in not so nice terms.

"Is there any chance that Robbie was kidnapped at home by two people dressed up like a monkey and gorilla?"

This question got the full attention of the agents. Just this morning a witness had revealed that he had seen a gorilla and monkey, driving down the road that led to the Dulik residence in Copley. They were in a black Lexus.

Dante spent the next hour and forty-five minutes relating his dream, his experience, with the agents. Lisa listened as her husband related the story of his own kidnapping, rescue attempt and eventual return to the Musketeers. He remembered every detail as the FBI agents furiously scribbled in their notepads.

He did not waste their time.

CHAPTER 67

Paul Pallibio had just loaded the last suitcase in the trunk of his Corvette when the unmarked car screeched to a halt in his driveway.

Special Agents Gill and Sweeney scrambled out of the car and approached the former owner of the Pallibio Machine Shop.

"What's going on?" he asked the agents.

"We need you to come with us for questioning about the disappearance of Robbie Dulik," was Agent Jim Sweeney's businesslike response.

Paul Pallibio lowered his head.

"Let me lock up, ok?"

They allowed him that, as they followed him into his house, making mental observations of its condition. It looked like he was going on a long vacation, nothing more. There were no boxes, no indication of Pallibio moving his residence.

"Listen, I have a flight to catch in two hours. Can you just question me here?"

Agent Jim Sweeney had some doubts about Dante O'Shea's story. His psychic dream. But he had to play this out. They had no other leads on this case.

"I'm sorry, sir," he stated. "You'll have to go downtown with us."

"You're not flying to Los Angeles, are you?" Agent Gill asked.

"Yes, I am," Pallibio calmly replied.

Len Gill looked at his partner. They both gave a hint of a smile to each other.

Paul Pallibio saw it but did not understand.

CHAPTER 68

Lisa O'Shea was amazed at how quickly her husband rebounded from the head injuries he incurred from the car accident. He was a lucky man to be alive. The police had told her that he hit the tree doing at least forty miles per hour. There were no tire marks revealing an attempt to slow down. The car was demolished. How he escaped with only head injuries was, in itself, a minor miracle. The fact that he seemed almost fully functional, mentally and physically, only hours after awakening from his deep sleep was, to Lisa, a major miracle.

"Everything has a purpose," her husband had told her many times. She was becoming a believer in his Divine Intervention philosophy.

"Lisa," Dante started. "I want to tell you something. It's kind of strange. Kind of scary, I guess. But something has happened to me. It's like I know more about life, more about you, than I did before the accident. But I was asleep most of the time. It's like some hidden power has been sparked within me. I'm not sure I can explain it."

His wife looked at him. He had been relating what he had considered the past year of his life to her, and she was amazed by the details he remembered. Especially about the kidnapping and his ability to tell of the conversations that others had when he wasn't in the room. And their thoughts, too. He told her that he dreamed she had prayed for him a lot while he was gone, and he knew she had prayed for other things, too. He relayed what he considered his out of body experience and seeing what he conceived to be God. He told her that he knew that she deeply loved him, but that she didn't feel complete.

"And that's what we need to talk about, honey," he continued. "About you, about us. I know you feel something is missing. I need to know more about your feelings, Lisa. I want to know more about everything about you. Lisa, you are my life. Believe it. Please open up to me."

Lisa O'Shea wanted to. She really did. But some things were just too hard to let surface. Too hard to talk about. Or explain.

She was afraid to tell her husband about her experience.

Chapter 69

Robbie Dulik strained against the nylon roped that bound him to the chair. His mind whirred with many thoughts about what might happen. And about Alise. Fortunately, she was gone the day they came. She was with Lisa at the hospital, keeping her company while she sat by his friend's bedside.

The queasiness from the injection had worn off, but the headache did not. There was total silence in the room. Not a word had been uttered. But he knew someone was there.

"Help me," he uttered to the darkness.

Vincent Burson laughed out loud.

"You are one helpless son of a bitch, superstar," he offered to the Musketeer player.

"W-w-where am I?" Robbie stuttered.

The padded door to the former office of Paul Pallibio crashed open. The sudden banging noise made both the captive and his captor cringe with fear.

"Police! Don't move!" shouted several Cleveland officers.

Guns were raised and pointed, ready to fire. Vinnie Burson didn't move. The room was soon crowded with police officers and a couple of FBI agents.

Jim Sweeney removed the blindfold from Robbie Dulik's eyes. Agent Len Gill worked on the binding ropes.

"Are you ok, Robbie?" he was asked.

The grateful All-Star guard of the Cleveland Musketeers nodded repeatedly.

The room quickly cleared as the police escorted Vinnie to the van waiting in front of his home on East Fortieth Street. Eddie and Big Carl were already passengers in the back of the Police Van. None of the boys dared to look at each other as Vinnie was loaded in the back.

Agents Sweeney and Gill remained behind in the room. To their amazement, it looked just like Dante described it would. It was all there. The tapes, the two tape players, the padded walls, the barely open window, and the thirty-eight special.

They became believers.

CHAPTER 70

Lisa put the paper down and poured Dante a second cup of coffee. She reseated herself on the swivel chair at the kitchen counter. The article that Ron Collins wrote for the Akron Journal explained the kidnapping story in full detail, including the role played by Dante O'Shea. A second article expounded the use of psychics by authorities to solve difficult cases.

"I really can't explain it," her husband stated. "It's seemed so real to me. It's like I had the experience, but it turned out to be someone else's life. It's so…weird. I mean, why me?"

Lisa shrugged her shoulders.

Dante swiveled his chair and looked into his wife's eyes.

"You know, Lisa, I love you more than anything else in life. You are my best friend. Yet, I keep getting the feeling that you're not happy with me. I know all of this happened for a purpose, but it's over now. I really am not a mind reader. I need you to talk to me about whatever it is that you are keeping inside."

Lisa stared at her husband, but her mind was elsewhere. Far away. A tear formed and rolled down her cheek.

"D-D-Daddy didn't really want me to go to college," she flatly stated. "He never planned for me or my sisters to want to make something of ourselves."

"What are you saying, Lisa?" her husband asked.

Her voice lowered into a barely audible whisper.

"I had to get out of that house," she continued. "It just wasn't a good scene then. Mom and Dad weren't getting along, and they were always on me about something."

"So you went to Ohio State," Dante concluded.

Lisa lowered her eyes. Her cheeks reddened.

"No, Dante," she stated. "I didn't go right to Ohio State."

"I didn't know that," he replied. "I always thought you were there all four years of college."

Lisa looked up at her husband and saw the confused look on his face. She had gone this far. For better or for worse, just like the vows they had taken not so long ago, she decided to tell him all.

Clearing her throat, she continued in as strong a voice as she could muster.

"Dante, I was there for four years, but, but I ran away from home when I was eighteen. I just had to get out of there. I went to Texas and," she stopped.

Her face flushed and her eyes focused on her coffee cup on the counter.

"I had to make ends meet, but I had no skills. So I did something I wish I never had."

Dante's mind whizzed with thoughts he wished he didn't have.

"I...became...a, a, a dancer," she blurted out.

The Musketeer player was stunned.

"You mean. You mean you were a stripper?"

He couldn't believe he was asking his wife such a question.

Lisa nodded.

Dante was dumbfounded. And confused. He rested his forehead in his right hand, not looking at his wife. How could she? Why did she? What else could she be hiding from her past? What did he really know about his wife's past?

"I'm, I'm sorry," she mumbled.

Tears streamed down her cheeks. She wanted to feel better at that moment for unloading this disappointing news on her husband. She wanted to let him know that she loved him. That she trusted him enough to tell him what no other person had ever heard.

Dante raised his head and glared at his wife.

"Why are you telling me this...now?" he wanted to know.

Lisa took a moment to collect her thoughts. This answer would probably be the most important response she had ever given to her husband. Thoughts of losing him, of divorce converged on her mind. She didn't need that. She needed his acceptance and understanding. Right here. Right now.

"Dante, I believe in you. I believe, no, I know that you are going to be a great basketball player."

"Yeah, so." Anger and disappointment showed itself in his voice.

"Your life is my life, too. As you become more famous, people are going to want to know more and more about you. About us."

"What are you saying, Lisa?"

"I saw the picture of someone in the paper today. Someone you don't know, but are connected with because of the kidnapping case. He probably would recognize me. And he would probably want to hurt you...through me and my past."

"Who are you talking about, Lisa?"

She grabbed the newspaper and pointed to the picture of the former owner of Pallibio Machine Shop. Paul Pallibio.

"He was kind of a regular at the club I worked in Texas. He flew down from Cleveland quite often on business trips. Dante, I don't want to have to tell you why he would recognize me. I just know he would. And since you played a role in putting him in jail. Well, I'm sure you can understand my fear."

Dante looked at his wife and shook his head. This was unbelievable. The woman he thought he knew, he was finding out, he really didn't. He had a decision to make. A major decision.

Dante left the house.

CHAPTER 71

Special Agents Jim Sweeney and Lenny Gill were given commendations for their excellent detective work on the Robbie Dulik kidnapping case. Because of Robbie's high profile in northeast Ohio, they were publicly honored by the Mayor of Cleveland.

Eddie and Vincent Burson shared a cell at the state penitentiary in Mansfield, Ohio. They did little talking. Big Carl Plath asked that he not share the same cell. He didn't even want to be in the same city as his former friends. He would spend his time at a similar facility in Toledo.

Paul Pallibio hated his cell in Cleveland. He did a lot of thinking. Too much thinking. Fred Durzak visited with him a few times. But eventually, Paul's depression was too much to bear. Fred would never understand his friend. Like in Dante's dream, Pallibio ended his life in jail. His suicide note included an apology to those he had hurt. A small confession that he hoped would grant him eternal forgiveness.

Robbie Dulik and his wife kept busy with a new project in their home. Renovating a bedroom. It would be their baby's.

Dante O'Shea didn't come right home after his last conversation with his wife. He needed time to think. To ponder.

He stayed at his parents' house. Told him he was tired of the calls from the press and psychics that had been pestering him since the case had broke. He needed to hide out for a few days. He told them that Lisa had decided to visit with her parents and sisters in Cincinnati.

She really was keeping busy at home. Wondering if her husband would return.

Dante O'Shea sat in the last pew at his church. It was five o'clock in the morning. Four days had passed since he had been home. His Bible was open to Paul's letter to the Corinthians. The one about love. Certain phrases played in his head.

"Love rejoices in the truth," the letter stated.

He didn't feel all that joyful about what he had learned. But at least Lisa was being totally honest with him. He could rejoice in that.

"Love is always supportive," advised Paul's letter.

Dante wanted to be just that. But his pride seemed to be hindering his effort.

He wanted and needed to do the right thing. For the past half hour, he sat in the silence, and meditated on the eighth verse.

"Love never fails!"

He made his decision.

Chapter 72

Dante O'Shea found his wife sitting at the kitchen counter. Pretty much where he had left her. Her eyes were red and puffy. She had been crying. A lot.

His entrance from the garage door into the kitchen startled his wife. He smiled at her and sat in the same chair he had occupied days before.

"Dante, I, I am really sorry," she stated as a greeting.

His response was a knowing look. A caring smile.

Dante walked around the counter and gently put his arms around his wife. She started to rotate her stool to face him. He stopped the motion. Leaning his tall frame over, he rested his head on top of her dark brown curly hair.

"Lisa, I've done a lot of thinking, about you, me, us. You made a bad choice. For whatever reason, you did what you felt you had to do. You know I don't approve, but I was not in your life then. I probably could not totally understand the circumstances, so I am not going to judge you for what you did."

"I feel like we've always have had an honest, open relationship. And I know that keeping me unaware of this, uh, situation probably made you feel like crap. I'm glad you think enough of me, of us and our relationship, to get it out in the open."

Dante O'Shea spoke no more. He wanted to say more. Say the right thing. He wanted to let her know that he accepted her for what she had become. He wanted to tell her that he loved her for who she is...now. How she got to be who she became didn't matter. It's the here and now that did matter. The last thing he wanted to do was state some cliché that she'd probably heard a thousand times before.

He gently grabbed his wife's shoulders and slowly swirled her around until she faced him. Looking deeply into her blue green eyes, he pulled his wife towards himself. He strongly embraced her, holding her closely, hugging her. A hug that reinforced his love for her. A hug that said, "I love you...no matter what". A hug that emanated from his innermost being and told her, "I am here with you and will always be."

At that moment, Lisa O'Shea learned a lot about her husband. Her arms reached around the Musketeer player's back, returning his embrace, letting him know that she accepted his understanding, his support, his love. Their kiss was long and tender. There was no more talk between them.

Sometimes, actions do speak louder than words.

CHAPTER 73

Lisa O'Shea sat in her usual seat, three rows behind the Musketeer bench. Her son, Dante, Jr., sat on her lap. Her four year old daughter, Veronica, sat on the edge of her seat next to Lisa.

"LET'S GO MUSKS! LET'S GO MUSKS!" reverberated off the walls of the Coliseum. Twelve seconds remained in the game. And the game was tied, 120 to 120.

The winner would be crowned the NBA Champions.

Dante O'Shea heard the final instructions of Coach Avery, but his mind was thinking of his friend, Robbie Dulik.

"Robbie would have loved to be in this situation," he thought.

His retirement, a year after his kidnapping, rocked the Cleveland world. Robbie was in his prime, a true superstar, but a better husband and father. He left the world of basketball 'for personal reasons' he had told the press. He left because he feared the safety of his wife and new son. He gave it all up out of love for them.

"I'm sure Robbie's watching," Dante shouted to his teammate, Henry Pickett.

Henry smiled.

"Let's bring it home, Dante."

They broke the huddle and hustled to their assigned positions for the inbounds play. Earl Seifert gave the ball to Henry and he quickly bounced a pass to Dante. Dante glanced at the clock, 10 seconds to go.

He dribbled one bounce to his right; cross dribbled to his left and smoothly bounced a pass toward Henry Pickett. Henry gathered in the ball and watched as Dante separated himself from his defender and glided toward the basket.

The old give and go. A play as old as basketball. A play hard to defend.

Four seconds remained as Dante received Henry's pass and made his move toward the basket. Two defenders converged upon him, but Dante had learned from the best and he would not let his old friend and mentor down.

One second before the buzzer sounded, he released his shot. A seven foot bank shot from the left side of the basket.

The ball caromed off the backboard at the exact spot that Dante wanted and banked through the nylon cord.

The scoreboard read: Time Remaining: 0.00. Cleveland 122, Los Angeles 120.

"Finally!" Bobby Hale exclaimed to his listeners.

And they all understood.

Printed in the United States
96111LV00004B/154-189/A